DARK INFERNO

ARLETA RAE

DARK INFERNO

CHILDREN FROM SACRIFICE
BOOK TWO

ARLETA RAE

BOOKS BY ARLETA RAE

Children From Sacrifice

Rising Ember

Dark Inferno

For my mom, the one who inspired the reader inside

For my dad, who was the first reader of this series, even before any edits

CONTENTS

CHAPTER ONE

THEA

*L*ife rushes by in an eruption of memories, painted in shades of viridian and drenched in abysmal black oil. There is pain in my mind with each step toward the unknown. To the place of fear that sat at the shores of my every action over the past month. Deep within my subconscious are emotions so primal, so earth-shattering that they tear at their rusty cage begging to be released.

Living, breathing fire. An inferno set ablaze with a single breath of hatred. It's what I did in the forest. It's the reason why my body feels as though it can break at any moment, stripped bare, with the abuse of my violent magic.

Thea, don't. Cole's broken plea still rings in my ear. He, who has become someone I cannot live without and would protect with my life, begged me not to go with the vampires who hunted me, even offered himself to them. The bloodthirsty Brais vampires. I had no choice though. I wouldn't have let them take him. I would do anything to keep him and Sarah safe. The two of them are the only people left who matter to me.

"Stop," the Brais General commands, one bronze hand in the air while the other rests on the hilt of his sword. That is the first word that spews out of Amaund's mouth since we left Cole and Sarah behind in the forest I set ablaze. His long and braided onyx hair glistens underneath the moonlight, the color blending with that of his cloak. He dons silver armor and a matching sword, a point to how long he has been a vampire. Only a couple other Brais within the group wear armor instead of modern clothing.

The forest around us seems to heed to his command as well. Insects cease their humming, and the leaves stop swaying. The silvery light of the full moon pokes through the canopy. It is past its apex in the sky, perhaps only a few more hours until the sun rises. I wonder how many of these vampires have their sun totems that allow them safety from the bright star. None of them appear worried, so wherever we are going must be close. Luckily for me, burning in the sun will never be a concern. My rare vampire magic somehow resulted in an immunity to the sun.

"What is it, lord?" A blond-haired Brais says tensely, his brown eyes searching the woods around us. The leaves underfoot crunch with his jagged, surveying movements.

I follow suit, sensing that there is something wrong. Something...*else*. The sudden silence of the forest and the tingling nerves down my back put me on alert. What little of my fire magic that remains sizzles underneath my skin in response. It is only a match compared to the inferno it was earlier. Despite how eager my fire is, my body does not feel the same. My limbs are heavy from exhausting most of my magic in the fight against Amaund and his Brais soldiers. Even though I gave it my all, it wasn't enough. The Brais wanted me for my ability to manipulate fire. The General hunted me for a month and killed people to get to me. People I knew and cared for. And in the end, his task succeeded.

The iciness of the chains that bind my wrists behind me bite at my skin. Nervousness pricks the back of my neck as thoughts of Cole and Sarah pursuing us enters my mind. Sarah, my over-protective witch best friend, would do anything to keep me safe. I left her with the vampire who turned me, Cole, who in the last month, has showed that he would be willing to sacrifice himself to keep me safe as well. They both were in rough shape before Amaund took me. Luckily, Amaund fulfilled his promise that he wouldn't harm them if I went willingly. That promise would most likely be null if they attacked or followed us. I don't think another fight would end well for my friends.

Please don't be them.

"We are being followed," the Brais General answers, and the grip on his sword tightens. "Alec, Mica, watch her." His gaze switches between the two vampires flanking me.

Mica and Alec nod their heads as they step closer in a shielding stance. I wonder if it is more for my safety from whatever is following us or if they think I might try and escape. The one on my left, Mica, is slightly taller than me with white, shoulder-length hair. His dark skin glistens underneath the moonlight. Glancing at his tense body, he isn't sure who is following us. His left hand clutches the sword at his hip, while his right holds a wooden stake. A stake like that is a far bigger threat to a vampire than a sword. Which means the sword is probably just for showing off.

Amaund, however, has no stake. But with the amount of magic I can feel radiating off him, I suspect he would have no need for it. He could probably rip us all to pieces without ever touching us. He stands fifty paces in front of the group with his gleaming sword unsheathed from its ornate scabbard, the point facing the darkness of the forest beyond. The silver metal reflects the light of the moon overhead. From here, he seems relaxed. It is unnerving to think about the number of times he has swung that sword at his enemies. The image of it impaling Cole through the abdomen causes a shiver to run down my spine.

The flare of a fire pulls my attention to the right. Alec, the vampire on that side of me, holds a wooden stake engulfed in flames. The sight of it could be intended to intimidate whoever is following us. He wears a checkered, blue dress shirt and black pants. His dusty brown hair is cut short, revealing wrinkles along his forehead and eyes. His movements and posture reveal no signs of tiredness, despite how old he appears.

Do they worry it could be the Essites? Their vampire enemies in this immortal civil war. My clan. The Brais fight for dominance and destruction, but the Essites fight for peace. Sarah said that the witches don't involve themselves with the war between vampire factions, but she was insistent that I stay away from the Brais. And with every interaction I had with a Brais vampire, I knew I could never be one of them.

In front of Amaund emerges a man, donned in leather armor. A golden medallion hangs from his neck. There is a symbol embossed in the center, but from this distance, it is too hard to see the shape. Six more people appear from the shadows of the forest behind the stranger, their features obscured by darkness and greenery. An acrid stench sours the air, like milk that has sat in the summer sun for weeks.

I wrinkle my nose, noticing that Alec is doing the same. A few others are covering their noses with their hands.

"A poison crafted from a witch's magic and that of a petrified monkshood plant," Mica whispers to me, his thin eyes never leaving the mysterious man. "A specialty of his kind. Won't kill a vampire but could do some serious damage."

A crossbow rests on the stranger's back, bolts set in a small quiver on his hip. He walks calmly from the trees with his hands raised, palms facing the vampire General. A familial smirk dances across his features, lit up by the various conjured flames from the Brais in front of him. His dark skin is covered in tattoos, the ink like thorny vines poking underneath the cuff of his sleeve and the top of his body armor. "I was not expecting to see you out in these woods, General." The man's voice is smooth as he keeps his dark eyes on Amaund. His comrades are watching the rest of the Brais, their weapons out, ready to defend their leader.

Amaund lowers his sword, the point resting on the leaf-littered ground. "The same could be said of you, *hunter.*" Amaund spits the last word like an insult, making me believe it isn't a name but a frowned upon title. The Brais soldiers respond to their General's movements by lowering their own weapons. A few shift on their feet.

The man waves one of his hands before dropping them both to his sides. His mouth moves, but I don't hear any words. Even standing in front of Amaund, his expression is relaxed, as if the two know each other well. Where there seems to be apprehension amongst the Brais, the man remains calm and arrogant.

I scowl, concentrating on the two, as I recall Cole's lessons on our vampiric senses. *Focus your mind to the sounds you want. Feel as though your ears have a dial, extend their range. Or lower it.* His calming voice is engraved into my mind, as is his smile and smokey eyes. Just remembering his words, my body heats to a longing for him. I still as the stranger points to me, his brown eyes are full of a hateful promise. Unlike a few of the Brais, Amaund doesn't move to follow his gesture.

"You can stop trying to listen in, Kindria," Mica says quietly as he leans closer.

Kindria. New vampire. I fight the urge to bare my teeth at Mica. I turn to him and notice that he has forgone his hold on the sword, though he still clutches the stake. "What is he saying?"

Mica scoffs. "None of us can hear their conversation."

"Mica, enough," Alec hisses. He also still holds his wooden stake, orange flames dancing along the weapon. His pale eyes are narrowed into slits at his comrade on the other side of me.

Mica smiles coldly at Alec before mumbling, "It's probably a silencing spell." The comment results in another glare from Alec.

I look closer at the new visitor's band of stakes, all various sizes strapped to a bandolier. A small leather quiver sits on the left side of his hip and inside, a multitude of wooden bolts. Sitting high enough on his back for everyone to see is a large crossbow. Opposite the quiver is an ornate pistol with numerous pouches on his belt that I suspect hold the putrid poison Mica referenced. Through the stench of his poison, he smells deceptively human. Was it him or Amaund who cast the silencing spell? And why would Amaund seem so casual talking to a human armed to the teeth in things that can kill vampires?

The stranger's assortment of items reminds me of that open panel in the wall of my childhood home. Crossbows and daggers were stored inside, along with old letters addressed to my father from my grandfather. There were decorative vials stashed in there as well, though empty, and were similar to a couple hung on the stranger's belt.

"Humans can use magic?" The words spill out, louder than I intended them to. Luckily, Amaund and the stranger are too engrossed in their own conversation to have heard.

"Not another word," Alec sneers at me.

"Some can," Mica says, his green eyes piercing his comrade's.

I swallow, trying to make sense of all this. "Why did he point at me?" I mutter, regretting saying anything. If the human did indeed cast the silencing spell, could he somehow use magic to track vampires? Even if he can, why would he single me out of the others in the group?

Mica's grin widens, showing all of his teeth. "So curious. You know, as a Brais, any questions you have will be answered. *Any* question. Even—"

"Mica, for once in your life, shut up," Alec cuts in. I watch as the flames that engulf his stake reduce to simmering embers. The sight of them seem to call to my sleeping flames, inciting them to wake up just a little. A tingling underneath my skin is the only indication that they are doing just that.

"I recall you being just as inquisitive once, Alec." The two vampires still at the voice. Amaund appears just a few feet from us. His golden eyes pierce mine, glistening with some sort of emotion that I can't pinpoint. "I would thank us if I were you, Thea. Those hunters were chasing you." A slight smile tugs at a corner of his lips. "If it were not for your alliance with us, you surely would be dead." Beyond the Brais General, the clearing is empty. The hunters departed, and I didn't even notice, too distracted by what Mica was telling me.

Hunters. Vampire hunters? When Cole saw the compartment in my family's manor with the weapons and vials, he called my parents vampire hunters.

My lips curl in distaste. "I am not in an alliance with you. Nor will I ever be." He is implying that the hunters didn't attack because they assumed I was an ally to the Brais. Or just to Amaund. It doesn't make sense to me for vampire hunters to align themselves with vampires—especially those who have no regard for the lives of humans. There is so much more to this world than just the existence of supernatural beings and their magic. I need to learn all that I can.

Amaund smiles at my statement, his fangs protruding from his upper lip. "We'll see, Thea." Amaund looks to Alec and Mica, the latter of which has paled to a ghostly color. "Let's go."

～

THIRTY MORE MINUTES of silent hiking through the forest go by before we stop again. My focus was either fixated on the ground or Amaund's back, hoping he could feel the daggers I was mentally throwing at him. Now, we stand in a small clearing surrounded by towering trees. Two bare, gothic looking pines are in the center of the clearing. The tops of their charred, scraggly branches touch and form an archway. We follow Amaund, who stops just short of the dead trees. He reaches underneath his cloak and pulls out a dagger made of black metal with a silver hilt and embossed with a spherical quartz crystal. I watch curiously as Amaund removes the bracer on his left forearm. A nasty burn is carved into the inside of his wrist. With the dagger, he slices through the circular shape of the burn and crimson liquid pours from the fresh wound. He sheaths the weapon and holds his bleeding wrist in between the threshold of the archway. As his blood drips onto the brown grass, he whispers words that I recognize as Latin.

"*Sol Invictus redit cum duobus.*"

Even with so many Latin classes between high school and college, I can't translate exactly what he said. Something about the sun returning. I think.

A faint, dark aura coils from the center of the two trees. Black waves of air ripple from that point and move toward the trunks. Within seconds, the forest beyond is no longer visible. Instead, a surface resembling black water stands vertical between the trees. It shimmers like a dark mirror, reflecting each of us in its murkiness. I almost gasp at my disheveled appearance. My brown hair looks matted, a smudge of mud has dried on my left cheek, and my hazel eyes are almost lifeless. Like the shell of a once lively person who has been stretched to a distorted shape. I grimace as I glance down to my black clothes. With a few tears in the fabric of the cotton shirt, there is no hiding that I have been in a fight.

Amaund puts his bracer back on, and I take notice of the wound that has already mended itself, much faster than I saw Cole heal. He turns to me, his expression emotionless, and grabs my arm.

I contemplate pulling away before contact, weary of what I just witnessed. I stand firm as he tugs me toward the blackness. "What is that?"

"You didn't think that the King lived in this forsaken town, did you?" He doesn't wait for an answer, just pulls my tired body through the obscure sheet of magic that seems to rip at my skin.

Instead of the familiar pine forest, I am met with the salty air and coarse sands of a beach. Amaund still holds my arm in a tight grip. One by one, the vampires traveling with us emerge from nothing. I look back and see them appearing through a large, stone archway. Twin pillars stand and bend to touch at a rounded tip, their bases engulfed by coarse sand. The top of the archway is just a smooth, flat circle, though a single crack crosses in the middle.

Winds whip around us, blowing my long brown hair into my face. Gray clouds stretch across the sky for as far as I can see. Waves crash violently onto the shore behind us, powered by a storm far out across the ocean. The ground is damp, as if we just missed the rain. Ahead of us, the golden sand morphs into pale grass before the landscape turns into a dark cluster of scraggly trees.

Someone unshackles my wrists. Amaund releases my arm and walks toward a path that leads into the trees. I find myself compelled to follow, my gaze shifting to the expansive quietness. There are no sounds of life here. No birds flapping in the ocean's winds or insects buzzing in the tall grasses. Just the sounds of our footsteps, the wind, and the waves. My chest aches as I can't help but feel how very far away Cole and Sarah are from me right now.

"Welcome to the land of the Brais," Amaund says.

CHAPTER TWO

COLE

They took her. Even with everything that I did to try and protect her, it wasn't enough. The sight of her being dragged away by Amaund will be burned into my memory forever. If I wasn't so tired and depleted of magic, I could have stopped them. I know I could have. Thea may have negotiated our safety before being taken, but she never should have needed to. I'm the one who turned her. It was my responsibility to keep her safe. Her absence is like a tear in my soul. Those hazel eyes I've come to love, not only because I'm her creator, but because of who she is haunts me. Will I ever see the way the green in her irises light up when the sun catches in them? Will I ever hear her subtle laugh again, or the one she lets out when she thinks no one is paying attention? I miss the pleasant shivers from her soft touch and that undeniable electric pull her presence has on me.

Now, I am only left with a horrible ache in my chest at the ghostly memories. And the resolve to do whatever it takes to bring her back.

The forest is quiet as Sarah and I use each other as a crutch to return to my cabin. We pass one of the small felt bags hung from a tree that denote the barrier's protection spell surrounding the cabin. Like walking through a spider's web, the spell's magic brushes my body like a curtain as we enter the safe haven inside. Neither of us have any words to offer the other. She lost her mother and her best friend was taken by the Brais, an enemy she has sworn to defeat. I lost an old friend, and…I'm not actually sure what to call Thea. She is so much more than just a friend. The Brais taking her fills that shattered part in my heart with a rage so wild and feral that it feels like a living, breathing beast, trying desperately to claw its way out. Even knowing that Amaund and his soldiers would have made quick work with me, I should have gone after them. If I could even catch them, that is. My legs are wobbling from exhaustion, my body aches, and nausea churns in my gut.

As we enter my silent cabin, Sarah mechanically sits on the couch, her skin stained with tears that have ceased falling. She stares at a single spot on the coffee table, her thoughts seemingly far away. Helios, Thea's cat, trots into the living area and jumps up beside her, not offering me a glance, as if he knows who is really at fault for Thea's absence. He places his chin on Sarah's leg and slowly blinks up at her. With mindless strokes, her hand moves over his russet head, her eyes still on that single spot on the table. No one would need Thea's second magical ability, her beta ability, to know what Sarah is feeling.

I rake a trembling hand through my short black hair, unable to shake the feelings of uselessness and guilt. I can't help Thea. I can't help Sarah. And Valeria…the memory of her body on the floor of Thea's childhood home haunts my mind. As does Thea's golden gaze of fury before her emotions took over. I wince as I remember how harsh I was with her reaction to what happened. She's a new vampire and was going through a tremendous amount of pain. Whether you're a human or vampire, it is hard not to be consumed by that degree of grief and anger.

I absently move into the small kitchen. Early morning light glitters across the countertop from the paneled window above the sink. I clutch the side of the cold ceramic as my head spins and tears burn in my eyes. A deep sigh wracks my body as I stare into the forest beyond the glass. The sunrise colors the clouds and tops of the trees shades of yellow, pink, and orange. It feels empty, lonely even, without Thea's presence. Her love of nature always warmed my heart. It refreshed my own adoration for the natural world.

After splashing water on my face, I fill the water dish on the counter for Helios and a glass for Sarah.

"Here," I say gently, placing the water on the coffee table. Her copper skin is discolored with smears of dirt and tear stains on her cheeks. The sight sends bolts of anger throughout my body. The glass clinks against the wood, the sound seemingly sending a jolt through her rigid body.

"Thanks," she breathes without moving.

A rain falls outside, drops pattering against the windows of the cabin. The sun is rising, fighting the clouds to brighten the world around us in its ascent. I light a fire in the stone fireplace adjacent to the couch before sitting in the armchair against the front corner of the living room. A symphony of the rain, crackling wood, and the cat's purring fill the otherwise silent room. Sarah's heartbeat adds a somber tune to the mixture.

"I'm sorry," I offer to the grieving witch. Not that condolences will put a bandage on her wounded heart. "I know that doesn't make anything better, but—"

"Thank you," she murmurs. Her chestnut brown eyes flick to mine. There is a noticeable sadness in the hues of her irises that seems to cut deep into her soul. Her fingers continue in circles on top of Helios' orange head. The cat's eyes are slitted in pleasure, his purring becoming louder.

I offer a sad smile, and we sit in silence for a while longer. The smoldering logs fight the strength of the flames. Though it will be inevitable, they resist succumbing to ash. Fire consumes. It is its nature to do so. And once the path of a wildfire is set, they can be difficult to extinguish. Like Thea.

I could only offer her a reprieve to their hostile nature. Juan, my friend and ally within the Brais, leaked so many secrets to my clan, the Essites, including their forms of "information gathering" from fellow vampires. And he paid the price for that secret, among others, with a stake through the heart.

Amaund would never have traded me for Thea. I knew that. She was his target. A strong fire user is what he wanted, not someone who can push air around. But offering my name as the person who turned her…at least that would save Thea some grief. I may have been given safety from being killed or captured at that moment, but if we encounter any Brais again, they won't be so generous. Being a defector of the Brais, the only successful one at that, is bound to catch up with me at some point.

"I—" Sarah starts. Her voice cracks. Tears well in her eyes, and Helios, as if he knew, crawls onto her lap. Sarah fixes her gaze on the soft feline as she tries to speak again. "I felt it. When they killed her." There is an unsteady movement to her hands that gently pet underneath the cat's chin. She sniffles before looking up at me. "They took my mother after she left the cabin that day. And they waited to kill her until they captured me." So that she was away from Thea and me. To inflict as much emotional trauma onto Sarah as possible, most likely. The Brais are ruthless in that regard.

"I-I was already contracted to become the next Coven leader when she stepped down." Her voice becomes a whisper, and I'm not sure if she is speaking to inform me or for herself. A storm brews outside, the sun having conceded to the clouds. Winds pick up some of the rain and pelt droplets against the glass of the windows at irregular bursts.

I lean forward in the chair, elbows on my knees. "So, the

magic that binds a Coven leader transferred to you upon her death."

Her expression is so sullen as she turns to face the fireplace that I have to resist the urge to move next to her and offer comfort. "Yeah." She exhales a long breath. "I don't even know what they did to her body." A few tears release at that, falling down her cheek and onto Helios. The cat's back twitches, but he doesn't seem to care.

I wince as I say, "Thea and I found her. She was left on the floor in Thea's parent's manor."

If it weren't for the cat on her lap, she might have jumped to her feet. Her eyes widen and she exclaims, "We need to get her!"

For the briefest moment, I contemplate withholding what Thea did from Sarah. Perhaps even to play it off as something that the Brais did. But a witch's wrath is nothing to shrug off. Best friend or not, if I lie and she finds out later how Thea handled the situation, things could get very dangerous. "Sarah," I say softly. Her sharp expression causes me to falter a bit. Telling her the truth is the best option, but deep down, I want to protect Thea from any fallout with the witches. "Thea, she…she burned the house down with Valeria inside. She was enraged and fueled by grief."

Her hands pause on top of Helios' head. Part of me wants to shoo the cat away in case the witch bursts with anger. I straighten and scoot closer to the edge of the chair. As if he sensed danger, Helios peers up at Sarah before jumping down and making his way into the kitchen. "Sarah," I say cautiously.

Her eyes sharpen and she stands abruptly. Instinctively, I follow suit, pushing the chair back with my calves. The wind from the storm outside stirs, letting me know that I can call upon it should a fight ensue. Sarah doesn't respond, only moves toward the door.

"Where are you going?"

She snaps her head to me, her eyes hiding pure rage beneath the composed expression. "I'm returning to my coven," she says curtly.

Despite her fury, I step closer, putting myself between her and the green front door. "That's understandable. Tell me though, is your anger toward Thea or the Brais?" Not the most empathetic question, but one that needed to be asked. I'll protect Thea against anything. Even her best friend.

She stares at me before answering, her face twisted into something mixed with disgust, grief, and anger. "Witches need a ceremony for our souls to pass to the ancestors." Though her voice cracks with her sadness, her rage fuels her to continue. "We can't perform it for my mother without her body." She tries to leave the house again, but I don't budge. "Move," she says through gritted teeth.

"Thea didn't know. She was grief stricken and—"

"Move, Cole. Before I make you."

I keep my eyes on hers, my attention noting any slight movement of her hands. The prickle of my magic pools in my palms. "Sarah, I just need to know you won't try and hurt Thea."

There is a storm brewing in her mind. I can tell by the subtle clenching of her fists and the sound of her teeth grinding. And the fire that burns in her piercing gaze. "She was my *mother*!" Sarah yells as tears well in her eyes again. "I don't even know if I'll be able to see her in the afterlife now." Her voice mellows to a bitter calm as she thrusts a hand into her dark hair. "And to answer your ridiculous question, no. I'm not about to set out and hurt my *best friend*, Cole. I just," she sighs, "I need to leave."

Despite the wariness, I keep my face neutral and step away from the door. A muscle feathers on her lips as if she was also fighting to hide her emotions. Neither of us say another word as she opens the door and exits.

CHAPTER THREE

THEA

The Brais and I stop in front of a large, stone mansion, Amaund's grip tight again on my arm. The building must be five or six stories high with twin spires on each end, rising far into the gray sky. In the center of the front wall is a round, stained-glass window. The symbol of a crimson flame sits as the window's focus. We walk over a lowered draw-bridge, the rusty chains attached to two separate columns. Underneath is patchy, muddy grass, not the typical moat that I would picture with this masterpiece of architecture. Decaying vines wrap around any structure they can, blocking many slender, arched windows.

Two enormous metal doors stand a hundred feet in front of us designed with intricate swirls that remind me of mist eddying around a river's bend. A guard is posted on each side, both with a sword at their hips and a long bow on their backs.

"Why do vampires need swords?" I ask no one in particular as we make our way to the grand estate. With a sidelong glance, I gaze at Amaund's lavish gold and silver weapon hilt. The scabbard is carved with elaborate symbols that resemble runes. The inky cloak on his back blows in the heavy gusts, revealing the armor beneath.

He keeps his beady, golden gaze ahead of us, not bothering to even look in my direction.

The two guards break from their posts to open the doors, which screech in the hollow halls beyond. The foyer inside could fit five of Cole's small cabins, maybe more, in each direction. It is massive.

As we enter, I hear some of the vampires stop where the guards stand, quiet conversations starting. I can't hear the words as Amaund continues to pull me forward. Gentle tingling sensations spread across the skin of my back, and I recognize it as my beta ability. Energy manipulation, Sarah called it. Like my sun immunity, this magic is another rare vampire ability. It lets me feel and see other people's auras, created by whatever emotions they harbor at that moment. I can even manipulate them to a degree if I am physically connected. During our training, this ability even enabled me to heal injured plants. I've never tried to heal a person though.

Without meaning to, my magic stretches from my back, reaching for two vampires who stayed with us as we entered the mansion. The energy of one feels stiff and closed off, reminding me of the gritty feeling of cement. The other feels smooth and warm, like the soft petals of a flower. It reminds me of Cole's inviting energy. My heart tightens at the memory. Stealing quick glances on either side of us, I notice that Mica and Alec are the two vampires I just read. The others stayed outside. It is Mica's aura that seems to call mine to mingle. Neither of them make an indication of noticing that I touched their energy.

Amaund tugs me to the left. Stone makes up the floor, ceiling, and walls here. A giant rug sits in the middle of the foyer with a few sets of soft-looking sofas, two lit fireplaces, and a long side table garnished with candelabras and dust-covered bowls. Across the room are giant windows overlooking a vast green estate. A menacing, dark forest looms far in the distance. Tainted, most likely, by the constant proximity of the Brais. I look up to see an extraordinary candle-lit chandelier hanging from the tall, vaulted ceiling.

My arm is released, though I can still feel the unpleasant remnants of his grip.

"Follow me," Amaund says as he takes a turn down a corridor. Mica's and Alec's energy gets farther and farther away. The different sensations of each, like unique fingerprints, is engraved in my mind.

I shuffle behind him as we walk down a dim, wide hall lit by tall white candles in holders. Wax has long since dripped on the floor and down the wall underneath the sconces. We pass countless rooms, many of which are devoid of furniture. One room appears to have been for dining because a large wooden table is in the center. Chairs sit all along the sides with a throne at the head. Some people—vampires—sit in the chairs, conversing amongst themselves. They watch as we pass the double wide doorway. Amaund gives them none of his attention.

At the end of the hall is a guard in golden armor, his posture stiffening as we approach. He stands in front of a massive set of closed doors. Amaund doesn't acknowledge the guard as we take another left. Another hallway. This one is narrower with a red runner along the floor. Slim windows are cut along the stone walls, too thin to be able to look out while walking at his pace. The sound of Amaund's armor clinks in the silence, masking the beat of my erratic heart. With all the stories that Sarah and Cole told me, meeting the fearsome Commander of the Brais is low on my list of things I would like to do, and the more we walk, the faster my nervous heart drums.

I stare at the back of my captor's cape, wondering if my

magic could penetrate his gear. Not that I would get far afterward, I think. Around every corner there appears to be a guard. Their watchful eyes follow us as we walk by. Even if I did make it outside, there is no way that I could find the path back home. I don't even know where that portal took me, or how to operate it.

I follow Amaund as we ascend a few flights of stairs. So far, I can recall the turns and patters of the corridors. After what I think is the fifth floor, we make all sorts of twists and turns, and I wonder if it is to confuse me, or if the layout of this old castle is just this much of a maze.

Finally, Amaund stops at a wooden door. It is curved at the top with large metal bolts protruding from its middle. The symbol of a shield—identical to the one painted on my window at home—is carved into the arch. It has three points at the top that meet in a single point at the bottom, a large "B" in the center. I scoff at the medievalesque qualities of the door alone. This entire building has never left the Middle Ages.

His fist pounds on the door before moving to unlock it. As it opens, a dimly lit, plain room is revealed. To the right is a wooden table with a stack of books and papers atop it.

"I see you have returned," a deep, gruff voice calls from the other side of the room, sending shivers of fear down my spine.

"I have," Amaund says as he takes a step to the side, revealing the rest of the room to me. And who stands beyond. "And with what I have promised."

My lips part as I watch whom I can only assume is the Commander of the Brais stand from a lavish desk. He is tall, like my captor, though bulkier. He dons a mostly black set of armor, a small golden Brais crest in the middle of his chest. A night-colored cloak flows behind him. Slowly, he makes his way over to me, studying with each step. I can't help but hold my breath as he approaches. His brown, shoulder-length hair is pulled back at the front. A thin line of facial hair trails from under his ears to his chin. Eyes, black like an abyss, pierce mine, causing me to instinctively want to lower my head. I don't, though. Instead, I stand firm, keeping my gaze matched with his.

He stops a few feet in front of me, and I hope he can't hear my heart pounding against my ribcage. Hopeful thinking. I know he can hear it because he's a vampire. I half expect him to strike me for not diverting my gaze. Instead, he just continues to stare.

"It is finally nice to meet the vampire who caused such a stir with her Unlocking," he says, teeth as white as a star. His tanned skin is flawless, a face sculpted into perfection.

I definitely cannot say the same about him as I still force my eyes to hold his.

A smile tugs at his lips. "I am Commander Kael."

I clench my jaw, partly to keep from spewing a retort that surely will not end well for me, and partly because I don't want to speak. A sliver of fear slips through that suddenly quiet cage in my mind, coating my tongue like ash. I think back to how I could smell Cole's fear in my family's manor. Can Kael smell mine in this moment too?

Kael's grin widens, confirming my suspicion. He glances back to Amaund who still stands to my side. The features on his face soften momentarily as he does so. A gesture that reminds me of the picture of my parents on their anniversary that sat on the fireplace mantle. In the house that I destroyed. I grit my teeth tighter.

"Well, Thea," Kael says, his words dragging me out of the shambled memory of my childhood home. "In anticipation of bringing you home, I have handpicked a generous gift for you."

Like a roaring waterfall, anger replaces the fear. Ash

turning to acid. "This is *not* my home." My nails dig into my palms as I squeeze my fingers into a tight fist. A subtle heat pools underneath my skin along my arms.

"We'll see," Kael replies without a breath. He takes a step back and walks around the inside corner of the room. A door opens and closes, then two sets of feet scuffle on the floor. One, a confident step, while the other sounds like dragging a bag of rocks.

A young woman walks in front of the Brais Commander. Her frail body shakes with terror, her clothes caked in dirt, eyes rimmed with tears. The aroma of soiled garments mixes with the spicy scent of a human's fear. Kael places his hands on her shoulder and pushes her along, stopping her just short of me.

The smell of her savory fear and the sound of her heart-beat awakens my drained body, messing with my clarity. My pulse quickens as my teeth elongate on their own, driven by that gnawing discomfort of hunger. I haven't fed in so long. Not since Cole's house… after Valeria… No. I can't think of that right now. Can't think of Sarah, Cole, Valeria, or Helios. *Helios*. My poor cat has never been separated from me since I found him.

"Come, Thea. Drink. You must be starving." Kael grins smugly as he takes a step back.

An understatement. It feels as though my veins are full of sand, clinging on to what little nutrients are left. I used so much of my magic when fighting Amaund, it left me exhausted and on edge. I rip my gaze from the woman's watery caramel eyes. "Until when?" I ask, my voice trembling.

"Until there is nothing left." His tone is full of concern, a trait that doesn't seem to fit him. The emotion almost feels forced with his stiff facial expression.

"But she'll die," I breath.

His expression doesn't change. "You are weakened, and we wouldn't want you to fall ill. Drink until she is dead."

I look back to the woman. Her face has paled and the water in her eyes falls freely down her cheeks now. The sound of her heart sings in my ears, a siren's call to the lone sailor—captivating. It draws that hunger out of me, as if it were its own entity. Peering into her eyes, I see her humanity, and I *feel* it. The fragility of a human life. I could do as he says and drink from her. I could kill her. My body tries to push for me to do just that, but I fight it, remaining still, despite the sudden rush of nausea. I don't just see this brown-eyed stranger in front of me. I see myself, a month ago. I see Sarah, my parents.

The Brais have no regard for human life. From the stories I have heard, they kill with no remorse, no laws. They would kill all humans if they didn't need them to live.

Not me.

I press my eyes closed and take a deep, steadying breath. My body loosens as I do so, less eager to prey upon the poor woman. "No," I whisper.

Kael's face hardens and the hand that grips his sword hilt turns white. "No?" He takes a step forward, and despite the slight trembling, I lift my chin. "Drink from this human until she is dead. Or you will be instead. You will not get another chance."

There are no second chances with us.

I've heard it three times now by various Brais vampires.

The assuredness of my decision does not falter. I straighten my posture just a little, keeping my gaze on Kael. "Sounds like I'll see you in Hell," I say again, pride flooding my thoughts.

The temperature in the room rises a little as Kael's nostrils flare with fury. He closes his eyes, as if taking a moment to think of his next move. When they open, I flinch. Pure rage, red as burning coal, blazes in the irises. His annoyance is palpable, a furnace radiating from his body. In a blur of movement, he unsheathes his sword and twists the woman before plunging his weapon into her gut.

All my unwavering pride vanishes as I watch her cry out in pain and collapse onto the ground, writhing in agony. I hold a shaking hand in front of my stomach, conflicted with the feeling of hunger as I stare at the blood pouring out of her wound and the shock of what he has done. The grief for this poor human who stood no chance.

"She will die slowly and painfully because of your decision," Kael hisses. "And you will stand there and watch." He walks by me, and my breath hitches though my eyes never leave the woman's. He speaks, not to me, but to Amaund who still stands behind me. "Thea can be led to her chamber when the human is dead. Snap her neck if she moves." The sound of the door slamming closed is all I hear afterward.

Blood spills out of her mouth, creating a trail that runs down the side of her chin. Her eyes are locked on mine, pleading for help. I could, with my blood, but there would be the risk of turning her into a vampire if she loses too much of her human blood first. There is also the threat of Amaund behind me. A faint warmth spreads into my palms. Not the sensation of my fire magic, but that of my beta ability. The energy manipulation that I've used over and over at Cole's cabin to heal dying—and dead—plants. The magical warmth itches to reach for the dying woman. As weak as it is, it doesn't reach my fingertips, simmering out like a mist caught in the wind. Would my beta ability allow me to heal her? Surely if I could heal a plant, I could heal anything, right? But if that were the case, why didn't Sarah or Cole ever mention anything while we were training?

Fear roots me in place. Fear, regret, and sorrow. Feeding on her until she died now seems like a kindness compared to slowly watching her bleed out. At least if I complied with Kael, her blood loss might be numbing. Maybe it would make her pass out before she died.

I stand for what feels like an eternity, watching as the life leaves her body. Brown eyes glaze over and stop looking, her body unmoving. Only then do I close my eyes. I let the sound of the churning storm outside be my anger, the drops of rain my tears. Here, I will show them no emotion.

CHAPTER FOUR

SARAH

Smoke fills the small alcove set in the darkened corner of the ritual space of my home. The light of a single flickering candle holds steady, illuminating the cloth-covered altar. A dried mixture of mugwort and bay leaves are scattered on a slate of smooth obsidian crystal, their aroma overpowered by that of the burning lavender. Her favorite plant to work with.

My mother enjoyed the softness of lavender leaves, the small blueish flowers, and the incredible calming scent. She loved when I wove the petals into my hair, having done the same when she was younger, she told me once. She'll never get to touch the silkiness of the silvery leaves again, or smile at the tall stalk of flowers, or breathe in their unique scent.

"Please, mother. Help me now." I bow my head at the photo of her resting against the wall. She never received a proper passing ritual. I don't even know if she can hear me.

But how do I move forward? The foundation of my life has crumbled. That which held my roots. I feel like I am spinning out of control into an endless darkness just waiting to engulf me.

The only other person alive who knows me as well as my mom did was taken. Thea isn't even a human anymore. The wound of Thea dying and being turned into a vampire hasn't even healed in my mind yet. I don't know if it ever will.

I want to be angry with her. For everything. For moving away after graduation, for not coming out with me on my birthday and getting into that car accident. For becoming one of my coven's greatest enemies. For my mother.

But I just can't. There is a gnawing anger inside of me, and I can't place any of it on my best friend. In all of this, she is a victim.

Instead, my fury settles with the vampires. The Brais. The Essites. My coven made a mistake hundreds of years ago with the first vampire. From that failure stemmed the deadly feud between species. And because of that, the strongest Demoix witch was killed. If our ancestors took care of things then, we would never have been cursed, and there would never have been a war. There wouldn't be any vampires. My hands grip the herbs so hard that they snap.

"You're thinking about it again, aren't you?" a soft voice says from my left, pulling me back into the present. "You're thinking about the past?"

I close my tired eyes for a moment and inhale the lavender. When I open my lids, the smoke from the herb slithers across the picture of my mom, blocking me from her smiling gaze. I sigh and look to my side. "Yes." Untouched by the light of the candle, my companion is shrouded in darkness. Her gleaming azure blue irises are all I see.

"Maybe something in the past is the answer you were seeking." Amelia's soft hand lands comfortably in mine.

"Maybe," I respond through a long breath. The weight of the ancient Demoix grimoire pushes against my leg. I don't know why I brought it down here with me. Perhaps because I came to honor my mother, and it was hers before it became mine. I've seen her write entries inside its crinkly pages, but I have yet to find anything that looks like her handwriting.

It is said that every coven leader leaves a piece of themselves in the bindings of this tome. But it doesn't feel like her. I can't feel the loving warmth that was my mother when I touch it or meditate with it. And I know that as much as she disliked vampires, she wouldn't condone the spells inside this book on how to deal with them.

I reach over and grab the book that sits on the floor to my right and open randomly to a page near the center.

"What does it say you have to do?" She squeezes my hand, probably because she has a feeling what the ancient tome says.

The candle on the altar begins to dance as I flip the pages. I have to be careful with how I speak about this topic. One wrong thought and the curse that binds us into silence will activate. The ghost of the curse's icy claws on my neck tingle as if it is just waiting for me to let it run wild. "To destroy our enemy, we have to first find the souls tethered to theirs."

CHAPTER FIVE

THEA

Three days.

Three, excruciatingly long days I have been stuck in this minuscule room that Amaund had led me to. No blood, no contact with anyone else. Only a tiny window that looks out to the forest far below. Day one was the worst. Hunger pangs ravaged my insides, and I was so furious that I punched a hole through the analog clock that hung on the wall. The bare, stone room is only large enough for a bed and a small night-stand, and to my credit, they still sit in one piece.

Now, I lie on the small bed, unable to move even my toes. With every movement my stomach roils with hunger, spiking my emotions. I have barely slept, and when I manage to fall asleep, it is a restless sleep, waking constantly in a cold sweat. Every possible reason that they have left me in here haunts my thoughts and dreams. Maybe Kael will be the first Brais to stay true to his word of giving me only one chance. Perhaps they never planned to do anything with me, furious that I caused so much trouble with my…what did Kael call it? My Unlocking. I think back to all the vampires who Cole and I killed after

Amaund made his move. Maybe they just plan to let me rot away in here.

In the silence, I close my eyes and picture Cole's kind, smokey eyes and gentle smile. The beautiful, silky color of his obsidian hair. I think about the short amount of time we spent together and how I grew so close to him. The lesson of controlling our emotions have me locking them back up in that cage I keep hidden deep within myself. *Our senses are heightened, our emotions stronger. They can be glorious, or they can be debilitating,* he said once.

And then I see Sarah. Not a single word was said between us when we saw each other last in the woods beyond Cole's cabin. Valeria…I couldn't tell her about her mother. Grief's icy cold nails creep into my heart.

"No," I mutter to myself, shoving it far, far down and wince as I roll over on the rock-hard bed. This is not the place for emotions like that. A place where I am alone. A few spots on the stone wall are covered in poorly spread plaster.

The second day of being locked in here, I kept an ear pressed to the door in hopes to hear something beyond this prison cell of a room. The only light inside comes from the narrow window. During the evening, I am mostly in the dark, as the sun sets on the other side of the castle.

A knock on the door has my body jolting upright, the bed beneath creaking. The remnants of my flames sizzle in my palms, like an ember compared to the firestorm it used to be. What it would be again if I drank from that human.

The door opens without invitation, and the vampire who stands in the entrance smiles pleasantly at me. Her cherry black hair falls in waves slightly past her shoulders. The color reminds me of my father's hair, and the silly childish tantrums I threw at not inheriting it. "Sorry for startling you," she says kindly. "I'm Morwen." She shuffles another couple of steps into the room, filling the space with an oddly comforting energy. She wears a semi-wrinkled, white dress shirt underneath a black vest and matching pants. I blink at this vampire who looks like she would be more comfortable in a library than here in this evil castle.

I clench my jaw and give her a curt nod, biting back a wince from what feels like tiny shards of glass stabbing at my skin. I don't trust the Brais in this castle, and I don't want to have a conversation with any of them either. Though Morwen looks like a polite librarian, something inside me wants to shrink away from her. Something deep and primal hidden within my body wants to slide onto the floor on my knees and beg for life. Her gaze is soft but being in her presence is like peering into Kael's furious eyes. Though, I'm sure I would have similar reactions to any Brais who walked in here with how weak I feel.

Morwen smiles, dimples forming at the corners of her lips. "I'm going to be your mentor," she says warmly, offering a hand.

I furrow my brows, my stomach rumbling in the quiet of the room. My mentor? What would I need mentoring for? My stomach churns again, though this time has nothing to do with how ravished I am.

"Don't worry, I brought a little bit of blood," she reassures, her voice lowering.

As if it had a mind of its own, my body turns off the bed and stands. If I weren't so hungry, I might have moved faster. That little movement makes my limbs shake from overuse. They feel like sandpaper surrounded by a pool of sludge, slow and uncomfortable.

Morwen pulls out a blood bag from the pocket of her vest. It is mostly empty, the sides caving in. "It's only a little bit," she adds with a frown as I reach for it. More words spill from her mouth, but I don't catch them.

I greedily snatch the bag from her hands and drain what

little is left. The roughness in my throat mostly subsides and the shaking in my body stops. There were only a few gulps inside but enough for me to be able to stand without feeling like a stone statue ready to crumble. I squeeze the bag, taking in the last drops.

Morwen nods. "I could only bring you that much. The Commander would be furious if he knew you had any at all." She shivers in a stiff movement.

I don't say anything as I hand her the remnants. Our hands touch in the exchange, and I feel a familial warmth wash over me. A sensation that has the rest of my prickly nerves calming. She doesn't seem to notice, and hands the bag to one of the two guards who is stationed outside my door. A waste of their resources, really. As if I could have escaped these past few days. I was too weak with hunger to even move on the bed.

Morwen gestures for me to follow her into the hall. Her scent fills my nose, citrus and cherry blossoms. My energy manipulation stirs. It reaches toward her and is met with a beautiful display of swirling blues around her body. The colors lull me into a peaceful calm.

We walk in silence until turning a corner at the end of the long hallway. Candles provide the dark corridors with light, and I wonder who keeps them all lit. "Am I being taken to the King?" I ask nervously, noting that this is not the way to Kael's study.

"So, she does have a voice," she answers, a mischievous smile on her lips. She shakes her head. "No, to Commander Kael." Her grin widens. "But first, a detour."

I let out a shaky breath the moment she says I won't be meeting the King.

"Do you want to see the King?" she inquires.

"No," I respond immediately. I'd rather not be here at all. Though, curiosity tugs at my thoughts. Cole once mentioned that the King is a shadow and that no one knows what he looks like. The idea is so strange to me. "Have you ever seen him?" I look sidelong at Morwen as our pace slows.

We stop at a double, stained-glass door. "The King doesn't typically get involved with those of lower power." She twists the knobs and pushes the gilded doors open.

Here, in this castle, there are shadows of death lurking in every corner, but when she opens the doors, all thoughts of calamity scurry from my mind.

My mouth drops at the expansive room that could be its own sort of mansion. The stone walls are lined with shelves containing mostly books. Smaller wooden bookcases are scattered throughout the room, holding both books and time-worn artifacts. Several antique tables sit in the front, collecting dust. In the center of the room sits a large spherical sun dial, the gnomon in the shape of a sword and its stone tip pointing toward the windowed dome ceiling. Four silvered chandeliers hang from the four corners of the room, candles flickering vigorously in their holders. Slate-colored clouds cover the sky, visible through the dome, and rain pelts the glass.

"This is incredible," I say, my hand itching to trace the numerous spines of the library's contents. The comforting aroma of old books fill my nose, and I wonder just how old each of these tomes are.

Morwen's red-painted lips curve upward. "This is my favorite room in the castle." She steps inside, and I follow her down the few carpet-lined steps. "I could get lost inside books for all of eternity," she adds quietly, her fingertips grazing a dusty stack on a mahogany side table. Next to it, flames dance on a grey candelabra, the color reminding me of Cole's eyes.

"It would take an eternity to read them all," I muse, mostly to myself. Like Morwen, I have always found a haven in reading. I once dreamed of writing and illustrating children's books, creating works that wove the mysteries of nature into story.

"You could, you know." Morwen's green gaze holds mine

in a playful and inquisitive way. There is an endless depth to her eyes, like peering into murky waters. At first glance, the water seems inviting, but a darkness sits deep below the surface, watching. Something with claws or sharp teeth that might reach out and pull you under. It reminds me of looking into my own reflection lately. There has been a darkness swimming in my own soul, born long ago but only recently awoken.

I look away. Is that why she is giving me a tour? Showing me all the pleasant things the Brais has to offer in hopes of changing my mind about them? Maybe Cole's assumption that the Essites are losing the war wasn't the right assessment. Perhaps it's the Brais who are losing, and they are getting desperate.

My fingers dance along the dusty cover of an old book. I brush away the layer of dirt with my sleeve. Not a book that I have read before, or even heard of. There are most likely hundreds, even thousands, in here that I have never known existed. The thought of scouring through each shelf excites the bookworm inside of me.

Could there be books in this library that I have read or heard of? Or maybe there are texts describing the supernatural world? Perhaps something that delves into the vampires and other species. Would they keep information on the Brais in here? Surely, only members of the Brais are allowed in this castle, so would they deem this room safe to keep documents?

A dangerous thought crosses my mind then. Like a heroine from a story, could I remain an Essite and appear to be a Brais? Perhaps it will make my stay more pleasant if I'm more agreeable. I have absolutely zero skills in espionage, but the opportunity might be too good to pass. Cole's friend, Mr. Esposito, did it. I shove the memory of my favorite college professor lying on the floor in my childhood basement. A stake through his heart.

But the only way to join with them is to do as Kael commands and kill a human. Nausea rises in my throat at the horrendous possibility of it. The necessity of it if I were to follow through with this plan to be a spy. For me, blood bags are a more suitable way to feed. At least I'm not harming anyone while I drink.

Whether I want it or not, I have been forced into this war between the Essites and the Brais. Gathering information on the Brais and delivering it to the Essites might aid the latter in the end.

After the library, Morwen showed me the immense training and weapons rooms. I hardly paid any attention, my mind still caught up in the emerging idea. She told me that there are feeding rooms within the castle, though with a sympathetic frown, didn't mention where they were. She did, however, promise to take me there when I am fully a Brais. She seems to have no doubt that I will accept Kael's human offer next time. That I will accept becoming a bloodthirsty Brais.

Morwen was planning to bring me to Kael, but on our way there we are stopped by a frantic short, blond-haired vampire. He acknowledges Morwen only, like my presence is a mere stain on his vision. After handing Morwen a scroll, she frowns at whatever news is written upon it. She nods him a thanks and we change our direction to my chamber. She won't tell me what the scroll said.

"I'll come back for you," Morwen says to me as she opens the door to my dreary room. "The Commander is busy right now." There is a subtle bite to her words. Just then, that deeply rooted instinct to flee from her comes crashing back with a quickening pulse. Maybe the fear isn't of her at all but stems from this small room. Should someone try to attack me here, especially being this weak, there is no way that I could defend myself well. The window is so small, only my arms could fit through. The door is the only entrance and exit. I'm trapped.

Trapped, alone, in a maze of a castle with powerful enemies.

I can only nod at her goodbye, my voice suddenly taken away. Only when she closes the door does that breath I was holding get released.

The reprieve from exhaustion I got from that small amount of blood she gifted me has faded, leaving me shaky and feeling sick. Moving incites nausea. With limbs like trembling rocks, I crawl on top of the bed and curl into a ball with my back pressing against the cold wall. The room has darkened with the setting sun. I wish I could feel its warmth on my skin, in my cells. I wish I could see Cole's smile, feel his touch. I wish I could hear Sarah's laugh, smell her lavender scent.

Sleep comes quickly.

A DEEP COBALT *sky stretches far in each direction. Veridian grasses and vibrant goldenrods tickle my arms. I furrow my brow and sit up. It's a field so expansive, I can't see where it ends. The warmth of the earth beneath me seeps into my body, and I feel myself melding with it. The bright sun shines on my skin, though I can't feel it. Sounds of cicadas singing underneath the sunlight fill every corner. This place is…pure peace.*

I close my eyes and take in a deep breath of the wilderness, untouched by anything other than nature herself. Only a few places within my journeys have come close to this beauty.

"Am I dreaming?" I ask aloud. The ghost of the sunlight answers. I raise my arm into the light of the day, frowning at the lack of warmth. Not even my energy manipulation has come here with me. Wherever here is.

It is like I am a human again.

"The happiest dream I've ever been in," drawls a familiar voice from behind.

Shivers, not from the cool breeze, skitter along my skin at the sound of that velvet voice. I turn, squinting because of the sun, and lift a hand to block the light. The silhouette of a person stands ten feet away. Without even being able to see—without even hearing his voice, I would know who it is. "Cole," I rasp. The sight of his entrancing smokey eyes and dark hair make my knees wobble. As does his muscular arms and chest underneath that black t-shirt. We both move to hold each other in a joyous reunion. Here, in this sanctuary, I am not plagued with the exhaustion of hunger.

We wrap our arms around each other, fitting together like two trees who grew alongside one another. His chin presses against the top of my head. When we pull away, my vision is blurry.

Cole brushes an escaped tear that runs down my cheek with his thumb.

I lean into his touch but frown. "I can't feel you." I realize then that I also can't smell his comforting scent of cedar. "Is this real?" I ask, again hoping that it is. In this moment, I don't want to consider that this is a dream, or worse, a hallucination. In this moment, I just want to hold Cole and feel this deep relief and happiness. A reprieve from the torment of my seemingly unending hunger.

His hand moves under my chin as if he were trying to tilt it upward. Even though there is no sensation of his touch, my head moves so that we are peering into each other's eyes. His grey ones are swirling like the morning mists over a serene pond. "It is. I'm here."

Despite trying to hold them back, more tears fall. Tears for both happiness of seeing Cole and the despair and loneliness that I have felt over the past few days. We kneel into the soft grass, our knees touching. Cole's hands are still on each of my cheeks. "How?" I ask with a shaky voice.

He searches my face, as if he can sense all the heavy emotions that have been plaguing me. "Sarah and I linked our magic. She was able to cast a spell that strengthened the reach on my psychic magic." His beta ability. A powerful ability that he has honed to be even stronger than most with the same gift. "It helped me get into your dreams." He brushes another tear away. "I told you that you will never have to be alone."

The words he said to me back at his cabin when I was ready to march by myself to my parent's manor. When Sarah and Valeria were taken by Amaund. We sit in silence for a few minutes, listening to the steady drum of each other's heartbeats. I didn't realize the sound of his was something that I missed so much. Despite not being able to feel his touch, those tendrils of electricity dance between us with hope.

"How are Sarah and Helios?" I ask finally, twirling a finger in a bent blade of grass.

He smiles gently. "Helios is all right. He meows a lot for you."

I'm glad he is safe. The little furball seemed to enjoy Cole's company. Though I miss him terribly, he's in good hands.

"Sarah is hanging in there," he continues, his smile faltering. My heart lurches at its absence and the reason why it wavers. "She is grieving, and she's extremely pissed."

"I would hate to be the Brais right now," I say, though the moment the words leave my lips, I remember that I'm currently in their midst. Perhaps this could work in our favor. An alliance between the Essites and Sarah's coven could prove to be a strong force against the King and his Brais.

Cole let's out a breath. "She has taken her mother's position as the leader of the Minuit Coven, and she's using all the power she has to find you and destroy the Brais. We both are." An ache pulls at my heart from their unending love. "We will take an army to them if we have to." He scrunches his face in contemplation. "Where did Amaund take you?"

I shake my head and hold his hands in mine. "No. I don't want you two to do anything for me. I'll figure a way out myself." I wish they wouldn't get involved with the war. It is far too dangerous living amongst the strongest of Brais. Morwen didn't say that the King lived at the castle, though she never said he didn't either. But still…if they attacked the castle, it would be suicide for the two of them.

"Thea, we aren't leaving you there. I am not leaving you there. And I know Sarah feels the same way." His voice is soft but firm. A bobolink, one of my favorite birds, flitters between the tall grasses, the white crown atop of its head a contrast to its black body and surrounding green vegetation. The sound of the bird's wings filter through our silence.

I look down at our intertwined fingers, wishing that I could live in this dream forever. "I did this to save you two." The words are almost a whisper, a plea for him to reconsider. "Don't let that be in vain."

"And you saved us, Thea. You did." His thumb brushes over the top of my hand. I focus on the touch but become frustrated that I still can't feel him. "You saved us, but who saves you?"

I look at him and see such a fierce determination in his smokey eyes, like a summer storm that is churning to create a hurricane. I know that there is no chance of taming that storm. Whatever I say, Cole will not change his mind about getting me out of the clutches of the Brais. And knowing Sarah, she has the same feelings.

"I save me." I let out a long breath. "I'll keep you updated." One of the first things I should do is to figure out if the King is actually here, and who he is. If the King likes to live shrouded in mystery, I'll uncover his veil. The Essites can do what they want with that information once I get it. If he is in this castle, then I'll have to be stealthy. I don't know much about the King's powers, but the things I do, I only know from the terrifying stories I've heard. Like how he killed the King of the Essites in a matter of seconds. If Cole and Sarah knew what my exact plan was, they would storm the castle immediately to get me out.

I barely finished the sentence before Cole's expression turns into a frown. To his credit, though, he doesn't say no. "If the King is there, you have to figure a way to get out." He runs a hand through his black hair, his fingers drumming lightly on my palm.

"Don't worry about me."

Cole watches me with a piercing gaze, a light wind brushing a lock of his hair onto his cheek. "Then know that the Brais King is a shadow. It is believed he is able to blend with them and even wield flames of their likeness."

I blink at him, wholeheartedly expecting him to say I should just remain somewhere secluded from the rest of the vampires and blend in until I can escape. Or be freed. "Okay. I'll let you know if he's here." I chew on my bottom lip, my mind churning. Cole watches me, his eyes darkening. "Had Mr. Esposito ever been able to pinpoint the King's location before?" The fire loving professor was a kind soul. I had no idea that my favorite teacher was a vampire. Not until I saw the stake in his heart and his sharp fangs.

He drags his gaze back up to my eyes in what appeared to have been a hard task. "No. Which is why doing this alone is a bad idea."

I squeeze his hands. "Trust me." If the King is there, then my plan of infiltration becomes more dangerous. It also becomes more important. To be able to identify the King would help us in the war against the Brais.

"I'd rather you trust me, Thea." There is a small amount of fear in his words. I can hear it in his tone, smell it in the wind. It is like his emotion seeps into the cracks of this dream. The scent of a human's fear is spicy, tantalizing. A vampire's is acrid.

The goldenrods bend in the light breeze, almost bowing toward the two of us. "Cole, I will do whatever it takes to stop the Brais. Especially if it helps protect those I care for."

He lets out a defeated breath. "I don't like that you are putting your-self in this position, but I will respect your decisions." He squeezes my hands in his.

I reign in the wince at his trust. For not divulging my plan to its entirety. The words almost spill out, but I keep them in. The unsaid truth tastes like ash on my tongue. "Thank you," I say with a gentle smile.

Cole stares at me for a moment before he gets to his feet and helps me to mine. Dirt and grass stick to our knees. "Just do me a favor and be care-ful. If something doesn't seem right, stay away. Survival is a must, okay?"

I nod and wipe the dirt from my pants, not that it matters since this is a dream. "Deal. Don't tell Sarah, please, or she'll do something rash."

He scratches the stubble of facial hair along his jaw. "Have they hurt you?"

"I'm fine." I watch him close his eyes, his chest rising with a deep inhale. The air vibrates around us, and the grass bends away as if there was a wind originating from where we stand. "What are you doing?"

He takes more deep breaths, his nostrils flaring with each one. After a few moments of silence, the light wind snaps back toward us as if it were an extension of him returning to his body. His eyes open and round as he grimaces. "You're in a castle."

I frown, needing to wake up before he can figure out more. "Stop."

He rubs a hand over his face, the light jagged line of a scar I've never noticed before runs from his ring finger to his wrist. "It just got a lot harder to get to you if you went through a portal."

I keep silent, willing myself awake. A gust of wind blows around us as the birds sing and dance, unaware of our tense conversation. I take a step away from Cole as he closes his eyes again. I need to get out of here. A prickly sensation washes over my body, and I notice that my skin is turning transparent.

"That castle sits in a pocket dimension." Cole opens his eyes. Fear crosses his expression before concern takes over. "Thea!"

CHAPTER SIX

THEA

I wake up on that too-small bed in that too-small room, my body still aching all over. Early morning sun shines through the narrow window, illuminating the cramped space.

Despite Cole saying that he trusted me, he searched for my location anyway. I just hope that I severed that connection before he figured more out. *That castle sits in a pocket dimension.* It may have been a clue for him, but it was a clue for me too. Hopefully the library has the information I need about both this dimension and the King. Then somehow, I'll relay that information to the Essites.

I take a deep breath, wincing at the sharp pain in my chest. I know what I must do in order to take that first step as a spy for the Essites. Follow Kael's command. My heart thunders in my chest at the thought of it. If I kill a human, I'm terrified of what will happen afterward. I can still remember the intoxicating taste of fresh blood when Cole and I fed on those hikers a month and a half ago. Luckily, I had someone who valued human life as a teacher. Stuck in this dreaded castle, will I become like the Brais? Vicious and heartless toward mortal life? If I don't feed, then I can't become a monster, and countless humans might stay alive because of it. But how would that affect the war? If the Brais win, how many human lives will be lost then? How much of the world that I love would be destroyed?

My mind drifts to that last place I sat and created art with. The moss-covered scenic beauty of the old forest. What would I be doing if I never returned home that day? Or if I went with Sarah to the bar? The most pressing thing in my life would probably be where my next adventure would be.

The wooden door opens and Morwen pokes her head into the room. "I wasn't sure if you were awake," she says softly.

I don't move or respond, too tired to do either. It feels as though the planet's gravity is pulling too hard on my body.

"The Commander is ready to see you again." Her hair falls over her slender shoulders in loose waves.

I swallow and wince at my dry throat. "Why do you follow him?"

Her brows pinch together and she blinks, taken aback by the question. She shrugs it off as she gently closes the door. "The Brais is all I've ever known. Honestly, my life before was a nightmare. I found sanctuary with them." She glances out the window, as if searching for her past.

A pang of sympathy crosses my heart for her, and I want to ask more, but feel it is too invading. Anger bubbles up in my chest instead. Anger directed at the Brais. To her, the Brais might be a haven, but after everything that I have witnessed or heard, I could never find that in them. If Morwen truly saw how they lived, I wonder if she would stay. Or maybe she knows exactly how they live and is with them because of it.

Slowly I sit up on the bed. With each shaky movement, it feels like my body is engulfed in a flame that isn't mine. "Lead the way," I say, biting back the soreness of my tired limbs. Show no weakness. Not to anyone. Even if they expect it.

Morwen nods, the ghost of a smile lighting her face. I follow her slowly back to the chamber where Kael waits, barely noticing anything on the way.

Standing at that arched wooden door, I swallow my nerves and exhaustion and force a straight posture. Her knock echoes down each end of the dimly lit corridor, illuminated by the flicker of various taper candles. I hear a mechanical lock releasing and the door swings open.

Still clad in that armor, Kael stands by the window next to the long desk, his arms crossed. He hardly glances at us as we enter, his attention on a piece of rolled paper. I shuffle on my feet, trying to stand without wobbling too much. Kael glowers at me as he finally turns his head.

"Good afternoon, Morwen. Thea." He nods at us both. I look behind my shoulder and see Morwen lean against the wall by the door, her arms crossed at her chest. "How are you feeling, Thea?" Kael stares at me, his hand on the hilt of his sword. It seems his pleasantries are forced.

I grit my teeth. No sense in lying about what he'll be able to hear, especially if I need to do this in order to survive. My stomach roils in an uncomfortable mixture of hunger and nausea. "Hungry," I respond, scanning the room. There is no sign of the senseless murder three days ago, not even a trace of scent. Outside, a steady rain blankets the glass windows. Most of the time, I have realized, it is raining here.

To this, he smiles. Not a warm smile, but a vicious one. As if he would love nothing more than to see me give in to the hunger that churns so wildly inside. "Let us fix that, then." He looks to his right, around the corner of the inside wall that I cannot see beyond. He nods once and lets his hands fall to his sides, one resting on the hilt of his ominous sword.

A young man rounds the corner, his movements stiff and forced, reminding me of that male hiker I drank from at Cole's house. The pain that came from drinking his blood. The nausea…the hunger in my stomach subsides, replaced with a heaviness. Like the woman before him, his clothes are dirty and torn. Dried blood cakes his neck and red shirt. This man has been fed from before. And by the stains, it looks like more than once. Anger blurs at the edges of my vision.

"Smell that sweet iron in his blood, the salt on his skin. Aren't you starving?" Kael says in a way that reminds me of a cartoon character's moral conscious sitting on their shoulder. In Kael's case, I don't think it will ever be anything other than wicked advice. He watches me as the male continues before stopping a few feet away.

Images flood my mind of the woman bleeding out on the floor. The room spins underneath my feet. The piquant aroma of his fear tingles my nose, igniting the hunger that roars inside me. I know what he expects of me but…

"Why do you need me to do this? What does this prove?" I keep my face neutral, not giving any hint of my racing thoughts.

Kael's eyes narrow into slits and slide toward Morwen who still stands behind me. If he could shoot fire from his eyes, I think he would do that right now. "Drink until he is dead," he orders coldly, ignoring my questions.

The scent of the man's fear pulls me from Kael's murderous gaze. I'm either a fool or an idiot for challenging him like that. Both most likely.

The pulse in his neck quickens under my stare, and I feel my teeth sharpen, dagger-like points rest on my lower lips.

My eyes shift as well, brightening the room around me. I can see the mess of Kael's desk in the back covered in many papers and books. A sword, daggers, and crossbow hang from the wall that was shrouded in darkness before. I clench my hands tighter, drawing blood from my palm. Kael smirks behind the man before taking a step forward. He leans into my ear, his voice grating as he says, "Do not let that foolish human mindset you cling to win." I scowl as he steps back, his hand returning to the hilt of his sword, a triumphant smile breaks his usual glower.

Astounding as it is, the hunger inside of me recoils at his words, lessening to a point that it is not so painful anymore. At least my hunger and anger can agree on one thing: we dislike Kael more than we want to feed on a human. The victorious look on Kael's face slowly fades as my vampiric features recede. The fury from before creeps back into his expression.

I call upon all the power that still resides within me. A blade to the gut is a horrible way to die. Knowing how the humans I have fed on winced and shook under my grip, being drained of blood by a vampire can't be that painless either. The idea that rushes through my brain should startle me, but it doesn't. This man before me will die in this room, but at least if I'm the one to do it, I can be merciful. I'm not sure which is worse, entertaining the idea of killing this man or that I had no reaction to conjuring it up. One more look at Kael's gloating face makes me move. I know I should be doing as Kael says in order to join them to be a spy. But I can't be here and continuously kill humans just for their blood. They won't break me or my morals. Neither he nor Morwen move to stop me.

A merciful death, that's what this will be. Quicker than feeding on him, and probably better than being impaled. I place my hands on both sides of the man's head and twist his neck so hard that it snaps. He never had a second to comprehend what was happening before his body falls limp on the cold stone floor.

A chilling energy runs along my limbs as I watch his body stop moving. It touches the sleepy beta ability that rests underneath my skin, waking it up enough that I feel its hum in my palms. A sliver of warmth travels to my tired heart from the man, a calming sensation flowing from it. It feels like gratitude.

Grief and hatred bloom like ice shards in my chest, overshadowing any appreciation the man might have had for the ending of his suffering. The Brais destroyed this man's life, their stealing of him was his death sentence. And I carried out the execution. I wish I could release every ounce of the fire that resides in my body and decimate all the Brais in one explosion.

The temperature in the room erupts. Heat slams into me, and I know that it is not from my own magic. I feel hands on my head before I can even look up to what is most likely a pissed-off Kael. A popping sound echoes in my skull and is followed by sharp pain exploding at the base of my head before the dark emptiness takes me.

CHAPTER SEVEN

THEA

With a startling gasp, I awake back in my tiny room. The sun sits in the middle of the window-pane, casting a blinding light into the space. I squint while my eyes sluggishly adjust and notice Morwen leaning against the opposite wall, a book with a silver and white drawing on its cover in her delicate hands. She wears a black turtleneck underneath a brown plaid blazer with high-waisted black pants. For a moment, I wonder if this fashion choice has always been hers, or if it evolved into it after spending so much time in the castle library. Cherry black hair falls over her shoulders. Her green eyes sparkle with a smile as she closes the thick book and tucks it under her arm. "Look who has finally risen. Kael snapped your neck like a twig."

I swallow and try to sit up, but the room is spinning, and the air is heavy. "How long was I…" Asleep? Dead?

I killed a person.

Dread floods my body at the horror. Bile rises in my throat, and the room spins. The memory of his spine cracking underneath my palms is imprinted in my mind. And then there is the way the life left his body. I lean over the edge of the bed and heave. Hardly anything comes out, which makes the queasiness worse.

Morwen pushes away from the wall and is next to me in an instant. She brushes my matted hair from my face and dabs my mouth with a handkerchief that she pulled from somewhere. I let her care for me, too weak to protest. I think part of me misses having a friend who would be there when I need it.

"Here," she says softly, leaning me against a pillow propped on the wall. When I am sitting, she carefully steps back and raps her knuckles on the door before cracking it open and whispering to a guard posted in the hall.

My hands tremble in my lap. I deserved getting my neck broken for what I did. That man lost his life. Because I took it. I murdered a person.

Maybe I *should* be a Brais.

The guard enters with a mop and bucket a few moments later. His nose wrinkles at the pungent scent in the room, but he doesn't glance at me, just moves to the mess on the floor. None of us say anything as he cleans it, which only takes a couple swipes with the mop.

As the guard leaves, Morwen mutters a thanks and closes the door before sitting gently on the edge of my bed. She places her book down next to her and rests a palm on my leg.

I hate the look of sympathy that crosses her face as she leans forward. At the same time, there is a swirl of appreciation for her that moves into that shard of bitterness. "You were unconscious for two and a half days," she says grimly, answering the question I asked before. Her voice is soft. "It normally would have only taken a vampire a few hours to recover from a broken spine, but you haven't fed in quite a long time." She tilts her head, a sad expression on her face. "It is actually quite amazing that you are even still alive."

Alive in the undead sense.

"I don't feel very alive at the moment." My body is heavy

like it is made of rock. Rocks that have been swallowed by a volcano, burning and becoming lava. Each breath is labored and sends waves of nausea rolling.

She chuckles. "Well, I suppose none of us are." I look to her, unable to form any response or emotion.

I killed a person. The thought cracks around in my skull like it is made of knives.

Morwen's hand squeezes my knee. "You really should feed, you know. After you do, I really don't think you'll have to kill another human if you don't wish to."

"What?" Despite the ache weighing down my eyelids, I blink at her and swallow, wincing at the sandpaper that is my throat. "I doubt that."

"Not all Brais are vicious killing machines." Morwen muses as she gives another squeeze. Her touch is soft and warm, somehow soothing a bit of the throbbing pain all over my body. Her lips thin, a slight frown turning them down. "The Brais are not what you think, Thea. I'm telling you."

But the stories from both Sarah and Cole... And the actions of all the Brais I have interacted with thus far say otherwise. The Brais vampire who attacked me when I fled Cole's cabin all those weeks ago. The death of that innocent man who the female Brais attacked outside of my apartment building. They were what I would define as a "vicious killing machine". I fight back the grief that emerges when I recall who Amaund alone killed. Sarah's cousin's boyfriend and Mr. Esposito.

Valeria.

I open my mouth to counter her statement when a calming sensation washes over me, so overwhelming that I get lost in its embrace. The pounding in my head and ravaging stomach subside enough that I uncoil and straighten my back with a deep breath. Morwen's green eyes twinkle in the light. "I've seen things that say otherwise," is all I respond with.

She smiles, removing her hand. A tingling warmness lingers, like the ghost of a friendly flame keeping you cozy from the cold. Her smile doesn't reach her eyes. "I've heard." A splash of red seeps into the faint aura of colors around her body. Her voice hardens as she says, "I can only hope that the King will reprimand those who acted against their orders." She looks to the floor, as if contemplating something. "I know the King will," she says with a terrifying calm.

A silence lingers. I don't know what runs through her mind as she clenches her jaw and takes a breath. Curiosity weaves itself into my own mind. Everything that I have learned from Cole and Sarah don't match with how Morwen is speaking about the Brais. Her emotions while she conveys her thoughts seem honest and bold. Swirls of vibrant blue slither so slightly around her body. The comforting color of the truth she holds about the Brais.

I mentally add another to my list of things to investigate while I'm here. To figure out the truth behind the Brais. Whose version of the vampire group is right?

I exhale a long breath and Morwen looks up from the floor, her gaze lightening. I swallow against the lump that is lodged in my throat. "What does Kael want with me, anyway?" My voice shakes as the painful memory resurfaces. My fist tightens around the gray blanket on the bed. "I-I killed that man yesterday." I let the pause after the acknowledgement speak for itself.

I killed a person. Like he wanted, I killed someone. Wasn't that what he wanted?

She sighs heavily, a long-lived weariness slumped on her shoulders. "Commander Kael doesn't like it when his commands are undermined. You need blood to survive, and he'll expect you—*want* you to kill a human by feeding."

The sharp pangs in my stomach intensify at the conversation. At the thought of blood. I close my eyes, hating that part of me that is so eager to harm someone. But she is right. I need to feed, desperately. "Okay," I say quietly, as if saying it low enough will keep her from hearing me, and I won't have to face Kael.

Killing a person…again. Is it really something that I will be able to live with? In order to be of any help in this war, I'll need to be alive to do so. If I undermine Kael again, I don't know if he would be able to contain his fury again.

Gather information on the Brais and their King and send it to the Essites. That is my plan. To do that, I'll have to feed from a human until they take their last breath. Fighting that primal, vampiric urge is exhausting, but if I allow myself to do it once, will I be able to stop?

Morwen offers a gentle smile as she rises and lends me a hand. "All right, then. You're quite frail, Thea. Let me help you." She ducks under one of my arms as I shakily raise it so that it rests on her shoulders.

We slowly make our way out into the hall. A single guard is posted outside my door. The dark-haired female straightens when she sees us exit. Morwen nods at her before we continue down the corridor. The entire walk there is in silence.

As we get closer to that horrible room that I wish I didn't have to set foot in again, my heartbeat begins to race. With each step, my body feels as though it is being stabbed repeatedly. In every inch. Part of me wants to stop the pain that moving causes, to just return to my bed and curl up until it stops, as if it were nothing more than a passing illness. If I don't feed today, Kael won't have to kill me. As weak as I am, I don't think I can last another day without blood. Morwen squeezes my hand reassuringly, as if she heard every thought in my mind. I realize then that my entire body is shaking, from fatigue or nerves, I'm not sure.

We enter the room to see Kael already standing with his hand clutched around the back of a young woman's neck. I stiffen at the sight, for both fear of what is to come and desire of fulfilling that raging hunger. For sympathy of the poor woman whose fate was sealed the moment she was taken by the Brais. Her blonde hair is tied into a messy updo, strands falling and brushing her shoulders. It looks like she was jogging prior to being taken, her athletic wear is relatively clean, save for the single stain of dirt on her hip. My nostrils flare with my growing rage.

Morwen let's go of me in front of the woman's trembling body. The air is ignited with the enticing scent of spices.

Kael doesn't say a word. He simply steps back from the woman, nicking her neck with his nail beforehand. A small trail of blood spills out of the wound, racing to her clothing. I stare at the thick, crimson liquid, entranced by its movement. The transition, usually smooth, is slow and strained. The usual vibrant colors that come with my reddish eyes are dull, hardly changing from what my hazel ones see.

With a shaky hand, I grab a hold of her arm. She doesn't move, her blue eyes the only thing that conveys her fear. That and her scent. As I bring my teeth to her neck, I steal a glance at Kael, my eyes like daggers at him.

With that single look, I make a promise to him.

A vow that I will make it a personal quest to end him.

The woman tenses as my teeth break her skin. The flood of honeyed nutrients crashes on my tongue like a tsunami. I wonder why I was so hesitant to drink from a human in the first place as all the body aches simmer away, like free-floating upon the surface of a still lake in the heat of summer. I close my eyes and drink deeply, bringing my other hand to hold her slouching body. As I continue, the fire inside my bones burns like a volcano, one that is a part of me, not meant to inflict pain. It melts parts of that cage deep inside that holds the anger and sadness I keep locked away, fusing with it. The promise made clings to every part of my reawakening magic.

Under my grasp, the woman's heart slows. Another greedy

gulp, and her trembling stops as her body becomes lead. This amount that I have already taken from her could be enough. I could—I should—stop. It has completely restored my body and magic. She could live if I stopped right now. But I can't. To be honest, I don't want to. And I don't think that has anything to do with Kael's demands.

So I take more.

And then her heart takes its last beat.

At the same moment, an addictive rush of adrenaline floods my veins. Like spiced honey mixed with a touch of salt. A heady concoction that my body is already wanting more of. Had there been another human in this room, I don't think I could hold myself back. I feel as though I could travel to all my favorite places on Earth in the matter of a single day, or maybe even take on all the Brais right this moment.

I killed a person for her blood.

The thought crashes into my mind and the electrified buzz from feeding wavers.

I am a Brais.

I lower the limp woman gently to the ground, not caring about the other two vampires in the room. I will not bend to their viciousness.

Kael steps forward, his large hand outstretched as I stand. There is a smug grin plastered on his lips, and I fight the urge to punch him in the face. "Welcome to the Brais, Thea," he says.

Not that I had a choice. I scowl at him, wishing I could slap his hand away or just turn around and ignore him. To live through this, I might have to pretend to be someone I am not.

I just hope I can keep the real me alive while I pretend.

The light of a candle flickers to my left and glints off the hilt of his sword. At the same moment, a rush of my revigorated strength and magic floods my cells. It pushes me to strike while he is unguarded. His weapon is in my reach. Fire flares in the palm of my left hand, pulling his gaze in that direction. A distraction. Kael's own magic responds in defense, the space between us igniting. He doesn't see my right hand as it reaches for his sword. The metal hilt is cool to the touch as my fingers wrap around it. As I pull the blade out an inch, the temperature in the room skyrockets.

Before I can register what is happening, Kael pushes me against the wall, his forearm across my chest. His palm is pressed against my collarbone with enough pressure that a little more might cause it to break. I hiss at the discomfort. My magic withdraws at the Commander's sheer power.

Kael's eyes are a deep shade of red, though his usual ire doesn't seem to be fueling the color change. Instead, a pleased grin is spread across his lips. Long, sharp fangs slide out from his upper lip, suddenly making me aware of my own heartbeat pulsing in my neck.

"Like a true Brais," he says.

With his free hand, he grabs my wrist and I wince under a sudden searing pain. Kael holds on tighter, his grin widening. The burning eases and he releases me, peering down at my aching wrist. I follow his gaze and see a subtle orange glow sizzling on my skin. It forms a triangular shape on my wrist, like a brand.

"What is this?" I sneer. The magic fades, leaving a reddish scar. The skin is raised and tender.

"The mark of the Brais," Kael replies stolidly. I look to Morwen who still stands against the wall, her face unreadable. It doesn't look like she moved an inch since we arrived. Kael steps back and resumes his typical stance, a hand on the hilt of his sword. His own matching mark sticks out of his sleeve. "A gift from the King. He will always know where you are." A not so subtle warning.

The mark that Amaund has on his wrist is also now on mine. He cut into that mark to make the portal. It wasn't a triangle at all, it was this. The lines seem to move as they settle into what will most likely be etched on my body forever. The outline of that shield—the symbol of the Brais.

One of the two things that I need to get out of this pocket dimension. And they gave me the key.

CHAPTER EIGHT

THEA

*A*n hour later, I'm sitting on the plush bed in my new quarters. It is double the size of the previous room with a single bed, a nightstand, and a closet, which is equipped to hold clothes and armor. An empty wooden mannequin stands in the corner with a small weapon rack on the wall behind it. A standard array of modern and medievalesque clothes are hung from metal hangers. Unlike the other room, this bed is an actual bed, not a rock in disguise. On the nightstand is a used candle, though covered heavily in dust, and an empty glass that once held blood. The stench of stale, dried blood mixed with dust burns my nose. I don't know who used this room before me, but it must have been a long time ago. Judging by the accents throughout the castle, it could have been centuries ago.

Morwen informed me where the feeding rooms are, which luckily are as far away from my room as they could possibly be. People who have been taken against their will and some who came willingly reside in two separate corners of the castle, each compelled to believe they are living in wealth instead of a dungeon. Since the Brais don't particularly want the attention of human authorities—not that the police or government would have any idea how to solve those missing persons cases —they keep those parts of the castle guarded by a few of the King's trusted sentinels who make sure no vampire takes more than they are granted. I'm terrified to tempt that part of me which craves drinking from a vein. I might be able to try and glean information about the Brais and the King from the people in the castle. Depending on how my research goes, I might have to try anyway. For now, I'll have to rely on the library for researching. As for blood…I am dreading the moment that I'll need some more. Locked in that gilded cage deep in my soul is the part of me that needs to drink from a human's neck. Hopefully, Morwen will be down there with me when I need to feed again.

A light rain taps the windowpane and trees below sway in a wind. Though the forest looks uninviting, my heart yearns to be within nature again. To feel the wildness on my cheeks and the grass under my feet. There is also a curiosity about the dimension. I'd like to explore the castle grounds and see if there is a finite boundary. Walking in the rain doesn't quite feel exciting at the moment, so I'll stick to exploring the castle.

Apparently, having the mark of the Brais means I won't need guards posted outside my door any longer. This room appears to be in a busier part of the castle compared to the other one I was stuck in. I hear conversations taking place, though not which direction they are in.

I walk down the wide, central stairs with an elaborately carved railing. Though most of the castle floors are bare wood, the stairs are lined with a faded red carpet. It makes me wonder why only this area that I've been to so far has this level of luxury, if you can call it that. Was this castle built after the creation of the dimension or before? Aside from the library, I wonder if there are any other rooms that might offer information about the castle and its inhabitants.

Gather information about the King. Send word to the Essites. That is my sole plan. Hopefully, I can survive long enough in order to fulfill it. At least I will feel like I accomplished something in this war. Help the Essites fight back against the Brais. Anything that might help, I will try to do, even if it means risking my life. Should the Brais win, all of humanity would be in danger.

"Hey, Thea!" a soft voice yells from one of the couches in the main foyer, dragging me from my thoughts. Morwen sits on the end, her arm waving above her head. Next to her is Mica, the vampire who escorted me here with Amaund. He leans his head of long white hair to Morwen and whispers something to her, which is acknowledged with only a nod.

Surprisingly, no part of me resents him. Unlike the others that day, he never sneered at me or acted like I was indeed a prisoner. No, he actually acted sort of like an ally, or at least, someone who wanted to help. My mother taught me to trust my gut when it comes to meeting others. For Mica, there are no alarms, only a warmth. For Morwen, there is a piece of me that wants to back away from her, almost trembling at her presence, but another part that reaches for her, consumed in the sincerity and calm that she radiates. When I'm with her, that part screams the loudest.

The foyer is large enough that the vast number of vampires within doesn't make it feel crowded. It is lit by candlelight and the multiple roaring fireplaces. One would think that with whatever mysterious way the candles stay lit, this place would also be magicked to be pristine. Layers of dust cover the table to my right, an opaque blanket on a bowl and small, abstract sculpture. There is so much on the piece of art that I can't even tell what the artist created.

I stop at the back of the couch across from Morwen and Mica. The former offers a gentle smile, the other a curious tilt of his head. Mica is dressed in a light gray, button-down shirt and black pants, one ankle crossed over his other knee. "Hello, Kindria," he says in a droll tone.

Morwen shoots him a glare. "No one likes to be called that, Mica." She doesn't give him a chance to respond before she returns her attention to me, her hardened features softening. "How are you doing, Thea?" She emphasizes my name by drawing out the last two letters. Mica never takes his eyes off of me, not even when she chided him. I can't tell if that is an intrigued expression on his face, or a suspicious one.

Uncomfortable under his stare, I glance to Morwen. "I'm okay," I lie. Hopefully, they can't read emotions, because I'm sure mine would give my true feelings away. Fear, anger, anxious, and sadness are just a few. I wonder if my beta ability can disguise what energies my emotions display, like a mask of sorts.

Morwen nods and uncrosses her legs. "That's good to hear." She stands from the couch. "Would you care for a walk outside? There is a path that winds through the forest which leads to a pretty pond."

Mica looks away to glance at the back of Morwen's head, an unreadable expression on his face. Only then do I notice the folded up paper in his hand. "That would be nice, but I think it's raining."

"Actually, I think it just stopped," Morwen says, pointing to the round window toward the back of the room. It must have stopped raining while I was making my way through the halls.

Though the rain has stopped, it is still gloomy outside. The lure of a scenic pond is too much for my curious mind. I wish I had my drawing materials with me. "A walk would be nice," I answer, trying to smile, though it might have come off as stiff.

"Sorry to ditch you, Mica," Morwen says as she walks around the marbled coffee table and links her arm with mine. The gesture catches me off guard, and I almost pull away, but her comforting energy soothes my own nerves, and I relax into her instead.

Mica clears his throat as he gets to his feet, swiftly tucking the piece of paper into the pocket of his pants. "That's all right. I have other things to take care of." He walks around the couch and stops at the backside, a hand resting on the top. "Enjoy your walk, ladies." With that, he turns and strolls down the hallway.

Morwen pulls me toward the opposite hall, turning to the right, past the giant doors. Again, a single golden armored guard stands in front of them, blocking the entrance. He doesn't gesture to either of us, only keeping his gaze locked forward.

"I'm so excited to show you the pond," Morwen says as we pass by various rooms. Some doors are closed, some open. Most of the rooms that have open doors are empty, no furniture or evidence of ever having any. The only things inside are lit candle sconces. "Aside from the library, it's my favorite place to be."

Another room we pass by has only empty shelves inside. "Do you ever leave the dimension?"

Morwen tenses and shakes her head. "I don't leave here, but most of the others do." There is no deceit, sadness or longing in her voice. She truly enjoys being inside this dimension.

"Why not?" I ask. After a while, being stuck here would drive me crazy. There is so much to see in the real world, so much beauty that this place could not possibly compare to.

She contemplates for a moment, her lips pressed together in a thoughtful expression. We pass a few doors that are closed. "It is just home to me here, I think. And the library is just the place I feel most comfortable, I suppose." She shrugs, her arm still looped into mine. "Besides, I am usually too busy doing research to do anything else."

I glance sidelong at her. "What kind of research?"

She waves a hand in a dismissing motion. "Oh, just boring stuff, really. Mostly for Commander Kael, but sometimes I research things the King is interested in."

My curiosity wins over the need to be discreet. "What does the King even need to do research on?" I keep my voice dull, my expression bored.

"Lately, it has been on magical bloodlines. How they have developed over the centuries and how some branched off and became diluted." Morwen smiles to a vampire we pass by, his copper skin gleaming with sweat. He wears a tank top and athletic shorts and returns her gesture. "I've been so busy late-ly," she pouts.

Cole once mentioned something about vampire magic lines. Like bloodlines, magic lines connect us with those who created us. I am connected to whoever turned Cole into a vampire. Is that what Morwen means by magical bloodlines? How do they become diluted? Or is she researching other species with magic, like witches?

"You are mentoring me, aren't you?" I ask, changing the subject. Later, I will ask more questions. For now, I don't want to seem too inquisitive.

She smiles at that, a warmhearted expression. "And you are my first mentee." Her grin beams as she winks.

Heat creeps up my neck. "Am I really?"

She chuckles, the sound a caress in the silent hall. "Yes. I'll try my best to train you well. There's probably so much untapped, magical potential inside you."

Her words, though kind, tug at my heart. Cole and Sarah were my first mentors. I know that nothing that happened is her fault, but I can't help but hate the idea of replacing them. Even though Morwen seems to have a gentle soul.

I open my mouth to change the subject when we pass the last room along the hallway. The door is open and reveals some sort of art museum. My feet stop on their own accord, and Morwen spins at the sudden tug. Like a child on the morning of a holiday, my eyes light up, jaw dropping. There are numerous paintings and sculptures, even a timeworn tome within a glass case. "This is beautiful," I murmur, mostly to myself.

Morwen releases my arm as I walk through the doorway. It doesn't feel like anyone has been in here for a while. Dust motes hover in the single beam of low light entering through the small window in the ceiling. The center of the floor is mostly open while the walls are covered with art. The side walls have statues of varying sizes. A couple are busts of different people, abstract sculptures, and the Brais symbol. Along the back wall are large paintings, each depicting a person in armor positioned in different settings. The largest painting is in the center and is almost the height of the room. It displays the subject in front of a red curtain, a sword in his hand.

A tremor slithers through my body. "Is that the King?" I ask, slowly moving toward the painting. The person is covered head to toe in black armor. His left hand holds a sword with its point in the ground, his other holding something covered in an inky black shadow. Whoever painted this didn't want the viewer to see what was in his hand. Or was it the King's wish?

Morwen's heels click on the wooden floor as she makes her way behind me. "Well, an artist's depiction of the King. All of these were created by different artists."

I point to his hand held out in front of his chest. "What is he holding?"

Morwen is quiet long enough that I turn my head toward her. She startles at my movement, as if I just pulled her from a disturbing memory. Her gaze flicks to the painting for a moment before she looks up at the window. "Have you never heard any stories about the King's magic?"

"Some," I answer. Stories I have heard only mentioned that the King's powers are nightmarish. Cole said that the King always seemed to relish in frightening his enemies with his magic, less so with his sword skills. The fact that he supposedly didn't use his magic when he fought and killed Eero, the King of the Essites, makes me wonder that he might have been afraid it wouldn't work against his enemy's own fire magic.

Morwen shivers, her hands rubbing her arms against an invisible chill. "The Commander doesn't like when people talk about it, but…" she glances to the open doorway before leaning in closer. "The King, like most Brais, can manipulate the fire element." Her voice becomes even quieter as she continues. "But the King is known to wield flames of black. They are said to not only burn but incite terror."

I swallow a lump in my throat, almost regretting that I asked. Tearing my gaze from Morwen's nervous one, I look back to the painting. There is a sort of dread that this piece conveys with the dark colors and somber tone. Not to mention that the vampire under the armor is huge. Unable to look any longer, I move to the painting next to it. Crafted with oil on paper, this art piece represents the King in a forest, sitting atop a gray horse. There are no flames in his hand, only the leather reigns. Even his sword is sheathed on his hip. In this depiction, the figure is slimmer, much less menacing than the other.

I move to the next, where the King is painted at the forefront of an army. His subjects are blurry, forcing the viewer's eye to look at him. The King is bulkier in this piece, though less so than the larger painting. "Why does he look different in each painting?" Morwen has moved to the doorway, her arms crossed, one foot inside and one in the hall.

She steps into the room again, her movement rigid. She doesn't seem to enjoy being in here. Though I love art, I can understand why. The art pieces feel as though the artists harnessed fear and coated the artworks with it. "None of the artists have actually seen the King, they only painted using information from stories."

"Oh." Super helpful…

Morwen drops her arms to her sides as she backs into the art gallery. A vampire in golden armor stops in the doorway and surveys the room before handing her a rolled-up parchment. Morwen takes it, her skin paling as she opens it and reads the contents. Without a word, the armored vampire returns down the hall, the sound of his armor clanking in the silence.

"The King has called for a meeting in the Great Hall." She folds the paper and shoves it in a pocket of her loose pants. "Everyone is to attend."

I feel the color drain from my own skin. "The King is coming here?"

"No. The Commander speaks for the King." She steps into the hall, and I follow. "The Great Hall is the one down there," she points to those large doors a guard is always posted in front of. "I have something I have to do first."

"You aren't coming?"

She gives me an apologetic look. "If I can, I'll come find you. My task shouldn't take too long."

Already, vampires are emerging more and more, making their way into those now open grand doors. When we reach the entrance, Morwen offers an apology and scurries to the stairs nearby. I am left in this cavernous room with dozens of vampires I don't know.

CHAPTER NINE

THEA

So many of us in one place. Different emotions race between each one, faint colors dancing and swaying together as more unfamiliar vampires filter into the Great Hall. The male in front of me is shifting on his feet constantly, his eyes flicking around the room. I notice his energy, an ebony-colored ribbon that swirls with dull yellows. A bit of fear in his overall cautious emotions. I find my finger mindlessly tapping on my arm, influenced by his projections. A dark-haired female across the room stands with her manicured hand on the hilt of a shortsword strapped to her hip, vibrant oranges dance around her body. She's eager for something. When she tilts her head in my direction, I find myself almost calling out to her. She looks just like Morwen. But where Morwen's eyes are soft and inviting, this woman's are hard and unwelcoming. With their sharp jawlines and narrow noses, they could be related. Even their hair is cut in the same fashion.

I would think that even with all these vampires in here, it would be hard to overlook Morwen's presence. I'll just have to wait for her though. Whatever task she was assigned, I wish I could have tagged along. Being in here with all these unknown

Brais vampires is making me nervous. An elbow to my side distracts me, and I look to my right to see a grinning Mica, his white hair tousled. Whirls of ochre move around his body in lazy circles. I can't quite tell the emotion that lies within the color, but it feels nice.

"Looking for someone, Kindria?" he asks in an amused tone.

"It's Thea. And no." I lie, shifting my gaze toward the front. An arched door is tucked behind the dais. On the back wall is an enormous painting of the Brais crest.

"Sure."

More vampires filter in from the main doors in the back, their mingling energies poking at my beta ability. One out of five I recognize. Alec's rigid body maneuvers around the others, stopping once he reaches a group of other well-dressed vampires. Each one is stone-faced and donning some sort of sword. The one standing next to Alec has a leather bandolier across his chest with an absurd assortment of daggers. I observe for just a bit too long and Alec turns and looks right at me. Bursts of dark red bloom from him as his brown eyes narrow at me. Embarrassed, I quickly spin and resume facing the front.

Mica huffs a laugh next to me.

"What?" I ask through gritted teeth.

He shakes his head. "She won't be here. Morwen never attends these." He says that as if these meetings occur often.

Confused as it makes me, I can't help the bit of disappointment that creeps into my voice as I say, "I thought this meeting was mandatory."

He laughs again, the sound a carefree melody. It is strange in a place like this, so dull and dark. "Is that what you were told? You shouldn't trust everything you hear, Kindria. This is not a meeting." He shoves his hands in the pockets of his pants.

I furrow my brows, ignoring just how close to home his words hit. "Then what is it?"

The door in the back of the room opens with a squeal, demanding quiet. I stiffen as Kael enters, clad in his impeccable armor. The metal clinks in the now silent room as he steps closer to the dais, his eyes fixed forward.

"A reminder," Mica whispers, his voice so low that it is hard to hear, even standing a foot away.

The sound of feet shuffling echo through the room. My spine straightens at the sight of a male vampire being escorted by a cold-faced Amaund. Heavy black clouds of emotion loom around the vampire's head as he continues toward Kael, who stands stoically with his hands clasped in front of him. Amaund releases the male's arm once they reach the Commander. The ghost of his icy grip on my own limb stings. I resist the urge to shudder at the memory.

Kael steps forward and wraps his hand around the hilt of his sword, the movement causing the male vampire's breath to become ragged. Everyone seems to have stopped breathing, myself included. Is this vampire going to be tortured for something? No wonder Morwen isn't here. She's the only Brais that I have met who seems to recoil at the thought of violence. Though I wonder just how she gets away with skipping. Her task must be important.

As Kael opens his mouth, he is cut off by a gold-armored guard. I didn't think the room could become any more tense. Everyone but Kael seems to straighten to attention as the guard walks right to Amaund and hands him a rolled-up parchment. The male vampire, whose hands are bound, gives a pleading expression to the guard. Gentle yellow hues appear like mist around his heart and chest.

A sharp, slicing pain erupts in my head. I flinch and rub my temples, forcing my beta ability to recede. The headache lessens as the energy manipulation returns to its slumber, only to be replaced with the gnawing emptiness of hunger in my gut.

The shuffling of paper pulls my attention back to the dais. Amaund bows his head to the Commander. "Excuse me." His previous confident gait has stiffened a bit as he follows the guard out the door.

Kael acknowledges Amaund's leave with a nod before turning his gaze back to the bound vampire, whose face pales at the retreating guard.

"Galland," Kael says in a voice full of strict authority. His tone commands the attention of the male vampire and the rest of us. "A sworn Brais. You have been found guilty of forming an alliance with the Essites." He draws his sleek sword, crafted of a black metal. "The punishment is execution."

My blood chills. Is this the fate of any Brais who decide to switch sides? The male vampire's face morphs into one that I know. Cole is kneeling up on the dais, Kael's sword pointed at his throat. I inhale a sharp breath of air and step forward, stopping only when a hand grabs the sleeve of my shirt. With a nervous swallow, I turn and see Mica holding me back, his attention never leaving the dais. I look back and see that unknown vampire kneeling again.

"I'm sorry," the bound vampire whispers with a shaky voice. He bows his head, awaiting the blow that will end his life.

Kael takes a few steps toward the male's side and lifts his sword. The black metal catches the light of the torches on the walls for a moment before he swings it down. In one swift movement, the sword slices through the male's neck. I shift my gaze to the back of the vampire in front of me, nausea rolling in my stomach. The thud of the male's head on the stone dais weaves through the silence of the room, snaking between everyone who witnessed the cruelty. The sound rests in my bones.

Kael turns toward the crowd, the blood on his sword dripping onto the dais. His gaze sweeps around the room, creating tension with the silence. Such a monstrous brute, enjoying the discomfort his actions put on others. "Come the Frost Moon, the Brais will begin the purge of the Essites. It is time that we finish this long, drawn-out war. Our efforts to find Vitamors has been proven difficult—" he cuts a sharp look to a vampire on his right, who shrinks at his cutting glare, "and we are adjusting our plans to continue without it. Prepare and be ready. Dismissed."

Purge the Essites? Ice-cold dread fills every cell in my body. I need to get this information to Cole.

Those around me begin filing out of the Great Hall. Casual conversations pick up as if they just finished watching a theatric instead of an execution. A few behind me are debating about where to train this afternoon. Another group are deciding to go feed in the cellars. Two vampires to my left are conversing about a hiking trip they went on a few days ago in the human world. The *human* world. They've completely separated themselves from the actual world, the realm in which we all came from.

"Mica," Kael's deep voice booms over the departing crowd.

It pulls me out of my head and the others from their conversations. Everyone keeps walking, though with less chatter than before. The Commander's tone wasn't demanding their attention, and their names weren't called, so they deemed it safer to keep moving. Their paces seemed to have sped up a touch, given the sound of the shuffling feet. Mica on the other hand became a statue at his name on the Commander's tongue.

"Yes, Commander?" Mica responds smoothly, inclining his head in formalities.

Kael is quiet for long enough that I dare to look up from

the tiled floor. His gaze isn't on Mica but on me. Even looking at Kael's cold blue eyes, I see the slumped, headless body of the vampire he killed. The blood stains the stone, a rotten aroma slowly filling the room. "Thea looks pale and Morwen is preoccupied at the moment. You should take her to get a drink." He takes a cloth from a table and wipes his sword clean before sheathing it. "We wouldn't want her to become ill." The ghost of a cruel grin splays across his face.

Kael doesn't want me to cave into the bloodlust. In those weeks that Cole, Sarah, and I were training, Cole warned me that not feeding can lead to a frenzy where a vampire may attack anyone at any time. Kindria are especially vulnerable.

Mica bows his head lower before straightening. "Of course." The white-haired vampire reaches across to my shoulder and turns my body away from Kael and the dead vampire. Only when we exit the Great Hall does the queasiness subside.

The corridor has mostly emptied, as if everyone fled the Great Hall once they left the doorway. Mica leads me to the left along a narrow, candlelit corridor. We walk in silence for a while, his hand on my back as a guide. I didn't notice how much my body was shaking until he removed it at the top of a dark stairwell.

"Are you aiming to get yourself killed?" Mica snaps. His hushed voice sounds loud in this area.

I'm not sure what he's referring to, so I only shrug before leaning against the curved banister of the stone steps. I let out a long, calming breath. There are no candles along the walls here, the only illumination coming from the narrow windows that are scattered about.

Mica crosses his arms. His green eyes glimmer in the light pouring in from the window behind me. As usual, it is an over-cast sky. "What were you going to do back there, march over to the Commander and demand he treat that vampire better?"

Irritation seeps into my blood, enough to stop my body from shaking. "Honestly, someone should." Somewhere on a level above, a door opens, the sound of feet ascending stairs follow.

Mica's nostrils flare as he glares at me. I think he is debating how to react to what I said but decides to shake his head before turning down the stairs. He puts a foot on the top step before turning to me. "Let's just go."

I push off from the banister and plant my feet. "I'm not going into the cellars to feed on a person."

When Mica looks to me again, his expression is of pure annoyance. Fine, that makes two of us then. "I was planning to go to the storage rooms." He must notice the confusion written on my face because he continues. "Where the blood bags are. Didn't Morwen show you?"

I blink at him. "I thought all you Brais preferred blood right from a person."

He lifts a brow and assesses me. "You're a Brais too."

Right. I glance at the brand on my wrist.

"You tell me. Do you still have your preferences?" I follow him as he continues descending. "I've overheard plenty of the others talking about their...preferences." My palms heat as anger bubbles in my chest. All those innocent people sitting in cold cells who have either been tricked into helping the vampires out or were captured.

We pass by a window that looks out to the forest that makes up the northern part of the dimension. Dark green blurs as I peer out the slim opening. A cool breeze caresses my cheek as I walk past the window, like it was waiting for me to do so. It makes me think of Cole. With him, comes the memory of seeing him on the dais about to be killed by Kael. I shake my head and run my palm along the cold stone wall.

Mica stops at the next level down, the landing dimly lit by a single flickering candle on the wall. "It is true that we may get a better source of power from fresh blood, but still, not all of us drink from a human."

I step down on the landing with him, noting how close we are. The space is smaller than I thought, so I step back on the last stair. "Really?"

He huffs. "You know nothing about this world. Did your creator not teach you anything?" The candle dances wildly as he turns down the next, darker flight of stairs.

I ignore the second part of what he said. "What is that supposed to mean?" I call out, following quickly behind him. My escort's only response is to stomp down the stairs like he hates that he's been assigned to babysit me. His footsteps echo so loudly that the sound bounces in each direction.

Still unused to my vampiric senses, the sound reverberates in my ear with anger and irritation. I try focusing on straining my eyes in this darkness to alleviate the sound. I can just barely make out his white hair and silver sweatshirt. Before I can study more of him, Mica stops so abruptly at the next landing that I almost slam into his back.

"Are you going to answer my question or just temper-tantrum stomp your way down another flight of stairs?"

No light is necessary to know there is a smirk on his lips. "Temper tantrum?"

"What else would you call your little stomping act?"

Light filters into the landing as the door creaks open. "So, you had no trouble seeing in the darkness of this stairwell then?"

I open my mouth to shoot a retort at him, but nothing comes out. I could see slightly better with every echo of his feet as it awoke my vampiric eyesight. His stomping was for my benefit? "How chivalrous," I snort.

He laughs and opens the door, revealing a large, cobwebbed room. Old white coolers line the walls. The air in this room is cool, borderline frigid. My human self wouldn't have lasted ten minutes in here. There are no windows, only a chandelier hanging from the ceiling, the coolers, and two doors. Mica closes the one we just entered through. The small door on the far end is also closed.

I move to a cooler on my left, kicking up dust as I approach. "This storage room doesn't get a lot of visitors, I take it." My fingers leave prints on the dirty door to the cooler as I open it and grab one of the few blood bags resting on the bottom. There are three other storage coolers in here and I wonder how stocked those are.

Mica grabs a bag for himself. "Those who don't drink from a human prefer the other storage room. I like the quiet that this room offers."

"What is more special about the other room?" I ask, popping the top from the bag.

"The blood is stored in glass bottles, stocked in shelves that line the walls. It looks more like a wine cellar than a blood storage room. Too boujee if you ask me," Mica says with a slight grimace.

I lift a brow to him. I don't think I could indulge in something like that. Drinking from a bag is a good reminder to me that the contents come from a person. Consuming from a bottle seems like it would make it easier to detach myself from that fact. "How do the rooms stay stocked?" The release of stress from the first sip washes over me. My shoulders relax, and I sit on the cooler, my legs dangling. As my eyes shift to their vampiric forms, the room brightens, and colors become more vibrant. I wish I could see like this all the time.

Mica's forest green eyes shift as well, turning a berry red. He takes a few sips before answering. "I take it you haven't indulged in the library yet."

"What do you mean?" I knit my brows together, annoyed at all the non-answers I get.

"Morwen did show you the library, right?" He runs a hand

through his shoulder-length hair, ignoring my frustration. Sitting on the appliance, despite what we just saw and where we are, Mica appears to be at ease. Perhaps it's because of our indulgences, though every time I have seen him, it is the same. Even when he was with Amaund the day I came here, there was a carefree energy about him. It makes my own body crave that.

I nod, taking another drink from the bag in my hand. The nausea and headache from before has completely vanished. Having the option that this room offers is incredibly relieving. I wonder why Morwen hadn't told me about it. Maybe her kindness made me forget that she is still a Brais and that she is one who enjoys drinking from a person.

"All the answers you seek are in the library," Mica says.

I sigh. "What makes you think I have questions?"

Mica studies me for a moment, watching as I drain a few gulps. Behind him, a spider spins a web in the corner of the room. I blink at it, wondering if I am imagining the scene or actually watching a tiny spider from more than ten feet away. "Are you watching the spider?" Mica wonders.

"How did you know?" I didn't notice him looking.

He smirks. "I can hear it."

My eyebrows rise in amazement, and I strain my ears to hear the spider's little feet, but I can't. I only hear Mica drinking from his bag like a child sipping through a straw when there isn't anything left in their cup. With narrowed eyes, I snap my attention to him and ask, "Really?"

He lets out that untroubled laugh again. "You need to learn to block noises out. When you start training your magic, train your senses too." He stands from his seat on the other cooler and wipes the dust from his jeans. When he straightens, he pulls his hair back into a small bun. Doing so reveals a tattoo on the base of his neck, just above his collarbone. It appears to be a plant of some sort, too hard to tell from this distance.

"Think of our senses like dials," he continues. "We need to find the right way to turn them in order to make the most from them." Cole's words said almost exactly as he did. Mica holds out a hand. "I can take your empty bag."

"Thanks," I say, watching his movements.

We exit the storage room, making our way back up the dark stairwell. "Would you like to stomp this time or should I?" Mica calls into the darkness, an amused snort following.

The blood rejuvenated my eyesight, and I can see the individual steps, as well as Mica's bright hair. It reminds me of a moonbeam in the night. "Neither," I respond with a chuckle. Still, I use all my concentration to keep the brightness, otherwise I might trip.

When we reach the landing above, there is more light filtering from the windows and candles. "Can I ask you what kind of magic you have?" When he doesn't answer right away, I add, "Or are you going to tell me to check the library?"

That earned another snicker. "I can manipulate water."

One of the vampires who attacked Cole and me in the forest could use water magic. I remember him pulling water from the ground and plants, creating a weapon from it. He didn't survive after my fiery explosion though. And if it weren't for Cole's air magic snuffing out my flames, the forest wouldn't have stood afterward either.

"What about your beta ability?" We reach the landing that enters the corridor to the Great Hall. When I think that Mica is about to enter through the doorway, he continues up the stairs.

"I don't have one," he answers with a shrug.

"Oh."

The female who I noticed in the Great Hall, the one who looks like she could be Morwen's sibling, trots past us on the stairs, a stern expression on her face. When she is out of earshot, I lean into Mica. "Who was that?"

"Elisz." He grimaces. "She is a General. She used to be one of the best fighters of the Brais."

"Used to be?"

Mica peers behind us as if she could be listening in. "I guess she did something to piss off the King. Now, she is in charge of the humans who are escorted into the castle. It's best to stay away from her."

He doesn't have to tell me twice. Nothing about that vampire made me want to go say hello. Seeing her reminds me of what Kael said during the "meeting". "What is the Vitamors that Kael mentioned?" I ask, lowering my voice.

Mica glances at me, a slight smirk on his lips. "So, you were paying attention. Something the Commander is obsessed with. He thinks it will help him destroy his enemies."

"His enemies, as in the Essites?"

Mica doesn't respond, his attention fixed on the hall ahead as we continue forward, his jaw clenching. It looks like he is either in pain or trying not to answer, so I don't push for more. We walk in silence the rest of the way to my room, my mind bouncing between the possibility that Cole and Mica might know each other and the barbaric execution. If I am to beat Kael, I'll really need to train with both magic and a sword.

"You didn't have to walk with me all the way here, you know," I say to him as I open the door to my chamber, suddenly feeling weary.

"I was bored." He shrugs again. "A word of advice. Do not trust anyone or anything here. Not a fellow Brais, not the things you hear, not even yourself."

"That's cryptic. And let me guess, you're the only one here I can trust?" For my entire life I have relied on my good sense of intuition. I don't know why he included myself in that list of things to not trust. Perhaps because I'm a vampire and he understands that primal, horrible desire to kill people.

Mica's gaze is unwavering. "No one."

I splay my fingers on my pants. "Right." A wonderful and warm greeting.

His expression shifts to an amused look. "Don't forget to check out the library, Kindria."

"Thea," I correct through gritted teeth.

He smirks and waves as he turns to walk away. I let out a breath as I close the door behind me. The sun has set, leaving my room dark, save for the small candle lit on the shelf above the bed. I wonder if the library will tell me how all the candles in the castle remain lit. With a shake of my head, I trudge to the half-made bed. Many vampires within the castle have changed their sleep schedules so they're tucked away when the sun is shining. I haven't been able to do that, nor do I plan to. My biggest advantage over them? I don't have to rely on a totem to survive in the sun.

But despite being satiated and feeling like I could take on the world, and despite my wandering brain, sleep comes quickly, the aroma of cedar like a lullaby to my tired body. Tomorrow...tomorrow I'll figure out who the King is. The last thing I see before falling asleep is the smile on Mica's face.

CHAPTER TEN

COLE

"Hey," I say into the phone as I walk into my bedroom. The green comforter is pristinely made, untouched by anyone other than Helios. Thea was the last one to sleep in here, and I haven't been able to bring myself to do so. During those weeks of training, I slept on the couch and the regret that sits heavy in my chest keeps me there at night. Sometimes Thea's cat joins me, but other times, I have found him curled up by the pillows on my bed.

"Hi," the witch on the other end answers. "Did you manage to get a hold of anyone?"

I pluck the laundry basket from the closet and place it on the dresser. "A friend. He has more contact with others within the Essites, so he should be able to gather a good amount." My friend never actually promised anyone, but he said he would try. "What about you?"

She scoffs. "Yes." There is a moment of silence between us. Since discovering what happened to her mother, Sarah has changed. She closed herself off from anyone other than her coven. The alliance between the Minuit coven and Essites feels more like two crumbling columns that are holding up a massive weight. And the columns are being held together by wet cement.

Without a proper ruler, the only vampires the Essites would listen to are the late king's inner circle. Out of the four who he appointed, my friend and I are the only ones who remain. The other two scattered or were killed. Even then, our words may not be good enough to convince other Essites to fight against the Brais.

"I checked out that house you mentioned. It is definitely one of the Brais' hideouts," I say. The item I was looking for in the laundry sits on top, waiting. Guilt washes over me at the sight, and the smell. Her smell.

Sarah says something to someone who is beside her, but I can't hear it. "Good. We'll move tomorrow then."

"What exactly is the end goal of this attack?" I ask warily. I wasn't there when Sarah and her coven decided that we would make a move to hurt the Brais. If I were, I might try and tell them that without a purpose, this attack would only incite a dangerous retaliation. The Brais King plays the long game. A single battle would do nothing to harm their forces in this war.

Sarah's cold laugh chills my bones. "You'll find, Cole, that the witches play at war a lot differently than the Essites." Her tone is chiding, like I was an ignorant student in need of a lesson. "We won't wait for them to strike. We need to know how they'll respond and what sort of defenses they have."

"It sounds reckless and not very well thought over," I grit out. Her jab at the Essites fills me with unease. I have to remind myself that Sarah is still a witch, and the vampires and witches do not get along. She might have love for Thea, but that doesn't mean she likes the rest of the Essites. "We should wait and think of a better strategy. One that involves the long term war."

"We don't have time," she responds quickly.

If Thea were here, she would tell me to reign in my irritation. Through the mirror on the dresser, I see Helios staring at me with indifference. There is something in Sarah's tone that implies she is withholding more information. I understand that there are things that she would prefer to keep within her coven, but if we are fighting side by side in a war against a dangerous enemy, we both should be open with each other. "Is there something you are not telling me, Sarah?"

There is a sputter on the other line before she hesitates. "I've told you everything that I can, Cole. See you tomorrow." She hangs up.

I glare at the call ended screen, unease swirling in my gut. For now, I'll keep my word about this alliance and our plan for tomorrow. But Sarah is going to have to divulge in whatever she knows. For Thea, I'll keep the peace with her friend.

I turn around, still holding the shirt that was in the basket. Helios has moved to the edge of the bed, his golden stare on me as if he knows what I am about to do. I arch a brow at the cat. "Are you going to tell on me if I do this without Sarah?"

I get a slow blink in response.

"Okay, then." I walk out into the dining room and turn most of the lights off before sitting down at the table. Folding the shirt, I place it in front of me, close my eyes, and envision myself traveling through space and time for Thea until I find that glorious pinprick of her mind.

CHAPTER ELEVEN

THEA

I awake, nestled into the swaying grasses of the peaceful sanctuary that holds our tryst. Gentle winds whistle through the leaves of surrounding trees, branches creaking in its melody. The ghost of the sun's rays dance on my skin as I run my fingers through the soft tips of the grass. Far away, a cicada sings.

"It will never get old."

A smile forms on my lips at his sensuous voice. I rise to my elbows and peer behind me to see Cole walking through the grass. "Hey," I say to him.

"Hey." Cole sits on the ground next to me and lies back. I do the same, our arms touching, as we both stare into the expansive blue sky. Clouds move idly across.

"What will never get old?"

He moves his hands from his stomach to the ground, our fingers just barely grazing each other. It's hard to focus on the beauty of nature with his hand so close to mine. "You and how much you love places like this." His voice vibrates through my body, sending pleasant shivers down to my toes.

I smile at his response, relishing in his peaceful presence. This is what will never get old for me. We lie there for a while, just sitting with each other's company, though the sun never changes its position from midday. Cole doesn't press for more information, he's letting me say as much, or as little, as I need to.

When a cloud passes over the sun, I sigh and sit up. A coldness is left from where our bodies were so close. I pluck a tall blade of grass and mindlessly run my finger over its smoothness.

He sits up, and I feel his concerned stare. "Is everything okay?"

In the distance sits a crystalline lake, its waters shimmering underneath the sun. I wonder how far we could walk in this space, or is there a wall somewhere, with life-like pictures for the background. My tone is somber when I finally say, "I killed two people." I hardly get the entire sentence out before my voice cracks.

Cole puts an arm around my shoulders and pulls me into his chest. He doesn't say anything as he holds me. The familiar sound of his heartbeat hums to mine, mending the ache that has been there since I have last heard it.

I don't know how much time this sanctuary can hold for us, but it must be coming to an end. We've already been here longer than last time, pleasantly consumed by the stillness of each other's presence. Still, Cole doesn't press for anything. I may not be able to feel the familiar warmth of his touch in this place, but just his company is soothing and brings me deeper into a place of peace. It also reminds me of what I don't have anymore. And if I'm not careful around the Brais, may never experience again.

I pull away from the comfort of his body and exhale a long, tired breath. The blade of grass between my fingers dances in the combination of light wind and my breath, and I stare at it, unable to bring my gaze back to Cole. "I've met vampires here that prefer blood bags." The words ripple through my mind, challenging what I previously believed about the evil vampire group. The stories I heard made me think all Brais wanted to destroy humanity. The few Brais members I ran into after being turned didn't help that belief, each one proved to be the worst parts of being a vampire. A part of me is irritated at both Sarah and Cole for helping implant that ideology into my head. If I knew beforehand that not all of the Brais were bloodthirsty murderers, maybe I could have been better prepared should I ever end up in their grasp. I don't know if it really would have made a difference, but I feel like it could have.

Cole pulls his knees up and rests his elbows on them as he leans forward. "There are some, yes. Their drinking preference shouldn't affect how much you trust them though, Thea."

I bite back the retort that I know better. The blade of grass tears in half between my fingers, and I release the pieces, letting them fall to the ground. They get lost in the sea of their kind. I turn to Cole but forget what I was about to say when I notice a small smear of blood sitting underneath his nose. My heart races with worry. "Cole, you're bleeding." I mindlessly reach for the spot, but he grabs my hand before wiping it away himself.

"It's fine. My body must be getting tired from using too much of my magic." He rubs his hand on his black pants and the blood is lost in the color.

My eyes widen. "That's not fine at all." Grabbing his hand, I hull him to his feet, ready to catch him if he wobbles. I'm not sure if him getting tired out in the real world would make him dizzy here, but I don't take any chances. "You can die from that, Cole."

He chuckles. "I know. Trust me, I'm nowhere near that." A wind blows the grasses, bending them to reveal their soft, silvery sides.

"What about Sarah? Is she helping you?"

He winces. "She was busy. Her magic was only a booster for mine. I wanted to see if I could get to you on my own."

I pinch his arm, but neither of us feel its effect. "Don't do this again, okay?" I soften my expression and rub my hand on my arm, brushing away a phantom chill. "I love seeing you, but if it's too taxing on your body, don't risk it."

"Thea, it's—"

"Promise me, Cole."

He sighs and rolls his neck. "I promise."

"Thank you. Most of the information I have can wait until next time. But, Cole…" I twirl a finger in my shirt, wishing that my next words didn't need to be said. "The Brais are rallying against the Essites. On the November full moon, they are planning to attack."

His face pales a little. "That's good information to have. That should be plenty of time to rally our own allies. We will be ready."

"Be careful."

"You too, Thea. The position you have taken on is risky. If they dig, they might be able to connect any information you share with us back to you."

A couple of blue jays call from the oak tree closest to us, flying off to other trees as if in a race, or if they were fleeing from something. "I know." I sigh.

"I'll try to come tomorrow night," he says. "Sarah and I, and a few others, are getting ready to hit one of the Brais' smaller hideouts."

"What?" My breath catches in my throat, a lump forming. "What if you're walking right to the King?" I shake my head.

"The place we found is too small for the King. There aren't many Brais vampires in there, we've done recon on the building many times."

"But—"

"Thea, we'll be okay," he interrupts. "It'll be Sarah and I and a few Essites and Minuit witches." When he sees my confused expression, he laughs. Oh, how I've missed that sound. "Sarah has done a lot already as coven leader. She has gotten many of her coven members to help the Essites."

Rain drops fall lightly on our heads. I look up to the sky, completely covered with dark clouds now. Geese fly away from the direction of the lake. I bring my attention back to Cole and suck in a startled breath. Crimson blood leaks out of his nostrils like a faucet being turned on. "Your nose is bleeding again."

He covers his nose with a hand. "I should probably go."

I nod in agreement, my fingers twitching to reach for him as he gets farther away.

"If I'm not here tomorrow night, then it'll be the next night." His *voice is ethereal, as if it were the first part of him to be carried back to his body.*

"Promise?"

He takes a few more steps, his body becoming blurry, before he says, "I promise."

Then, there was only me. Even the storm decided to leave.

I WAKE JUST after sunrise the next morning to a knock on my door. I contemplate ignoring whoever is there when a thought bounces in my sleepy mind. Rolling over, I let my energy manipulation reach out toward the door and creep to the bottom like a phantom limb. Sweat beads on my forehead as I concentrate it to slip underneath the slim crack. Joy mixed with a familiar calm presence greets my magic. With a grunt, I pull my magic back, toss the covers from my body, and walk to the door. She'll most likely keep knocking, or even barge in, if I don't answer.

"Good morning, Thea," Morwen says happily. Her cherry black hair is pulled back into a messy bun, a few strands resting on the shoulder of her tan cowl-neck sweater. The small lavender plant in her hand stops me from telling her that it's too early for her cheeriness. She peers behind me, into the small, bleak little room. "I brought you this. It smells so good."

I take the fragrant plant from her, the smoothness of the terracotta pot reigniting the slumbering gardener in me. A pang of guilt creeps into my heart when I remember my favorite roses and other flowers that were destroyed in my apartment when I blew it up. "Did you go through the portal to get this?" Gesturing for her to enter, I place the small herb on the nightstand then turn it so the fullest part bends toward the pillow. The window sits just behind the table and sunlight covers the pot like a gentle blanket.

Morwen sits at the end of the bed and crosses her legs. The black dress pants she wears are immaculate, not a wrinkle on them, though she picks at something on the knee. "No," she responds with a laugh. "I had someone get it when they went." Her ice-blue eyes study me as my fingers run along the soft lavender leaves. "You look well rested."

I lift my gaze, settling them on the bedpost for a moment before turning to look at her. "I had a drink yesterday evening with Mica. Then, I slept like a log. So yes, I am." In the closet, I pluck out a cotton shirt and a pair of jeans that are spilling from the armoire and throw them on the bed to change into. Thinking of Cole from inside that dream sanctuary warms my skin. I pretend to rummage for some more clothes so that she won't see my reddening cheeks.

"Do you like Mica?" she asks, her tone soft.

I whirl around, startled by her question. "I mean, he's nice and all. I don't really know him that well though." Cole's image flashes in my mind as I say the last sentence, my heart-beat skipping. Morwen might be the only person I semi-trust in this castle, but I won't tell her about my feelings toward Cole. Not that I even know how I feel about him exactly.

She nods as if in agreement, her attention on the scenery beyond the windowpane, then asks, "Do you believe in eternal love, Thea?"

I chew on my lip. "Like love that lasts forever?"

Morwen's gaze slides to mine. "Yeah. Or love that can break through all barriers. Even space and death."

With a deep breath, I walk over to the clothes on the bed. Morwen lifts a perfect brow before turning to face the door. I slip out of the clothes that I never changed out of for bed and replace them with a fresh set. "I don't know. I guess." When I throw the old clothes into the basket in the closet, she turns back to me, an unreadable expression on her face. "Why do you ask?"

She shrugs, a corner of her painted lips pulling up. "I'm a reader. I fantasize a lot, I suppose." Standing from the bed, she adds, "And I like to ask others the questions that I contemplate."

"That's fair," is all I manage to say. Had someone asked this before I met Cole, my answer would have come quickly. No. But now…isn't that what Cole and I are doing? We are defying distance between us so that we can still see each other. The death part might be just pure fantasy though.

"Ready to get some training in?" she asks as she makes her way to the door.

"Ready as I'll ever be, I suppose."

Morwen and I exit my room and head down the hall. "I figured we could go outside to do some training since the sun is out for once," Morwen chimes into the silence.

"That would be nice." I haven't been outside in a while. How fortunate that the rain stopped on the first day of my training. I wonder how long that will last for. "Do you have a sun totem?" I ask, wishing I didn't. We wouldn't be going out in the sun if she didn't have one.

She pulls a long, slim chain that sits around her neck. It must hang down to her mid abdomen. I've never noticed it before and wonder if I've just been that oblivious or if she only puts it on when planning to actually go outside. "I have this," she says. The silver, tarnished charm sits in her palm. A tawny circular stone sits in the center with lines extending out all around it.

"It looks like the sun," I muse, admiring the jewelry. My fingers itch to trace the smooth stone.

She drops it back underneath her sweater. "It does, doesn't it?" We walk down a couple flights of stairs, passing a few vampires on our way. She nudges me in the side. "I heard that you don't need a sun totem."

My cheeks burn. "No, I don't." Sun totems are created by a

witch's spell and an object that has sentiment value to the vampire. If I needed one, I would probably have used the necklace my mother gave me when I was little. It still sits in the spell bag on Cole's front door, along with his old house key.

When we step out the doors that lead to a small side courtyard, I ask, "Where were you yesterday? You never showed up." I debated whether to bring it up, but my curiosity got the best of me.

Morwen hangs her head with a frown. "You mean for the meeting?"

I scoff, irritation seeping into my veins. "It wasn't a meeting. It was an execution." A traitor to the Brais. I wonder how long that vampire was aligned with the Essites before he was killed for it.

"I know." We walk through an opening within a hedge of boxwoods that could really use a trimming. Dull green grass stretches to make a small garden lined within the bushes. On either end are plants with white and pink flowers. "I'm sorry I never made it. I had things I was asked to do in the library."

The frustration at her ignorance of what occurred in the Great Hall subsides at her apology. Without even using my beta ability, I can sense the distress with her hushed tone and bowed head. Dark clouds pass overhead, as if the nature of this place also feels her regret.

Morwen sits in the grass and gestures for me to join. It is so quiet here. There is an ocean in front of the castle, yet I can't seem to hear its crashing waves. There is no wind to stir the trees or birds calling out from the forest. No insects buzzing around the flowers. I can't imagine living in a place without the touch of nature. This manicured space of the courtyard feels too fabricated. There is that same subtle, gloomy sensation that I felt by the forest of my apartment building. It feels of death. Cole said it was the Brais and their stain on the natural world.

"Why stay with the Brais?" I ask Morwen who sits, crosses

her legs and closes her eyes. Her chest rises and falls in slow, even breaths.

Her voice is calm. "You already asked this before."

I inhale a deep breath and scrunch my nose. The air is stagnant here. "I know, but…the Brais," I pause, searching for the right word without offending her. A cloud passes in front of the sun, cooling the area. Images flash in my mind, of the people who have died since I became a vampire, all because of the Brais. "The Brais are barbaric killers." There really isn't a way to sugar coat what they are.

To this, she opens her eyes. But it is curiosity, not anger, that glimmers behind her irises. "Do you really think that the Essites aren't killers?"

The only one who I know is Cole. "I've never seen one kill ruthlessly like I've seen Brais do."

"We are all vampires, Thea, driven by the same desires. Has the vampire you have been with ever done anything that seemed off to you?"

"No," I answer immediately.

She tilts her head. "No? Then you must have been lucky." Her manicured nail draws circles on her knee. "I've been around for a long time, and I've never known a vampire who hasn't stalked or killed a human, nor have I ever known a vampire who hasn't killed a fellow vampire."

I still at her words. Cole has done all of those, either to me or in front of me. Before turning me, he said that he followed me for months. He was a Brais when he killed Valeria's friend, but he was with the Essites when he killed me. But if it weren't for him, I wouldn't even be alive right now. At least, that's what he said. *You were much worse than your friend was. Even vampire blood would not have healed your human body.* My chest tightens at the thoughts bouncing in my head. Could that wound in my chest have been healed with vampire blood? Cole did say that he needed to help fill the ranks of the Essites…

I shake my head, unable to entertain those thoughts any longer. "No." Cole is not a liar. Not to me. That, I know in my bones.

Morwen places a hand on my leg, her expression soft. "I'm sorry." The tightness loosens a little at her touch. "Vampires should be honest with those they create. We don't have to talk more about this, but you should give more thought to it. Has your creator ever killed other vampires?"

"We both have," I whisper. "When Amaund came for me."

Morwen shrugs, her hair falling over her shoulder. The dark red glints under the light of the sun. "I suppose if that is the only time, then perhaps your assumptions about the Essites are not stemmed from deceit. In a time of battle in war, it cannot always be helped. But there are other ways to disable a vampire other than killing." Like snapping their neck or using a wooden stake made from a dead branch.

Despite her warm touch, chills spread down my spine. That night Cole and I infiltrated that house and fought off a couple of vampires, we both killed members of the Brais. The one who attacked me could have killed me with his poisonous beta ability, but I stuck a stake through his heart first. Cole…he had the upper hand on that vampire he fought. Out of anger, he killed his opponent.

"Have you ever meditated, Thea?" Morwen's serene voice pushes my thoughts away like the ebb of a current. Her eyes have closed again, though she still touches my leg.

"Yes, but not in many years." The surprising calmness in my own voice forces the rest of my body to lighten.

She takes a long, slow breath. "Close your eyes."

I do as she says, my mind zoning in on her hand. Her touch is warm and gentle.

"Breath in and out." She pauses, our breathing becoming synchronized. "Let your mind rest on the air as it moves in and out of your nose. Notice how it is pulled from the space around you, how it flows into your body before returning to your surroundings."

The air enters my nose and slides into my lungs. I picture it moving throughout my body. Morwen's hand seems to be a magnet for my attention as it slips there with each inhale. I have to force myself to remember to focus on the exhale on every breath. Her warmth reminds me of Cole's. The thought drags my mind to his touch. To the exhilarating feel of his skin on mine. The memory of his hand on my cheek sends fire to my center. On the next inhale, that image vanishes, replaced with the memory of him killing that Brais vampire in the garage of the house. That pale vampire in the woods tried to kill me shortly after I was turned. My body tightens and I remember the first time I ever saw Cole kill. Is taking the life of another vampire, regardless of them being a Brais, something that comes easily for Cole? A simmering heat churns in my gut.

"See how your magic reacts to emotion." Morwen's voice cuts through my mind. "Magic incites chaos, it manifests our emotions to the outside world. It is easy to succumb to them. Return your mind to the air around you when you become distracted, releasing all thoughts. Be creative with your magic and control it, don't let it control you." Her tone is tender. There is no judgement.

With a deep breath, I readjust my seat. My hands rest in between my crossed legs, fingers grazing the softness of the clovers and grass underneath. I bring my attention back to the air that fills my lungs. This time, it moves into the cracked, gilded cage in my mind. I've been ignoring the emotions and memories trapped within since coming to the Brais, afraid that being here would incite them. The air whirls around the bars, coercing the anger that resides within. Red hot fury bites back, rumbling the enclosure. One of the bars loosens and the temperature around me becomes fiery.

I open my eyes in time to see fire explode from my body. Flames engulf the garden and charge at Morwen like a tsunami. "Morwen!"

CHAPTER TWELVE

THEA

The fire erupts from me with such force that I wonder if it indeed has a mind of its own, feeding from the emotions stashed away. Swirls of dull black mix with the color of the flames. Fear. Her fear. It screams at my beta ability, its icy grip latching onto my own. The force of magic pushes me onto my back, the ground an unforgiving barrier. When it passes over me, I sit up again, my breathing ragged. The flames are gone, somehow never igniting the shrubbery around us. Then, I spot her. Morwen was pushed back as well, her charred clothing sticking to her body. Rising to my feet, I rush to her. "Morwen!"

"I'm okay," she breathes. She motions to get up but grunts and looks at her arm. A burn that covers her entire forearm is seared onto her skin.

"I'm so sorry," I repeat, feeling sick at what I've done.

She offers a faint smile. Her hair is messy, a few leaves are stuck in the strands. A grass stain is smeared on her sweater. "I'll be okay." She begins to stand and I help. "I'm just going to get a drink and some rest." The back of her fingers on her good arm graze my cheek, and I realize that tears have fallen from my eyes. "I'll be fine. You're strong, Thea. Both with your magic and your inner strength. Your emotions, all of them, are valid. We can only become stronger if we work through our blockages."

I nod, unsure if I'm worthy of her compliments. "Okay."

We walk back to the castle. Once inside, Morwen insists on getting to her room alone. After many attempts of offering my help, I surrender and watch her trudge up the southern staircase.

THE LIBRARY IS QUIET, peaceful. A light rain has begun outside, droplets hit the glass ceiling in a symphony. Candles are lit everywhere; their gentle fire seems to dance with anticipation. It almost feels as though the room has a spirit of its own. Perhaps it does. The castle seems old and there might be spirits of those who loved these books dwelling within, if there ever has been anyone who enjoyed them here before. Morwen mentioned that she's the only one who truly uses this place. Other vampires come to her when they need research. Having an eternity to live, collecting knowledge on all manner of topics seems like a good way to pass the time.

I never did ask Morwen what kinds of tomes are sitting on these shelves. The wooden floor creaks under my slow steps as my fingers graze the various spines. A book with a faded red cover sits on a table to my right. The dust on the surface of the table is disturbed, as if someone recently slid the book around while they were reading it. An unlit candle sits a few feet away. A silver embossed title reads *Gwenna Trethaway, A Memoir*.

I tap the chair, deciding whether I should crack open the book or continue my search for something else, not that I have a clue of what I should be looking for. I doubt there is a book titled *The Identity of the Brais King and Where He Hides*.

I snicker at the thought, turn away from the table, and stroll toward the back of the library. There are so many tomes here, how one even begins looking for information is beyond me. I wonder if there is some sort of catalogue around. The musty smell of old books and stale air grows more intense the deeper into the library I explore. These mismatched, uneven shelves must rarely get visitors. It seems like there is a calm sheet of dust floating around in the air, not used to disturbances. Some of the spines are so worn that any letters have long been faded away.

A shelf that sits against a wall holds only two books and a painting of a sword. The hilt is golden with an amber stone embedded in the pommel. Like the books in this area, the artwork is faded, but it looks like the sword's guard is carved with circles that have a horizontal line through them. The symbol, though not elaborate, seems familiar somehow.

The point of the painted weapon is aimed right at the other objects on the shelf. Two books sit stacked, their spines and covers heavily used. With a gentle finger, I wipe a streak of dust from the top book's cover. The title is in Latin. *Vita Moresque.* Life and death? Maybe one of these books have a clue to what words need to be said to make the portal work. There are probably more books written in Latin than English in here, though. I hope I can rely on my dull recollection of the ancient language to be able to find what is needed. If I can find it today, then I'll be able to share that information with Cole when I see him next.

The glint of something to my right catches my eye. Beyond the next bookshelf is a portion of a large statue. There is a droning purr emanating from the direction the statue stands, as if it were beckoning me like a siren's call. My curious feet move on their own accord, padding on the wood floor. A low rumble of thunder fills in the space between steps. Candles in sconces dance to the sounds of the storm outside.

A large statue indeed. Made from some dark-colored stone, a massive humanoid work of art stands against the back wall. It must have gone through some travel to get here, as pieces are chipped off, and it is missing its head. The stone person stands, one foot on what could be a rock. Its left hand is down at the hip, though the palm faces outward. A few fingers are broken off, and there must have been something in their crumpling hand. Some parts are chipped, and others look as though they were deliberately shaved. At the angle the hand is facing, I wouldn't think that it could have been an object. Perhaps this effigy is of a vampire, and they were depicted with magic? The other hand is closed around a sword, the blade pointed at the ground. The statue is dressed in smooth clothing with little design, though the elbows and knees appear to have some sort of padding. I tilt my head, examining the strange outfit. Would someone be wielding a sword in normal clothing? I suppose one could, considering I've seen plenty vampires in this castle do just that. But still… Leaning closer, I notice that it isn't as smooth as I thought. There are designs carved into waves along the breastplate. In the center is a circle. I step back. The symbol matches the one from the painting of the sword. Not clothing at all but armor.

Could this be a statue of the King? There is no plaque on the massive base, nor is there one hanging on the wall. He must be vain to have had a statue of himself made and placed within the castle. Or perhaps its purpose is to remind those who dwell here that he is their commander-in-chief. But why would it be stuffed into a place that seems so abandoned?

In other words, he may or may not be in this castle…

This is getting me nowhere. I release an exasperated breath as I place a hand on the circular symbol on the statue.

Pain and terror shoot through my body, a searing and suffocating pain. There are flames everywhere. They lick at my skin as they devour the furniture around me, none of which I recognize. I am crouched against the corner of a charred wall, my small, wobbly knees scrunched against my chest. The heat is unbearable, and it stings my watery eyes. The smell of wood burning mixes with something else…something horrible that churns my stomach. There are screams echoing all over, or maybe that is me screaming.

The flames burn my skin, blistering and unkind, though they don't touch me. No, they stop just short of me, as if there were an invisible barrier cast in a circle around my frail figure. This body feels like mine, yet unfamiliar all the same. I tuck my knees in closer, the movement revealing what lies just beyond my feet. The charred remains of two adults, their hands clasped together. The remnant of a sapphire glow pulse in the space between their palms. Though their bodies are blackened by the violent flames, the expressions upon their faces reveal only contempt. Strange.

The shattering pain of grief rips at my heart, tearing from my chest and escaping up through my throat and out of my mouth. A scream so heartbreaking roars into the storm of the all-consuming fire.

"Thea!" a far away voice shouts frantically as hands grasp my shoulders. "Thea! Open your eyes!"

The burning world around me shakes. Darkness creeps in, devouring first the splintered home, then the burnt furnishings, and lastly, the lost souls at my feet. The scorching heat and flames remain, along with my trembling and still screaming body.

"Thea, please!"

The voice becomes louder as it rattles in my mind. The dreaded scene disperses like ashes in a hurricane, violently and with a vengeance that seems to mix with my fading body. With a gasp, the darkness fades and books surround me once more. Morwen is kneeling next to me, her eyes lit with concern. I'm lying on the floor of the library. Rising to my elbows, I look around. The statue stands as still and broken as ever. Though there is no head, I can feel its tormented gaze peering down at me. "What happened?" I ask, my voice hoarse.

Morwen runs a delicate hand down my arm in a calming motion. "I forgot something in here earlier and came to retrieve it. When I came in, I heard crying in the back. Then you started screaming." She stands and offers me a hand. "I ran to you, only to find you prone on the floor."

What was that? A vision or a dream? "I'm sorry for scaring you," I say as I take her hand and clear my still aching throat. "Thank you." There is no fire, no burns. The air, though thick with dust particles, is free of smoke. I place a hand on my heaving chest and run the other through my long hair.

She smiles, though it doesn't reach her eyes. "I'm just glad you're okay." With a glance to the statue, she shudders.

I rub my hands over my face, trying to shove away any lingering effects of whatever it was that I saw. What *did* I see? Was it a future vision or a past memory? Or was it just something that my mind conjured?

Those two bodies in front of me and the way they held each other in the face of inevitable death… Images of my own parents flash in my mind. I can't recall too many details about the car accident that took their lives, but I feel like I can remember them holding each other like that as well.

I shake my head. No.

I let out a long sigh through my nose and gesture to the statue. "Do you know who this is? Is it the King?"

Morwen turns away from the stone and glances at a stack of ancient looking, leather tomes on a shelf across from it. The spines are faded and uneven in height. One of them has a few layers of cobwebs atop it. The book farthest on the left appears to be relatively free of dust and other debris. I make a note to check that book out at some time. "I was informed it was once a depiction of the first vampire."

"What happened?" My fingers, as if on an invisible tether, crave to roam the jagged pieces of the shoulders, but the gleam of the symbol stops them.

She traces a painted red nail over a discolored book cover. "To the statue or the first vampire?"

I shrug, trying to appear as genuinely interested and not at all as someone looking for answers. "Both, I suppose."

A slight smirk tugs at her lips as she picks something from underneath a nail. "Why so curious?"

"History has always been interesting to me," I lie.

A muscle feathers in her cheek. Somewhere in the library, wind howls through a cracked window. The storm outside intensifies and rain drums on the domed ceiling. "The first vampire was once a witch who craved vengeance on those who wronged her. I've read multiple theories on how she transitioned from one species to the other." Morwen moves down the aisle, her finger slicing through the dust on the shelves as it roams. Her heels click on the wood floor, echoing with the sounds of wind and bursts of rain on the glass above. "In general, the stories say that she was betrayed by her own kind once she became a vampire. The witches disagreed with her new abilities, particularly the living eternally part."

Sarah told me that some supernatural species vowed to protect the balance of nature. When I pressed about what she meant by "species", she would only mention witches. Then, there was Cole who had mentioned that there are more than just vampires and witches out there. Maybe Morwen would tell me more.

Before I have a chance to ask, she continues. "Again, the written history is vague about what happened to her. Some claim she was destroyed by the witches while others say that she was imprisoned." She lifts a shoulder and glances back at me, her hand dropping to her side. "The statue was erected in her honor long ago. Weathering has done its damage, so it was brought in here."

A shiver runs down my spine and I'm unsure why. I place a hand on the back of my neck and roll my shoulders. Perhaps it is because the vision still lingers in the back of my mind. Morwen notices the stiffness within my body. "Are you all right?" She stops her retreat from the statue and turns to face me, a worried expression on her usual calm face. "What happened while you were over there?" She points toward the dark corner.

Even though there is no head, no eyes on the stone sculpture, I can still feel its gaze on my back. "I-I'm not entirely sure." I shove my hands in the pockets of my sweater. "When I touched the chest of the statue, I...saw some things," I say, quieting my voice.

An eyebrow inches upward on her face as she tilts her head slightly. "What sort of things?"

A curved window sits on the wall at the end of this aisle, its glass cloudy with age and rain. The tops of trees sway in the brewing storm, the sight obscured by the worn panes. I don't notice Morwen moving closer until she places a gentle hand on my arm, her fingers grazing lightly on my skin as they move up and down in a soothing motion. I offer a sad smile as I exhale a long breath, allowing a bit of comfort to seep into my body from her touch. "There was fire. And death. A lot of it." My voice sounds distant. I think of the screaming and the corpses at my feet and shudder. "I saw two people who died in the fire."

Morwen's hand pauses on my forearm briefly before she drops it to her side. "That's awful, Thea. I'm sorry. If you want to talk about it more, I'm here to listen." We begin walking again toward the path between the two tall, wooden bookcases with contents that are old and dust covered. "You think you saw that vision because you touched the statue?" Morwen asks after a beat of silence. The only sounds have been a symphony of our feet and the rain.

I shrug. "If not, then it was a strange coincidence."

"Curious," she contemplates.

I shoot her a puzzled look. "How so?"

"I don't think I've ever heard about anyone else getting visions from touching the statue. Maybe it was trying to tell you something." She spins around when I don't respond. "Don't you want to figure it out? Oh, I love a good mystery." Her eyes gleam with excitement as she presses the palms of her hands together.

I let out an amused but tired breath. "If I have to relive that vision, then no, I don't want to figure anything out." There is a part of me that wants to know why there was that blue light between those two people's hands. Just like my parents. But I could stave off my curiosity for a while if it meant returning to that horrible scene from the vision. It's bad enough having the memories of the night my parents died stuck in my mind.

She pouts. "What if I do the research? You won't even have to think about what you saw ever again."

Her childlike exhilaration reenergizes my tired body. I rub the back of my neck as she interlocks her fingers and stares at me with sad eyes. "All right, all right." A sliver of me is eager to find any connection to my life before. Especially after finding those weapons in my parent's basement, locked away and hidden from me. Another part is terrified to find anything.

"Yay," she says as she grabs my arm and tugs me toward the center tables. "I'll warn you before I tell you anything scary, okay? There are a few places I think I can start with. Will you keep me company?"

Even through the rain-drenched glass ceiling and dark clouds beyond, there is no mistaking that the sun outside has mostly set. "I would, but I'm actually getting tired, and I want to stop by the coolers first."

"You can sleep after! We don't have any training tomorrow, so we can stay up late reading." She laughs quietly, as if only to herself. "Not that any responsibilities have ever stopped me from reading all night." She stops pulling when we reach a long, empty table toward the front corner. The furniture and shelves seem better maintained here.

"Okay," I respond with a laugh.

Morwen yips with excitement as she darts off toward a stack of tightly shelved books.

CHAPTER THIRTEEN

COLE

How can something feel so weightless but heavy at the same time? My tired mind wanders the black depths of my magic, unaware how to get back to my weakened body. The thread that connected the two parts of me must have snapped from overuse. The price to be paid for reaching out to Thea without Sarah's extra boost. Still, I would do it again. Without hesitation.

Her intoxicating scent of sage and cinnamon linger somewhere in this void. Strange, since I couldn't smell her in the sanctuary. If I follow it, would it bring me to her? Knowing that she's trapped with the Brais is torture. The way I handled that interaction with Amaund that day was stupid.

Despite not feeling my body, subtle sharp pains emerge from below my consciousness, mixing with the heaviness of a weight. The sensations feel fuzzy, as if an invisible wall stands between my mind and body. Being in this strange hollow place, I suppose there is. Where did I leave my body when connecting to Thea? Right, in my cabin, holding her favorite shirt for a bridge between our minds. What are the chances that my body is still sitting upright in the dining room chair?

The black void vibrates, emanating from a point straight ahead. Unsure if it is the path I need to get back, I float forward anyway. It's the only path, after all. The only indication that my consciousness is moving toward the vibrations is that the invisible wall seems to dissipate. There is no light and no movement of air to guide me. The more I move, the more noticeable the sharp pains become. They're a beacon in this maddening place.

Slowly, the sensations my body is feeling emerge. A hard resting place underneath my back, the light buzz of the refrigerator. A weight sits heavily on my chest, as do the alternating sharp pains.

Like an elastic breaking, my wandering mind snaps back into my body. I'm staring at the ceiling of my small dining room, the wooden chair I started in pushed back against the wall at an irregular angle. The pains have stopped, but the weight…

Golden, slitted eyes stare at me. "Helios," I breathe, scratching Thea's orange-furred cat on the head. His purring becomes louder, and he rubs his chin and cheek on my chest. Helios cuddled against my legs the first time that I used my psychic beta ability to connect with Thea's mind. Maybe he can sense her. "I need to get up," I whisper to the feline, wincing at a pulsing headache.

As if he understands, Helios slides off my body and trots over to my kitchenette, sitting in front of the sink. His water bowl has apparently never been good enough, as he always demands water from the bathroom or kitchen faucet.

Slowly, using the dining table for stability, I move to my feet. A wave of dizziness washes over me as I do so, and I have to grip the wood to keep from falling. When it subsides, I wipe the back of my hand underneath my nose, pulling it back to see dried blood. I grimace at the sight, noting the metallic taste on my tongue, and scrub the rest of the blood off with a towel from the kitchen counter.

Everything hurts. The sun shining through the window that I have been meaning to put curtains on for months, the feel of the floor on my bare feet, and even the air current—who's presence I am usually grateful for. My black hair that brushes along my forehead feels like a razor. A headache pounds against my skull and nausea roars in my stomach.

Opening the refrigerator, I wince at the light and cool air as I grab the last bag of blood. With a frown to the empty shelves, I trudge to the couch and sit, my entire body screaming at all the movements. It feels as if there are grains of sand scratching against my deprived veins. The first sip of blood lessens that roughness to a tolerable but uncomfortable feeling. The second drink relieves it entirely.

Helios trots over and plops on the floor at my feet, his golden eyes staring intently at me. With a sigh through my nose, I pat the cat's head. "I'm sorry, bud. I'll turn the water on for you. Though you could just drink from your bowl."

He returns my words with a slow blink and a twitch of his fluffy tail.

The front door squeaks open and I tense as Sarah enters. Her black hair is pulled back into a tight bun at the crown of her head. Honey eyes pierce mine like a burning sword. "What the hell, Cole?" Her words are clipped and hiding her true irritation. She waltzes into my cabin with an air of superiority, and I do all I can to keep a level head.

A light wind howls in the chimney, echoing down to the cold fireplace. My mouth tightens as I furrow my brows. "A knock would have been nice. Just because the Minuit witches and Essites have an alliance now doesn't mean we should disregard formalities. This is still my house." Helios leaps onto the kitchen counter behind me, his tail thumping impatiently against an empty box.

Her nostrils flare, and she clenches her jaw before speaking. "The alliance is hard to maintain when the one at the head of the vampire side doesn't show up to the raid that we have been planning for *days*."

I open my mouth to retort, but a bright sunbeam catches my eye. When I contacted Thea, it was late evening. We were supposed to raid the next night. I was unconscious for an entire day. The almost empty blood bag, having been forgotten, falls out of my slacked grasp as I stand. Too fast. A wave of dizziness washes over me, blackness creeping into the outskirts of my vision, and I place a hand on the fireplace mantle to steady myself. How close to depletion did I get? I was too careless in the use of my magic.

Sarah doesn't say anything, but her eyes are narrowed when I raise my gaze to her. "I'm sorry," is all I manage to say.

"What happened?" she asks, her voice losing some bitterness. Gentleness softens her features, though her fury is still evident in her creased brow.

Sarah has been adamant about me not using my magic to contact Thea alone. Was it because she didn't want to miss any information or because she was genuinely concerned about the toll it would take on my body? I rub a hand over my face, my body stabilizing enough for me to stand on my own. "Nothing," I lie. "Everything is fine." I'll have to mention to Sarah about the Brais plans to move on the Essites soon, but not this moment.

Her fingers tap on crossed arms. She clicks her tongue in annoyance and runs a hand through her black hair. "Sure. We will hit them tonight instead then. I have already spoken with the coven on the matter."

"Wasn't the entire point of executing our plans yesterday to ensure the leaders of this particular Brais group would be absent?" I told Thea I would reach out to her tonight, but there's no way that I'll be able to see her if we do our attack. Though, it will be a good win for the Essites if we succeed.

She lifts her chin. "We accounted for them returning as a backup. We will just have to adapt our main strategy."

I hold her gaze for a moment before turning toward the kitchen. Helios shifts happily on his front paws when he notices me. "Why are you so adamant on hitting this group? I'm sure we could find another one." When she doesn't answer right away, I shift my gaze to the corners of my eyes in time to see the flash of anger across her face. "The leader of this group—"

"Is one of the King's generals. I know," she hisses.

"Do you?" Turning the cold water on, I stroke Helios on the top of his head before shifting to fully face Sarah. "It could be Amaund." My voice lowers as if the tracker himself could hear us. It would make sense if this place belonged to him. He was close enough that he felt Thea awaken her fire magic that day. An uncomfortable thought sends a shiver down my spine. At the closeness that a Brais has been to me all this time.

Sarah's expression hardens at the mention of his name. "If it is, then we make him give us information and we destroy him," she responds, her voice unnervingly calm. A fire burns in her heart, one crafted of pure hatred. I just hope that hate is directed only to those who deserve it. Like Amaund and the King. Not Thea.

My body tenses at the ripple of power radiating from the young witch. A reminder of what a coven leader possesses. Despite it, I remain leaned against the counter in a show of trust, though my fingers twitch with the air currents within the room. With the breath that hovers in and out of her mouth. "All right then. Tonight it is."

She gives me a swift nod before making for the door. "Once the sun sets, meet at the chapel ruins by Lewen Lake." Her steps fade as she closes the door and walks toward the path in the forest.

A DEEP ROYAL blue sky stretches over the canopy of the forest. The song of the cricket has joined that of the bird as the sun finishes its descent. The Hunter's Moon illuminated the wilderness yesterday. According to Sarah, full moons intensely fuel a witch's magic. Tonight's second day full moon will have to do, I suppose. I wonder if the moon shines in the realm of the Brais. And if it does, does Thea enjoy its silver gleam? For all that he has done to her, I hope Amaund will be there tonight. Torturing him for information will be satisfying.

I will remind him why I was named the Tempest.

As I round the corner of the path, the glittering sight of the lake sprawls into view. Somewhere on the other side sits the ruins of a manor and the last resting place of a valiant witch. I wonder if Sarah chose this spot to keep what happened that night fresh in the minds of those who Valeria's death has impacted. For her, it would be a reminder of how cruel the Brais are. For me…I can't help but feel as though she wants to remind me of how Thea and I wronged the coven by burning Valeria's body. I look up to the rising moon and sigh.

The oak and maple trees give way to large patches of birch, their silver bark dark in the dimming light of the day. It's just then that I realize how similar the birch and moon appear to the eyes. Both dotted with tones of gray and silver, of darkness and the light.

"You're early," Sarah calls. The anger from earlier appears to have mostly slipped away, at least on the surface. She stands with those of the Minuit coven who joined. Mostly young members it seems. The witches all wear silver cloaks and a gold medallion around their necks. The woman standing beside

Sarah is the only one without a medallion. Her umber-toned skin glitters in the moonlight and pale blue eyes narrow at me as I approach.

None of the vampires I called upon have shown yet. "I figured after my unexcused absence yesterday, it was better to be early."

"Good," she says. A cloud passes over the moon briefly, plunging us into inky darkness. "Thank you," she adds, her voice a bit softer.

"Where are the rest of the vampires?" The woman next to her asks in a clipped tone. She stands with her arms tightly crossed at her chest, her legs hip width apart. There is a unique aura around this woman, unlike anything I have felt before. Many vampires can sense a person's presence, like two energetic fields mingling as others get close. It takes time to develop this sense, though. Most species typically have the same general feel. She doesn't feel like a witch, human, or vampire. A witch's presence feels jagged and vast with glimpses of roots that reach deep down toward the core of the earth. Humans have a wavy, unimpressive energetic field. With vampires, it is more like a variety of needles, always putting my body on alert. This woman's feels fierce, like it has a mind of its own.

I survey her, deciding whether I should be extra cautious around her. Her blue eyes seem to glow in the darkness, a hungriness in their gleam. Sharp features on her angular face give her an unfriendly impression. Light colored hair is pulled into a bun at the nape of her neck, loose strands curling around her dimpled chin. "They're coming," is all I say in response.

Sarah puts a hand on the woman's shoulder. "Cole, this is Amelia. Amelia, Cole."

Amelia uncrosses her arms and puts her hands on her hips, pushing back the cloak that hangs around her. The movement reveals the two stakes strapped to her brown leather belt.

Though it is expected that everyone here has at least one stake, her showing them off while being introduced to me is a threat as much as a warning. With a bored expression, I bring my gaze back to hers. "I would say it's nice to meet you, but it appears that you would likely see through that lie." I jerk my chin at her. "Not a witch or a human. Definitely not a vampire."

A corner of her lips turns upward. A smirk with absolutely no amusement behind it. "Wouldn't you like to know, vamp?" Two sets of fangs flash as she speaks, one set in her top teeth and the other along her bottom. A vampire only has the one set along the top. I fight the urge to take a step away.

"You're a werewolf." I've never met a wolf shifter before. Stories are told about them, and I assumed that they simply did not live around here. I wonder what aspects of all the stories are true and which ones are myths.

Amelia opens her mouth to respond but is silenced by Sarah grabbing her hand. They lace their fingers together and Amelia rips her predatory gaze from me. Her features relax as she looks to the witch. A lover's gaze. My heart aches at the emotions that swirl between them, and I look up to the moon that pokes through a spindly cloud. Here, away from the city, the night sky is dotted with stars of various brightness. Even at my secluded cabin, I don't see this many.

A familiar aura filters into my awareness, and I turn around to see a few Essites making their way to the group. Fewer than I was hoping for. The vampire's steps are cautious as they take in everyone who is here. Witches are dangerous to cross. Being around this many within the same coven can be extremely lethal.

"Everything all right, Cole?" the one leading the approaching vampires asks. He is wearing the only thing I have ever seen him in, brown leathers with a bandolier across his chest. Equipped on him is a simple steel dagger and three wooden stakes and a pouch at his hip, presumably holding throwing knives. Though I have never actually witnessed him kill another vampire, I've heard stories about his favorite method. All I can say is that I hope he and I never become enemies.

Shifting to face him, I say, "Yes. Good to see you, Oba." We clasp wrists in greeting. He is almost a foot taller than I am, so I have to tilt my head back to peer into his striking brown eyes. "There are less of you than I was hoping to see," I add with a grimace. With four vampires in total and teaming up with almost a dozen witches and werewolf, we should be able to put up a good fight, but I would feel better if there were more of us. The only worry settling in my bones is if Amaund ends up being there. As the King's best general, he is a force not to be underestimated. Hopefully with all of us, we can still overwhelm him and take him as a captor.

"Yes, well, many that I spoke to think this is a horrible idea." He lowers his deep voice. "Witches and vampires working together has never ended well."

"Maybe in the past. This will be different," I say, keeping my tone steady. This time has to be different. The animosity between the witches and the vampires never made sense to me. We've been at each other's throats for centuries for a reason that no one ever speaks of, if anyone alive even knows anymore.

Oba pokes me in the side just above the dagger in my belt. "How'd you manage it?" When I lift a brow, he clarifies. "The truce between the Essites and witches. And nice dagger, by the way. I've long lost mine." A gift from Eero, the late King of the Essites. He gave every member of his closest allies one as a symbol of his trust.

"Lost?" I huff. "Knowing you, it was probably because you wagered it in some contest or gamble."

Oba chuckles. "A downright stupid contest it was."

I smirk. "Let me guess, it was either a game of Hazard or knife throwing." Probably the latter in which he used the dagger. Oba has excellent technique for throwing weapons, but if alcohol is involved, he is just horrible.

He runs a thumb underneath the strap of the bandolier along his shoulder, testing the snugness of it. "The knives. Damn barmaid was loading me with ale too."

"They're called waitresses, you know."

He nudges my arm, a gleam in his eyes. "You haven't changed a bit, old friend. Still avoiding questions you don't want to answer."

Shifting my gaze to the leaf-littered ground, I let out a long breath. "I turned someone a little over a month ago. Her name is Thea."

"Oh?" His tone is light, filled with the amusement I've always known him to carry. I cast a sidelong glance at him and notice the movements of air around his fingers as he wriggles them slowly. The magic that spins the air is a song to my own. When he sees me watching, he closes his hand in a fist, the magicked air vanishing. "I think you might be the only one of us who managed to be successful in Eero's last wishes."

I press my lips together. "The King certainly enjoyed giving us four the hard tasks." We share a laugh, the sound a mix of cheerfulness and sadness. One of remembering our fallen friend, killed by the King of the Brais within the past year. "The one I turned is a fire wielder. And she is intertwined with the Minuit Coven. Her best friend." I jerk my head at Sarah who is conversing with a few of her witches. They watch her with reverence. "Sarah is the coven leader, appointed recently after the Brais killed the previous one, her mother."

Oba's eyes widen. He looks to Sarah and watches her, the corners of his lips turned down. "Valeria Demoix." He shakes his head, still observing the young coven leader. "She was a witch I would have never liked to cross. That the Brais managed to get the better of her…" A cricket chirps some-where beside us as his sentence trails off. The other two vampires behind us shuffle on their feet. I almost forgot they were here. "She must not have been paying attention," he murmurs.

That or she was distracted. I can still see the bleary-eyed gaze that Valeria tried to hide from us that day. When she apologized for how things turned out since that last time I saw her. Not that she even needed to apologize. "And my gut is telling me that the Brais who killed her will be at the base we are infiltrating." From there we can question Amaund, torture him if we have to.

He whistles, a short, descending tone. "If he's lucky, Valeria's daughter will kill him quickly."

"After we get the information that will lead us to Thea and the castle, I don't care what she does with him," I say after a moment. The witches break away from each other and as Sarah looks over to us, I walk forward.

Oba follows a step behind. "I don't see your vampire." His voice is solemn, as if he already knows the answer.

The coven is Thea's ally. The leader was killed by the Brais. She is a fire wielder and is nowhere to be found.

"Because she's not here," is all I say. He doesn't press for more. Too many Essites have switched over to the Brais, either because they were forced or because they feared for their lives and didn't think there was any other way to live. Even those who did not wield fire magic switched sides. The Brais King likes to play the long game. I wouldn't be surprised if he waited to make his grand move against the supernatural world once the Essites have completely crumbled under his grasp.

"Calm down," Oba whispers in my ear. "Maybe no one else here can tell that the sudden wind is magic, but I can."

Indeed, a chilled wind has picked up, the leaves on the trees and ground dancing in its music. "Sorry," I mumble. Oba grumbles something that I don't quite hear. Not over the roaring in my head and the ice-cold stare of the Minuit coven leader.

Her look is a warning: *do not waste your magic*. The battle is about to begin.

CHAPTER FOURTEEN

COLE

"Whoever is in there will come out once we make ourselves known," Sarah says as the group moves along the slender path. The grove of birch trees slowly thins, giving way to goldenrod and ferns. Golden leaves dot the ground, signaling nature's start to autumn and her beautiful colors. "In which case, they'll be bombarded with the rest of the group. The Brais shouldn't know anything about our alliance yet." Sarah steps through a thicket of ferns, careful to not crush any stalks. The plants seem quite ready for a winter slumber, their leaves droopy and browning.

The evening's chill is another indication of the coming season. A few of the witches wrap their cloaks tighter around themselves. After a half hour of standing around, watching the witches clutch their medallions in one hand and a birch tree in the other, we begin our trek. They spoke the language of the witches, words that sound eloquent and almost musical. Amelia watches with awe as Sarah leads the chant. I am informed it is a call to the spirits of the earth for a blessing in their endeavor. It makes me wonder if they are to choose, would the spirits of the earth oppose all vampires? Or do they just dislike the Brais?

Or perhaps they simply answer those who acknowledge them in earnest.

A smile dances on my lips as I think about Thea. No wonder her and Sarah became friends. With her love for the environment, Thea would have made a wonderful witch. The sparkle in her eyes when she beheld a vibrant flower or an inquisitive bee always warmed my heart. It is clear that her curiosity for the natural world stems from deep within her soul.

"You know, I never told you this, but before you joined the Essites, I once had a run in with Amaund," Oba says after Sarah finishes speaking and begins a low conversation with Amelia and another witch.

"How'd that go?" I ask, keeping my attention warily on the wolf. Her arm brushes against Sarah's as they walk, their fingers occasionally grazing as if they would latch on to the others.

Oba snorts, the sound harsh against those of the quiet meadow. "Well, I'm still alive. He and one other vampire slaughtered almost a dozen of us." My friend shudders next to me, his hands formed into fists at his sides. "I swore that I would repay them one day."

I nod in understanding. There are so many of us who would like to owe the Brais for their horrible deeds. "Who was the other vampire?"

He is silent long enough that I look away from Amelia to see his face pale underneath the moonlight. Finally, he says, "The King."

I almost stumble on a half-rotted log. There is a roaring in my ears as fear and anger mix.

"He wore black armor and a matching helmet. Not once did he use any fire magic. His movements with a sword were…" His expression turns grave, as if he were remembering each strike and maneuver the King made. "We never stood a chance. And when I was the last one left, he stood in front of me, his armor and sword dripping with the blood of my comrades. He hacked them to pieces, too fast for me to even follow." All other conversations have ceased, all ears on Oba. "He sent me back to Eero with a message."

I swallow and take an even breath. "What message?" I ask, though I'm sure I already know what it was.

"Amaund spoke then. He said that traitors to the King will die, along with their allies." Meaning all traitors to the Brais King since they never recognized Eero as a leader.

Ahead of us, Sarah continues walking, her body rigid. She keeps her gaze on the ground in front of her. No one says anything else as we walk through the long meadow. Crickets stop chirping as we interrupt them and jump from plants to avoid getting trampled. The house we seek is just beyond this stretch of open wildness. Magic hums in my veins, growing louder with each step. The threat of the King showing up tonight was something we all considered. The King has always won when faced with other vampires, his powers too great to go against. But to face a group of three different species. Could we do it?

A two-story Tudor style manor sits behind a row of tall hedges. An immaculate lawn stretches beyond and around the home. A paved driveway, lined with elegant streetlamps, curves from an iron fence to a wide doorway. The house is secluded from the rest of the area with its enormous property, all devoid of landscaping and furniture. All the better to spot intruders early.

"Cole, I've already discussed Thea's appearance with the witches and Amelia. They know not to touch her if she happens to be here." Sarah nods to the vampires behind me. "Make sure they know." Her words come out as a growl, a warning.

Without acknowledging her, I turn to my comrades, my beta ability roaring to life. "I'll send an image into your mind of the vampire we need to look out for. If you see her, get her to safety."

"What if she is trying to kill us?" one of the vampires who I haven't met asks. He is tall and slim with beige skin. His brown hair is cut short and out of his dark eyes.

I stare at him, trying to calm the irritation seeping into my pores. "She won't. She is one of us." The two vampires flick their gaze to Oba who stands just behind me. Whatever he does seems to ease their worries enough that they both nod and look back to me. I close my eyes and pull the memory of Thea forward. With a calming breath, her shape materializes in my mind. Her long, toffee brown hair outlines her oval-shaped face. Twinkling hazel eyes gleam underneath a conjured sun. There is a slight tug of a smile on her full lips.

With the image engraved in the forefront of my mind, I open my eyes and touch each of the vampires on the side of their heads. With my beta ability, I send the image into their minds. Each of them bobs their head in acknowledgement. When I send the image to Oba, he has a curious expression on his face. I don't ask about what he is thinking, because I don't want to know.

Sarah dips her chin at Amelia who nods and darts through the bushes to the right, her footsteps pounding until they disappear. I hope that when she returns, she can tell friend from foe. Next, Sarah casts a glance at me. I step back and the vampires follow suit, hiding in the shadows beyond the manor's lights. Sarah crouches down and removes her medallion from around her neck and clutches it tightly, her other hand splayed on the grass. The other members of the coven crouch behind her and form a link of sorts. The two behind her place their hands on her back as the three behind the second row do the same, forming a triangle. The four in the rear place one hand on the shoulders of their comrades in front of them and their other hand on the ground.

The witches close their eyes as Sarah murmurs that melodic language. The air around us becomes energized and Oba shifts on his feet behind me, cursing under his breath. A cloak of shadow drapes over the witches to conceal them. Even though vampires can see in natural darkness. Sarah told us little about how exactly she plans to get their attention. As we wait, I call upon my magic, delving into the deepest parts. A tight stream of air whirls around my body as I test it.

Sarah stops speaking, and I freeze to look at her. None of the witches move. Then, the lights along the driveway explode. One by one, the glass domes of the streetlamps shatter, starting with the ones closest to us, moving in a line toward the manor. Darkness rolls in, as if the spell was an army on horseback charging into battle. The explosions don't stop at the house. The lantern on each side of the double front doors explodes, then the lights that are on inside. Slowly, room by room, the house is plunged into darkness.

When I think she has finished, the windows shatter. A window, stained with the shield of the Brais, crumples into tiny shards. The second-floor windows shatter at the same time, a boom of glass breaking, rumbling like a crack of thunder.

Then, silence.

Minutes pass with no movement from either side. The Brais didn't take her bait. Or they are gearing up for a hard strike.

Sarah remains crouched but lifts her head and glances back to me.

All right then.

With a deep inhale, I pull air from all around us, careful not to pull from the space that the witches are breathing from. The air is like an extension of my body, like a blade to a swordsman. It heeds my command. With a swift forward move-ment, a ferocious wind pushes through the hedges. It picks up momentum, dragging more air with it, and slams into the house. White painted boards break, leaving gaping holes in the exterior walls. The left front door breaks off its hinges and crashes into something with a thud. The wind howls through the gaps in the house, the only sound echoing around us.

We wait for any movement. Each second that ticks by feels like an eternity.

Over the whistling of the wind, a bone chilling howl cuts through my soul. Several more follow. Something deep within me wants to recoil at the sounds. Oba curses behind me.

Knowing that one werewolf lives in this area is frightening enough. I guess I shouldn't be too surprised that there are more, so I let the fact that an entire pack of werewolves have been hiding in these woods disappear from my mind. It is not something to be thinking about at this moment. It is something, however, that I'll be speaking to Sarah about. As one of the leaders of this orchestrated attack, I should have been informed of the plan in its wholeness. Did she think that I would have been opposed to using werewolves for this? As long as they are on our side, I would never have disagreed.

A few vampires emerge from the manor, all with frightened expressions on their faces as they look behind them. To the destroyed manor and the creatures that lurk beyond it. A blast of fire roars from the left side of the house. Its heat is so intense that I can feel it from a hundred feet away. The cloak of darkness vanishes from around us. One of the vampires behind me steps forward as a wall of water emerges, pulled from the ground and plants around us.

I reinforce his barrier with one of air. The impact of the Brais fire strains on our combined magic. The wall of water dissipates almost immediately, leaving a hiss of steam in its wake. Already weakened, the fireball disperses once it collides with that of my own defense.

Sarah stands and the other witches follow suit. Anticipating Sarah's next command, their hands conjure a faint silver glow.

"Break off and do what you must to survive. Our target is the one in charge." She speaks with the witches, though her eyes land on mine when she finishes.

Oba moves quickly in front of the witches, his hands rising to send a gust of air that disperses another blast of fire. Without even a flinch, the witches break away from each other just as the first wave of Brais reaches the outskirts of the property.

I have the vague sense that Amelia and the other wolves are meant to scare the vampires in this direction as not a single wolf has come this way. My wooden stake is stained with fowl smelling blood as I poise myself for another blow from the Brais who decided to pick a fight with me. Unless necessary, I have no desire to kill any of these vampires. In the past, anyone against me was an enemy, and I wouldn't hesitate to ensure my survival. I've done enough of that. The one in front of me looks young, though his appearances mean nothing about his age. Like most Brais, he wields fire magic.

My opponent swings a flame-engulfed hand toward my chest, hoping to catch me off balance no doubt. An aura of wind circles me like a vortex, snuffing his flame. With a twist of my body, I grab his attacking arm and use his own forward momentum to shove him away. He stumbles on his own foot-ing, collapsing to the ground. Focusing on the metal behind me, I drop to a crouch and send the iron gate soaring. The vampire's eyes widen as the points of the gate pierce his abdomen, pinning him to the black SUV that was tucked in the corner of the stone driveway. Before he has a moment to register what happened, I'm on him. With a snap of his neck, his body falls limp.

"That'll be a nasty headache when you awake," I say to him, turning around just to see Oba pounce on another Brais vampire.

His opponent pants as she stalks closer to him, a bronzed,

curved sword in her hand. Eyes the color of blood darken on her face as she snarls at him before darting forward. In a swift movement, Oba throws three knives at her chest. She stumbles at the impact, distracted for just a moment. And that moment is all Oba needs to finish her. There is a flash of green light, and her skin sizzles as if she was just doused with acid. She screams as the burns quickly spread about her body, dissolving her leather armor. Her scream is stifled as her skin and muscle and tendons melt to a sickening pile of remains.

Nausea roils in my gut, and I turn away from what is left of her. "You didn't have to kill her," I scorn.

He picks up his steel dagger and wipes it on his pants before sticking it back into the bandolier. Two of the wooden stakes are gone from his arsenal. "She just killed Elijah, one of my comrades." One of the other Essites who came with him. "They're lacing their weapons with poison." He jerks his head to the woman's curved sword that is now resting on the ground.

When I open my mouth to respond, his flaring nostrils and low growl stop me. I turn in the direction he is facing and my heart stops. Amaund waltzes onto the blood-stained grass, a wicked grin on his lips. His long onyx hair is tied back into a braid, revealing those menacing deep golden irises. Like the night he took Thea, he dons a silver set of armor with a sword at his hip.

"Tempest," the general muses.

A wolf, most likely Amelia, given the same shade of ice-blue eyes, leaps from a pile of debris on the side of the house closest to us. She barrels straight for Amaund, her lips curled in primal fury. She is three times the size of a regular wolf. Her sheer black coat glimmers underneath the light of the moon. For a heartbeat, hope spreads through my body as she closes the distance.

Then, without even a break in his step, he turns with a raised fist that collides with her jaw. Something cracks at the impact. The giant wolf's yelp cuts through the noise of the other fights. She skids across the ground and slams hard into the cement foundation, motionless.

Amaund continues toward us unfazed. "Did you think that the agreement I had with your siree would extend indefinitely?" The promise he made the night he took Thea that kept Sarah and me from being killed.

Cold fury boils in my blood. A wicked wind picks up around us. Amaund's smile only widens.

Oba snarls beside me. "Let me fight him, Cole." He pulls out two throwing knives from the pack strapped to his hip. "I owe him for my comrades."

"No, not until we find out where Thea is."

Amaund flicks his gaze to Oba. A curious expression flashes across the General's face as if he was just noticing him. "Interesting. I don't remember you at all." He tilts his head in an assessing gesture. "But I will gladly take you on first."

"Oba—"

"Stay back. Let me do this alone," Oba snarls. He throws a knife at Amaund with lethal speed. The Brais general leans to the side to avoid the blade, his steady step never wavering. If I know anything about Oba, the right-hand vampire to the King of the Essites, is that his first throw is never intended to hit. Only ever to assess. In a two-pronged attack, Oba throws another knife then fires a blast of fast-moving air afterward. With this attack, Oba's enemy usually would only be able to dodge either the dagger or wind-knife. The compactness of the wind and its shape could cut right through someone, so they usually dodge that.

Oba's attempt makes the Brais unsheathe his sword. He dodges the wind-knife, and, in a too-swift movement, Amaund strikes the knife out of the air. It clinks against the steel of his sword before embedding itself in the ground. He takes the moment that Oba is distracted by his anticipated magical strike to close the gap.

With loose footing, Oba pulls out his dagger and takes one step back. Metal hits metal as the two weapons collide. Oba is strong, but Amaund is too. And the Brais vampire has a longer weapon. Sweat gleams on Oba's brow, his body trembling slightly. Why isn't he using his magic? My own magic whirls eagerly in my palm. Adrenaline courses through my blood. Oba wanted to fight Amaund on his own, but I won't stand by if things go wrong.

The sudden sharpness of someone approaching me from behind pricks at my senses. I turn quickly and almost stumble when a vampire attacking me is within striking distance. How did I not sense him sooner? I clench my hand around the hilt of my dagger and swing it at his chest. Except it only hits air. The vampire disappears as if my mind conjured him.

His presence returns to my left, and I spin, dagger raised. His stake is pointed toward my chest, too close and fast for me to block.

My breath puffs in front of me as the temperature around us plummets. The vampire attacking me stops moving, his skin tinted blue. It is like he is frozen in place. I blink, still clutching my dagger, and step away from the Brais in front of me.

Behind him, stands an unfamiliar vampire. He wears a cloak, the hood pulled over his head, shrouding him in cloth and darkness. He brings his hand to his forehead and salutes me before quickly darting into the gardens beyond the property.

I turn and observe the frozen Brais in front of me. My blood chills at the sight. There is only one vampire with water manipulation that I know who is strong enough to freeze a target solid. My feet start on their own to follow him, but Amaund's voice brings me back to the fighting.

"Come to think of it, I do remember you and your

friends," Amaund croons to Oba. "I also remember feeding their dismantled bodies to the crows as you ran like a coward back to your false King."

Rage burns in Oba's eyes. They transition to a cherry red as he bellows and pushes on the crossed weapons with both of his hands. Fire pours from Amaund's arms like water would through paper. They creep toward his fingers, to where they can reach Oba.

Without a thought, I unleash a whirlwind on the General. Magic sizzles from my veins, pouring out of my body as it entwines with the air around me. Careful to avoid my comrade who is still within ten feet of my target, my magic slams into Amaund, pinning him in place and snuffing out his flames. He struggles to keep upright. One hand lets go of his sword and points to the ground. Fire emerges from the grass and spreads quickly toward me, leaving a trail of charred earth in its wake.

I drop my dome of wind, jumping back and to the side to avoid the lethal flames. I toss another blast of air, this time at Oba. He is safely pushed far back, away from Amaund and his sword. My friend drops his weapon to reveal a shaky hand.

Amaund writes Oba off and turns to me. "Your Kindria is fitting in with the Brais nicely. She drinks from humans and—"

"Shut up," I say through gritted teeth. I know he is only trying to get this reaction from me, but I can't help the anger that rises at his words.

He clicks his tongue. "It's almost a shame that I won't be able to fight you while you're at maximum strength. Being separated from the one you turned must be awfully draining."

It is true that I haven't been as strong as I usually am. Having never turned anyone before Thea, I've never experienced the troublesome setback that is being apart from the vampire you create. Magic from my body ignited the magic in her veins during the transition. Part of me is with her, always. "I have more than enough strength for you, Amaund."

He barks a laugh before lifting an arm. A sheet of flames moves to me, and I have just enough time to throw a wind barrier at it. He used the firewall as a way to hide his movements. When it disappears, Amaund is in front of me, shoving the tip of his sword at my gut. Considering that one of his other vampires had a poisoned sword, I assume this one is too.

With a forward shove of my hands, a pulse of my energy connects with that of his sword as if on an invisible thread. I sidestep to the right and push his blade away with my beta ability. A confused expression crosses Amaund's face momentarily, but he recovers quickly, shifting his body to face me again. He drops his sword arm, and I lunge at him, grabbing the stake from my belt as I do. I see the slight smirk on his face too late.

A wave of flames erupts in front of him. It catches on the stake in my hand, which I drop right before it slithers onto my skin. In that moment, Amaund lifts his weapon. Mindlessly, I reach up to grab the blade, hoping to stop its advance. The honed edges slice through my hand before he thrusts the point deep into my stomach.

I grunt in pain, nausea building as a throb pulses from the wound. The scent of my blood fills the air.

"I was impressed with what you did to the house." His golden eyes shift, a deep red mixing in. "That must have been all you had, no? Oh, how Tempest has fallen."

My bloody hand still grasps the base of the blade, my other on top. I try and force it out, but he is too strong.

"I'll make sure to inform Thea of your death," he says as he leans in, still pushing on the sword. He slowly slides it up, and I fight to stay on my feet as the blade slices through my body. "I've never seen a vampire with such volatile emotions as hers before. The King has use for them and your death will surely aid in her increase of power."

Ice-cold fury burns in my bones, red filtering into my vision at all thoughts of the King wanting Thea. Without averting my gaze from him, my beta ability reaches out beyond my body, beyond Amaund. My grip on the sword tightens, and I ignore the lashing pain from the blade. I push against Amaund's strength, and the sword stops its creeping toward my heart. Still impaled, I take a step to the left, Amaund steps with me instead of releasing the weapon. My mouth curls in a fury as I say, "You will never harm her or anyone else again. And after you? I'll kill the King myself." My voice becomes so feral that I hardly recognize it. "No one will harm her again." An invisible tether of my magic finally connects with its prize and yanks with deadly force.

That poisoned, curved sword of the vampire Oba killed, silently flies through the air and stabs itself right into Amaund's back, the bloody point sticking through his front. The Brais general stumbles back, releasing his hold on his own sword. He drops to a knee, his breathing turned ragged as he tries to reach behind him to pull the blade out. The poison must be spreading, his skin pales and limbs shake.

With a grunt, I pull his sword free from my body. Blood pours from the wound, though I can feel it already starting to mend. I was lucky that Amaund didn't poison his blade. The pain subsides substantially. Holding my wound, I take a step toward the fallen general, my body heavy and tired. I stand over him, and he snarls up at me, his bloodied hand clutching the sword tip.

"If you think that you can get anywhere near the true King, you're mistaken. He is everywhere, and he will conquer all of you and this pathetic place." Sparks ignite from his fingertips and jump into the night air, disappearing before they reach me. His magic is depleted too then, perhaps courtesy of the poison running through him.

I put the point of his own sword to his throat. "Where is—"

"Cole," Sarah says, her voice brittle. She stands behind me, her footsteps and presence lost in the chaos of everything around. I don't move, unable to take my attention off Amaund. Sarah stops beside me, her hand on mine. Her skin is cold.

Amaund stares at me, ignoring the witch. He is one of the few vampires who knows who the Brais King is. He should be kept alive. But everything that he's done...to Thea, to Oba, to Valeria. To so many others. He also deserves to die. But he knows how to find Thea and the Brais King. Despite the labored breathing and stiff body, a muscle feathers in Amaund's cheek, as if he can read all the thoughts that are racing through my mind. My knuckles have turned white from gripping his sword so hard, it's a wonder the hilt hasn't broken off.

"Cole," Sarah says again, her tone softer.

I step back, conceding to the coven leader. She deserves to question him. Even though I want to tear his head from his body, it would be more advantageous to try and get at least something from him. The fact that he hasn't given in to the poison already is amazing. And troubling.

Sarah puts herself in front of the Brais vampire, her face unreadable. Despite the fury and grief that undoubtedly runs through her heart, she looks at him passively. And he just stares right back.

"Witch," he says callously, his fangs flashing. He shifts from amused, to disgusted, to angry as she continues to stand there without moving or speaking. The trembling of his limbs ceases just a little, and I ready myself for Amaund to lunge at Sarah.

The air becomes electrified, minuscule tendrils of power tickling my skin. I see no movement from Sarah, but Amaund is suddenly on the ground writhing from some unseen force. Blood oozes from the sides of his body, at his ankles, abdomen, his arms, neck, and head. His fingers scratch at the earth below him, and that's when I notice. Thin, thorny plants have emerged from the ground and entered his body. They move as if alive, slithering and arching. One pokes through the top of his arm then reenters into his chest.

"Sarah, what are you doing?" I ask, but the witch does not respond. A suffocating, dark aura emanates from around her. The air too heavy for me to connect with.

Amaund screams, but a vine cuts through his throat, stifling anything but a gurgle. Then, more bloody dagger-like thorns tear out of his body. One at an angle just above his left knee. Another comes from the ground by his boots and pierces through one ankle into the other.

Finally, Sarah moves. She leans over his torn-apart body and whispers, her tone full of acid. "For my mother." The silver shard of a plant plunges from the ground through his back, right through his heart.

CHAPTER FIFTEEN

THEA

Unburying my head from the plush quilt, I curse Morwen's name for keeping me up so late. The sun's warm glow filters into the small room, waking my senses despite the tiredness that still lives in my bones. If someone told me just a year ago that vampires were real and that they still needed to sleep, I wouldn't ever believe them. Not only do I still need sleep as a vampire, I need even more than as a human so my magic can replenish and continue to strengthen. As Cole and Morwen like to point out so many times.

A smile forms on my lips as I think about the two of them. They would most likely get along, both strive for growth and knowledge, both kindhearted. I think that if Morwen were to meet Cole, he could talk her into joining the Essites. I've never seen where the Essites' King once lived, but perhaps there is a library that she could oversee there. I wonder if that is the true reason she remains here in this dull castle. The glee never left her face for a moment last night as she was pouring over book after book. The only thing we discovered though was that it won't be so easy finding out information on my connection to the first witch. If there even is one. Cole would most likely advise us that there are more important things to be worrying about at this time.

I turn over and squint as the sun beams into my eyes through the window. As if the sunlight implanted the thought of Cole, I burst from the covers. Where was he last night? He said he would call on me. Did something happen during their attack? Fear burns in my heart, my stomach twisting. It feels like hunger, but I know that it isn't. Just that primitive vampiric urge to destroy. I shake my sweaty palms out before rummaging through the closet for something else.

Maybe I just stayed up too late and he couldn't wait. Sarah and Cole should have told me where they were going. Perhaps the library has some insight into all the Brais' locations. I mentally note to look for anything relating these places when I can. What if they were outnumbered? It didn't seem like there were any less vampires within the castle, but from what Cole mentioned the other day, there must be many other bases the Brais use. Could the Brais have been expecting an attack there? What if they captured Cole and Sarah and whoever else joined them? I'll kill whoever hurts those I love.

A light wind drums against the old panes of the slender window, pulling me back from the abyss of thoughts. Perhaps the fight took more magic out of both Cole and Sarah, and they need extra time to recover. I will see Cole tonight. My reassurances calm that roaring in the cage that pushes me to find a way out of this prison. I relax enough to realize that the metal doorknob to the closet has bent under my grasp. I step away and throw on clothes before heading to the library.

WITH A DAY OFF, it is likely that Morwen is in the library. I wonder how many ancient texts she has her nose in already, if she even left. She probably walked right back to the library after walking me to my room. Having her in there will make it slightly harder to research things about the King and the Brais.

When I open the door, I see Morwen at one of the tables. The noise of the door startles her, and she jumps in her seat, half closing the book she was reading. "Oh, good morning," she says with a smile before returning to the book.

"Good morning," I reply, closing the door and meandering toward a shelf to the right. Last night, I only read what she brought to the table. All dull tomes, none that had any useful information. They were about reincarnation, soul bindings, descendants of the first vampire, etcetera. I think Morwen forgot what we—she—was researching and was only grabbing random texts that interested her. She's probably read everything in here already. Today, I'll look for some books that have nothing to do with me and that weird vision. I need a brief break from those topics, and I still need to find more information on the Brais.

I take a turn down an aisle with shelves on each side. Dust motes dance in the light movement of air, glimmering in the light of the sun above. Just as I look up to the windows, a large cloud rolls overhead, leaving us to the light of the candles.

A book with matte black lettering on the golden cover reads *Dimensions of the Universe*. If it weren't for the little nagging voice in my head to pick it up, I would walk past it. It looks like an inevitable headache with all the information that is most likely written inside. In school, I loved all the science classes, but given everything that I am learning about my life right now, I don't know how much of it I can delve into at the moment. I pull the book from its shelf and tuck it under my arm when my eyes catch another interesting title.

Magics of the Undead. The sickly white lettering blends with the tan leather cover. My hand stops before touching the spine, my face twisting with a grimace. If this book is about to tell me that zombies exist, I will never recover. War be damned, I'll never leave this castle.

I peer over the books and see Morwen hunched over the one she's reading. Her long hair hangs over the wooden chair and is tangled at the ends. She casts an occasional glance toward the door then to the back of the room. I pluck the creepy book from its shelf and walk over to the table.

"Are zombies real?" I ask.

Morwen jumps at my question and turns to face me, a quizzical expression on her face. "Gods, I hope not." She glances back to the doors of the library before focusing on the book again, which appears to be a thick, pictureless read.

"Why are you so jumpy?" I slide into the chair across from her and put the two books down in front of me. The sound startles her again, and she winces as she lifts her gaze.

Her painted nail mindlessly caresses the edges of the page she's on. It stops when she notices me looking. "I didn't read a single word from this book," she says apologetically.

"You're almost halfway done with it," I observe.

"I've just been turning pages. I'm sorry," she repeats.

I shake my head. "About what?" Colors of charcoal and lead mix around her, overtaking the usual calm of blue hues. My own leg bobs up and down, affected by her contagious nerves.

Her voice lowers as she says, "I…did something last night." Another glance to the door.

I can't help but flick my eyes to the closed double doors to the library as well. "Oh?" A brief spike of worry pokes its unwanted presence in my mind. Did she have something to do with Cole and Sarah? A completely ridiculous thought. I've never seen her leave the castle, nor has she ever mentioned doing so. Not to mention the fight was supposed to be the other night. Unless they were captured…

"I freed some of the humans from the cellars." She winces again, as if she were expecting me to yell.

I stare, my mouth agape. Of all the things she could have said, that was certainly not what I expected. I feel bad about immediately assuming that she had something to do with fighting the Essites. And when I think I know exactly who the Brais are, I'm proven wrong. I suppose that while some are indeed bad, others might not be. Perhaps some are just like me, trapped within these stone walls because there is no other choice. I wonder if there is anyone else here that chose to sacrifice themselves for those who they love. Would they turn on the Brais? Could there be an army of rebels right under the King's nose? An army of Brais who have no real allegiance toward the King. Those like me.

I swallow, choosing my next words with care. "If the King finds out…I can't imagine it would end well." Morwen once said that the King never required his vampires to feed from humans, but it was Commander Kael who desires it. But to release humans from the King's dungeons…

"The King would destroy those who take without asking," she says quietly. I swear she shivers as the sentence leaves her lips. She picks at a drop of wax on the table before smearing it across the smooth surface. "I just—they've been here for so long. They were so frail. They hadn't even seen sunlight in years."

I put a hand on hers and conjure a memory of the calming blue sea. A memory of a vacation from so many years ago— the last vacation with my parents before they died. My hands warm as the magic flows like water into her body. Like the waves returning to the ocean, my magic pours into her with a loving embrace. Morwen's shoulders relax, if only a bit, as she releases a long breath.

"Thank you," she says.

I offer a solemn smile. "Will the King just replace those who were freed?"

She looks to the table, contemplation written on her face. "Perhaps. I've heard the war with the Essites has become more intense. The Essites have been using more aggressive and offensive tactics. They used to only defend against the Brais." She tilts her head and watches the rain pelt the glass ceiling. "I think the Essites have finally realized that the Brais are aiming for domination. The King might be too preoccupied with all of that to care about missing humans. Plus, I only freed some. There were those who volunteered to stay so that the others could leave."

"They decided to stay?" I ask with disbelief.

"Yes." Morwen lifts her chin to the windowed ceiling. "A sacrifice, of sorts, in hopes that maybe one day the luck would be in their favor."

A sacrifice to save others.

Images of the vision floods my thoughts. Of the two people with clasped hands at my feet. A faint memory of something that I have long stashed away in the deepest parts of my mind rises to meet me. The night that took everything from me. When I couldn't even say goodbye to my parents. I remember the flash of the headlights from the oncoming vehicle. But there was another light that pulsed from inside our car. A beautiful, sapphire glow that gleamed from between my parents.

"Thea?" Morwen's concerned voice tears me from the haunting memory. Her azure eyes are warm, despite their color.

"Sorry, I missed what you said." I lean back in the chair and place my hands on my legs.

"I was thinking about going to the other section of the cellars tonight. To free more. Do you think that's stupid?"

"No," I respond without hesitation, the muddled fog in my brain dissipating. "I think it is admirable. Would you care for some help? Two ears will be better than one." Hopefully good enough to avoid being caught. And if we do, I hope any guards could be coerced into not caring. My fire flares at the thought of a fight.

She bites her lip in contemplation. "Are you sure?"

"I would help you a thousand times over." The thought leaves my lips before I can retract it. No matter. It feels good to have someone like this again, to be around a person who is kind and good. Whose ideals seem to align with mine.

A grin spreads across her face. "Be careful what you say, Thea." She leans forward, and I find myself doing the same. Her smile widens. "You might find yourself in over your head."

With that, she stands from the table, closing the unread book as she rises. Her heels click on the timber flooring. Only then do I realize the cold spot on my foot where hers was touching mine. And the breath that lodged in my throat as I unknowingly held it.

"I'll come by your quarters once the sun sets. I'm going to get a drink." She turns at the top of the three steps. "Did you want to come?"

I clear my throat and shift in my seat. The offer stirs the slumbering hunger within me. I shove it down and shake my head. "Not yet. I wanted to look for one more book I saw yesterday. I'll join you in a few minutes."

She waves a hand before turning back to the door. "I'm taking it to my room. I've got a letter to write," she says, as if I knew all along that she was writing correspondences to someone.

"A letter to a lover?" I muse.

She laughs, the sound warming the room. "Something like that."

❧

THERE WERE ACTUALLY a couple books that I wanted to check out. Both snuck into my dreams last night. In the absence of Cole, there were images of golden hilted swords and a mysterious leather-bound journal that I could never quite reach. They constantly remained a distance away that my arm could not touch, and if I jumped, they jumped. A game of cat and mouse, but I didn't feel like the cat. I've never felt so taunted by books before. Unfortunately, one that I seek is by that statue, and I'm not sure if I want to go near it again.

The painting of the sword still sits in the same spot, pointing to that dark corner in the back. An uncomfortable sensation pokes at my side. I ignore the urge to face the end of this aisle and what sits in the shadows. Still, the golden hilt gleams in the candlelight, as if it is waiting for me to return. It is exactly what appeared in my dreams last night, which is unnerving. Morwen and I haven't even begun to train with swords, and I'm not entirely sure I want to. Magic is my weapon.

I trace the frame of the painting. My mind is pulled into another place. Unlike the last vision I endured in this library, this one comes in snippets. I'm still aware of my own body and where I am, but I can see images as if I were pulling them from my own memory. An altar of stone, a red cloth set atop. Candles flickering in the darkness. The sword sits on the altar, nestled on a pair of silver hooks. I trace the paint that depicts the pommel. A robed figure places a copper bowl on the altar and utters words in a language I have not heard before. A feminine voice. She dips her fingers in the bowl and raises them above the pommel. A thick, dark liquid drips onto the sword and seemingly disappears as it does so, as if the sword was devouring it. An iron aroma fills my nose. That liquid...its blood.

The images cease the moment I remove my hand from the painting, the scent of blood slowly disappearing with them. I let out a long, shaky breath. Two visions, both revealed to me in this library. Before Cole turned me into a vampire, he erased my memory so I wouldn't remember meeting him. My heart still remembered though, deep in my subconscious, as it conjured images in hopes of reminding me. Could these visions that the statue and sword revealed to me be similar somehow? I've already learned that my family was connected to vampire hunters. How far does that connection run in the supernatural world? Or maybe these visions are trying to show me that I have always been destined to become a Brais.

"The sword of all swords," a deep, curious voice says from behind me.

I jump at the sound and swivel, suddenly frozen at who stands just a few feet away. Commander Kael is poised in the archway between two shelves, his frame blocking the entire space. His expression is light, a contrast to what I have usually seen. I could have sworn there was a flicker of a smirk on his lips as I turned around. His long chocolate hair falls loose around his face. The sight of his armor causes a flutter of my nerves. Black with gold accents. The King's armor. My blood freezes and I fight myself to remain unfazed. Has the King always been right under the Brais' nose? Surely, someone else would have considered him being the King. Unless everyone is too frightened to suggest it.

Commander Kael takes a step forward, his cobalt eyes moving to the painting. "An heirloom of the first vampire. It is said to be the last piece of her legacy." He lifts a brow as his gaze turns back to me. "It is said that her will haunts the castle's walls."

"Morwen isn't here," I blurt out of irritation, or stupidity, before my brain has a moment to decide whether that was a good idea. I have no desire to hold a conversation with him, let alone have a chat about ghosts. Did he come in here to taunt me or to give Morwen something to research?

A short, low laugh. "I see that." He surveys me for a moment, and I resist the urge to squirm under his intense stare. "I will look for her later," is all he says before turning away.

I am just about to sigh with relief when he half turns back. "And Thea, if that sword is calling to you, best not to ignore it." He looks to the back of the library, his gaze so intent that I wonder if he can see through the shelves of old books, right to the statue with that stone sword. "Like the rest of the relics within this castle, the sword once belonged to the first vampire. Now, it all belongs to the King." His smirk widens into a devilish grin, his attention roaming the library around us. "Do be careful."

I watch him leave until his muscular figure disappears behind the shelves. Nerves prick down my spine like nails, and I remain motionless until I hear the click of the library doors. Even then, I don't move. Not until my feet hurt from the lack of movement, and my body aches from being so stiff. Every bone, every muscle and cell screams at me to run away. To escape this horrific dimension. Why did I think that I could be a spy? Because I've watched countless action movies where the heroine prevails despite their lack of experience? But this is real. Real life, and I've already seen a vampire be killed for being considered a traitor to the Brais. How can I do what that vampire could not?

A clap of thunder rattles the windows above and startles me from the spiral of thoughts. I tilt my head and watch the droplets of rain smack the glass.

Real life.

This isn't some fantasy where the good always win. The Brais are old. If Amaund is old, patient, and strong, I can only imagine what the King is like. Lightning races across the clouds, stretching from the windows above the door and past those above the dark alcove in the back. The haunting presence of the statue pushes against my mind, as if it knows how much it terrifies me. Just the thought of the vision petrifies me. I don't want to know why it felt familiar. Why that blue light was so reminiscent of the one I thought I saw when my parents died. I don't want any part of this.

Another crack of thunder booms against the ceiling. Something behind me glows a ghostly cerulean, its light casting a shadow from my body. Forcing myself to turn around, I clench my teeth and twist on my feet. Somehow, my hand itches for a weapon instead of calling upon the flames. My heart sinks at the sight.

The painting of the sword is glowing.

Actually glowing.

A faint blue light in the shape of the blade outlines the sword before shifting to a golden one at the hilt. I feel the pull of something tugging me back to the shadowy alcove.

Thunder rolls and the candles begin extinguishing.

"Nope," I mumble to myself into the growing darkness as I snatch the tome with the Latin title and scurry out the door as quickly as possible.

CHAPTER SIXTEEN

THEA

Sitting on my bed with extra candles to light the room, I take a sip from the blood bag and let the liquid calm my unease. The book I took from the library sits open in front of me, its words seemingly screaming into the stillness of the room. I've read the same page over and over, unable to understand anything helpful. The only thing I was able to comprehend is that the vampires took and adapted a tradition that was used in some witch cultures. A *Necaut Necare*. It means a fight to the death, typically for the power and title of leader. A swirl of fire emerges on my fingertip and slithers around my finger. If I could use my fire on the King, I wonder if I could overwhelm and devour him in it.

The storm has only gotten worse. A terrible wind started up, each gust rattling the panes of glass in every hallway I walk through. Even my slender window by the nightstand bends to the wind. The rain pours from the clouds in sheets, and I can only see about ten feet out.

I curse at myself for leaving those other books on the table in the library. But until Morwen is with me, I'm avoiding that room. As much as my bookworm-self hates the idea.

The scent of the lavender that Morwen got me wafts into my nose, further calming the nerves stirred from the library. With every dark corner of the castle, an unnerving presence lingers. At least my room is safe.

My hand mindlessly moves to the pillow next to my leg, aiming to stroke what would have been my cat's fur if I were home. Helios was always my reading buddy. Any time he crosses my mind, I shove the thoughts away. My heart can't handle being away from him and his raspy meows. My fingers crave the silkiness of his orange coat, and my ears miss the heavy vibrations of his purring.

Again, I reach for the pillow, my eyes staring blankly at the scribbles of words in the book. I close my hand in a fist and throw the pillow against the front wall. Anger sizzles in my chest, in my blood. Anger at the ache in my heart, at the absence of a life forgotten. A life where my biggest concern was selling my art and finding a place to set up camp.

I slam the book shut and push it off the bed. It lands on its spine on the cold floor with a thump, opening again just to spite me. I toss the wool throw blanket on top of it and lie down, staring at the ceiling.

Despite being empty, the blood bag's aroma entices my senses. If it weren't for not wanting to walk back down to the storage room, I would go get more. Instead, I shove the hunger away and close my eyes, listening to the raging storm outside.

A fist pounding at my door causes me to jump out of my skin, my heart thundering against my chest. Smoke from a burnt-out candle slithers around the room, moving swiftly with my abrupt change of position.

The pounding continues, the loud noise vibrating through me.

A familiar presence, mixed with unusual fear, pulses with each aggressive knock. I get up and frantically move to open my door, stumbling on the blanket crumpled on the floor.

Morwen pushes past me when I let her in, her eyes wide and strained.

"What's wrong?" I ask, concern flooding my thoughts.

She moves to the other side of the room and waits until the door clicks closed before she opens her mouth. "The Commander is furious." Her words come out shaky. "Can I hide out in here for a while? I don't want to be anywhere near him."

I still at the information, my own nerves pinpricking down my spine. Sweat beads on my back and in my palms. The last time that I saw him angry, he killed that vampire. Though that wrath manifested in a terrifying calm. And before that, he snapped my neck when I didn't do what he wanted. "Of course, you can stay in here as long as you need to. But why is he mad?" I ask, my tone hushed as if he could be on the other side of the door listening in. "I just saw him not even a half hour ago. He seemed happy."

She crinkles her perfect brows. "That can't be right. He just came back from going outside the portal. He was gone for a couple of hours."

"Oh." The candle that burned out sits on the windowsill. The wax has melted and left a trail halfway down the stone wall. "It must have been a dream then," I say, mostly to myself. "Why is he mad?"

She swallows and looks out the window, her slender fingers caressing the lavender petals. Her gaze looks far beyond the forest behind the castle. Past the wind-blown treetops. She whispers when she says, "Amaund is dead."

I practically choke on an inhale of breath. "What?" Though I trust and feel safe around Morwen, I don't think that jumping for joy about the horrible General's demise would be a good idea. In whatever manner he died, he deserved it. For what he did to those he killed. There is a small part of me that sinks at the thought that I was unable to see his face when he realized he was going to die. The glee turns sour in my mind at another thought. "Who killed him?" I ask, trying to keep my voice calm. Could this be why I haven't heard from Cole?

Morwen glances at the plant between her fingers. "A witch." She turns to me, her narrowed eyes scanning my reaction. "Your friends are okay, by the way."

I can't help the sigh of relief. Sarah killing Amaund was good. She deserved the vengeance for her mother's heartbreaking death. Still, I wish I could have been there to console her. "How do you know my friends were responsible?"

She casts her gaze downward, a red tint blooming on her cheeks. "I'm sorry I didn't say anything before. Word travels fast around here usually. Most of the castle probably knew what vampire created you once you arrived. And it's hard to keep a battle between the Brais and Essites secret." Her expression shifts so slightly to a suspicious irritation. I reach with my beta ability and only find her usual calm energy. "Though, this battle appeared mostly to be with the witches of the Minuit coven and the Brais. Most likely a retaliation for killing their coven leader." Her drifting gaze snaps to mine, and she winces. "I'm sorry."

I ignore her words, swallowing my rage and the jab of magic that wanted to lash out at her for saying that. "Were the Essites not there?"

She runs a hand through her long cherry-black hair. "Including the Tempest, there were only a total of four Essites who fought the Brais. Most of their force were witches. And," now her expression turns curious, "werewolves."

I blink at her. "Werewolves? Fighting together?"

She nods. "I think they were with the witches. So, it is true then, that your friend is the new Minuit coven leader."

Sarah mentioned that she was slated to take her mother's position as leader during the weeks that I was training at Cole's cabin.

Morwen is seeking an answer. But can I trust her? She has shown only kindness to me these past weeks. Even so, she is still a Brais. And she seems to work closely with the King, even if she has never met him. Panic rises and my pulse pounds under her gaze. If I tell her, how long will it be until the King knows as well? The attack and death of Amaund undoubtedly made the Minuit coven a threat to the Brais. I wonder if my allegiance with them would force the King's hand in some way. Sweat beads on the back of my neck, and I flatten my clammy palms on my pants.

Morwen's eyes soften in my silence, and she places a hand on my arm. Her touch feels like the coziness of a fire or the warmth of sunlight. It reminds me of being around Sarah and Cole. It feels like the Essites. Safety and goodness. Like the receding tides revealing the wonders hidden underneath the ocean, my fear washes away to reveal a friend. A friend who worries and has shown that she will be there to help. "She is," I confirm.

Morwen smiles, her fingers moving slowly down my arm in a comforting gesture. "That's a powerful ally to have, Thea." She looks away as she drops her hand. "It could also be a terrible enemy to have."

Strangely, the worry and fears I had when first meeting Morwen creep back into my mind. It grows with each step she takes away from me and to the door. She turns to face me, and I realize she is most likely expecting some type of reassurance. I shove the fears down, sticking them in that cage. "Sarah and I would never become that." In all our years of knowing each other and living together, we have never really gotten into a fight. Sure, we disagreed on things, but we have always had good communication. Sarah always has my back no matter the situation. And I always have hers.

Morwen cocks her head. "If your friend has declared war against the Brais, which you are now a part of, would that not make you her enemy?" I can't make out the tone under her words. There is a layer of curiosity, but also something else. Something that my body wants to tremble under.

Somehow, I keep forgetting that Morwen is still a Brais. Something in that gilded cage rattles.

I swallow, acutely aware of every muscle and movement in my throat. "I suppose it does." My mouth has gone dry. "Though I hope our friendship runs deeper."

Morwen nods. "It is said that the Minuit coven will stop at nothing to protect those they love. They would destroy anything that poses a threat." Her gaze rolls over the entirety of the room. "I wonder if they would be able to destroy this dimension."

I almost ask if that is possible and have to bite back the eagerness. "What would happen if it were destroyed?"

She rubs her fingertips on her shoulder, hidden underneath the neck of her sweater. "Everyone still residing within would most likely be killed."

A heavy silence settles in this now cramped space as a flash of lightning brightens the room. The storm still continues, though it doesn't seem as much of a torrent. If what Morwen says is true, and Sarah finds a way to destroy this dimension, could that end the war? Cole mentioned that the Brais have many places they reside, but there are so many Brais here that if it were destroyed, surely the hit on their forces could change the tide in favor of the Essites. If the King is here, then I hope the witches wouldn't second guess the destruction of this dimension.

Morwen clears her throat and drops her hands to her sides. "I think I might try and get to my room. You should get some sleep, Thea."

"I will," I say.

She turns and exits the room, no typical smile or pleasantries on her face like I'm used to. I get a sinking feeling in my chest and can't help but feel like I revealed too much of my thoughts.

~

*T*ALL *GRASSES and golden dandelions tickle my bare feet. I wiggle my toes in the softness of the earth, tilting my head back to embrace the glorious sunlight. Though I still can't feel its warmth, I relish in the glow. A light breeze wraps around my body, and when I look ahead, I see him.*

"Cole." Leaves crunch underneath my steps as I run to him. His warm smile that I have missed stretches across his chiseled features.

"Hey," he says as we embrace. I take a deep breath, hoping to be greeted by his cedar scent. Still, there is nothing. "I'm sorry we couldn't meet sooner."

I pull away enough to look up at him. "It's okay. I'm glad you're here now."

"Me too," he says, squeezing me tighter. After a few moments, we release each other and sit down in the grass. The meadow stretches far, no trees or lake in sight.

"Is Sarah with you this time?" I look behind him to the deep blue sky beyond.

He snorts a laugh, the sound sending tingles all the way down to my toes. "Do you think I would risk your wrath again and come here alone?"

"Tell her I miss her."

He turns his head and casts a side glance behind him, as if listening. His smile falters just a fraction. "She said she misses you."

"Is everything okay?"

"Of course. We are just tired," he winces.

I lie my head on his shoulder and listen to his steady heartbeat. I let it calm the growing worry in my chest. "I heard you had a busy evening fighting Amaund."

Cole stills. "You heard?"

His tone is full of enough mixed emotions that I have to look at him again. Even here, in this peaceful sanctuary, his skin has paled. "Did something happen?"

His mouth opens, but he closes it almost immediately, his attention flicking over his shoulder. "No. It was just a draining fight." He brushes hair away from my face, his hand resting on my cheek. "I'm sorry if I worried you."

I lean into his palm. His smoke-colored eyes seem to sparkle in the beams of sunlight. "It's okay."

He frowns, lowers his hand, and looks behind himself again, his jaw clenching. "Sarah wants to know how you found out about Amaund."

I turn around as if Sarah is sitting behind us. "One of their leaders died, everyone knows." A dandelion bends over from a burst of wind and brushes my hand.

"Who told you?" Cole asks, his voice almost a growl. Not directed toward me, but to the Brais. A warning.

"Her name is Morwen." Perhaps Cole knows her. He was a Brais once, after all.

He opens his mouth to say something but is cut off. His eyes widen, and he twists to look around. His body flickers for a moment, like the image from an old projector. "Sarah? What's wrong?" Cole motions to stand but fades away before completely rising.

"Cole? Sarah?" I yell, frantically getting to my feet and turning in place. "Sarah!"

The worry in his voice before vanishing sits like a rock in my body. I shove a hand through my hair, scraping at my scalp as I pace back and forth. The meadow is still here, which means the link must be intact. I've never been able to come here or stay without one of them. Still, not being able to be with them... What if they were followed? What if Kael is hunting them down? What if they're being attacked—

"Thea, I'm here."

I whirl around and see Cole, his expression calmer though still tainted with exhaustion. "Is Sarah okay?" I ask, my fingers twisting in my lilac cotton shirt.

"Yes." He frowns and takes a deep breath. "She's tired, but she is fine."

My shoulders drop in relief. "I'm glad you're okay," I say, tilting my head to where Cole looked before.

"I'm not sure how much longer we can keep the connection here." He takes a few steps forward so we are an arm's length away. In other words, he's asking me to tell him any information I can before he disappears again.

I shove my hands in the pockets of my loose pants. I still haven't been able to figure out who the King is. Kael's image flashes in my mind, of him and his armor. Of his warning. "I don't have any information for you yet."

Cole eyes me for a moment before softening his voice and saying, "Stay alert. And please, be careful."

"I am." I almost wince at the words, having remembered that I left those books on the library table. Before what happened earlier, I always assumed that Morwen was the only one to use the library. A foolish mistake, considering the number of vampires in the castle and that I'm not always in there. Hopefully, if someone sees the books, they'll look past them or just assume it was Morwen's research. Or perhaps they'll just think nothing of a new vampire being curious about this new world she's been submerged into.

I consider not telling them about the other things that have happened. The statue and the sword. Kael said the first vampire's soul rests within the castle's walls, but also that all the old relics belong now to the King. So, which one is trying to taunt me? "What do you know about this castle that I'm in? Did it belong to the first vampire?"

He scratches the stubble on his chin, his attention fixed on a swaying flower. "I've never been to the castle and there are so many stories revolved around it and her. If you let me see more, I can help you better."

I shake my head. "No, Cole. All you need to know is that there's a castle involved."

His expression hardens as if he was about to argue with me on this. Instead, he sighs and runs a hand through his dark hair. "I have heard that the first vampire resided in a castle before she became a vampire. It's also said that the castle is where the witches killed her centuries ago. How it became the center of a separate dimension, I'm not sure."

I really need to get back to that book I left behind. "It's at the center of the dimension?" I wonder how large the dimension is. If I were to travel into the forest in the back, would I hit an invisible barrier? From my window, it looks to be an endless landscape.

"All magic made dimensions require an anchor. A tethered object that keeps the dimension stable." He rubs the back of his neck, the muscles in his arm and chest flexing. When I realize that I'm staring, I snap my attention back to his face. Luckily, he was looking at the sky. "I just assume that it's the castle, but I suppose it could be something else. Maybe even a person."

"I think there are vampires here who would fight against the King." Even though we are alone, safe from any ears within the castle, I whisper the words. Just the thought of sparking a revolution from within the King's domain sends my magic on defense. A chilled spider walks down my spine and over my arms. If I thought being secretive around their library was a difficult task, infiltrating their ranks will be even more so.

But there are Brais vampires who have fought back. I witnessed it the day Kael killed that male. And my old college professor. Whether they were once Essites who have switched over to save themselves or others, or just too scared to stand against them…

Cole keeps my gaze, a contemplative expression on his face. His jaw tightens, and I imagine thoughts racing through his mind. Knowing him, he understood the meaning in my statement and is trying to figure out if he can dissuade me from any further action. "I know there are," he finally says in an equally hushed tone. After a long breath through his nose, he takes a few steps forward, closing the space between us. "Thea, no vampire who has stood against the King has survived. I'm the only one who has escaped. I didn't fight." The muscles in his throat move as he swallows. "There have been attempts at revolutions in the past, but any vampire connected, no matter how little that connection was, was executed."

"Should we just sit and wait for him to destroy everything then?" I *ask, my tone sharp. The King is at the center of it all. If he were elimi-nated, could we stop the war from continuing? Would those who oppose him step up to create a better world in the aftermath?*

"No," Cole answers. He lifts a hand to my face, his thumb brushing my cheek. "It terrifies me, you know? To know that you are in the most dangerous place, and I can't be there to help. But," he loops a strand of hair behind my ear, "you are strong, Thea. And I trust your judgements."

I place my hand on his that still rests on my face, a smile on my lips. "I learned from the best."

He chuckles. "You have always been strong. I know that in my soul."

I fight the burning in my eyes. "I miss you," I say with an ache in my heart. "You, Sarah, and Helios." I run my hand down his arm. "I wish that none of this happened, me being here. And I wish that it wasn't neces-sary for me to stay."

A caressing wind dances between us, leaves picking up with it. The realization of missing my favorite season causes another ache in my chest. A small price to pay for working toward stability. In a world I didn't even know existed until a couple of months ago.

"You'll come back to us. I know that in my soul too," he says softly. He closes the distance some more and moves his hand so that his fingers trace over my lips. "And when you do, Thea," he purrs, my name almost a prayer on his tongue, "I want to kiss these lips."

I think I stop breathing. All I know in this moment is his promise and those endless, beautiful gray eyes. Here, in this sanctuary, we are floating in space. There is no meadow, no loving winds. No mental bridge where Sarah can eavesdrop. It's just us.

A smirk cuts across his face, revealing a pointed tooth. Flecks of red glitter in his irises. Two indications of his desires manifesting through his vampiric being. His hand moves slowly down my chin and to my neck. If I could feel his touch, I think I would melt into a puddle on the grass. "I have to go, Thea."

Finally finding my voice, I say, "I know." The words come out shaky as I try to hold myself together. The weight of everything that I haven't told him yet is heavy on my tongue. He and Sarah should know about the visions. But I don't want them worrying too much, especially if they are going out and fighting. Sarah might be able to provide insights on it all, but that would just add to everything that she already has on her plate.

Cole rests his forehead on mine. "It might be a while until we can reach out again. I don't want to leave you wondering where we were, but we've already used too much of our magic in too short of a time."

I close my eyes and breathe him in deeply. "Okay. Take care of your-selves, please."

"We will. Stay safe, Thea." His words come out more in a plea.

"I will." We embrace before releasing each other. Every cell in my body craves his touch, to drink in the warmth of his body. We break apart too soon, our fingers laced together as he takes a few steps backward. "Give Helios some love for me," I say, biting back the tears that threaten to break free.

"I will."

We don't say anything more. No words are necessary to convey our emotions as he slowly dissipates into mist. I can still see his smokey eyes holding mine as he vanishes.

CHAPTER SEVENTEEN

THEA

A few uneventful days pass with the same schedule. I wake up, feed from the storage cellars, train with Morwen, then research with her. Meditation is still difficult, but we sit for hours in the eastern garden. Luckily, I haven't burned her or anything else. My brain usually wanders first to Cole and Sarah before it shifts to the missing books. The ones I took out and left on the table vanished. When I went back the next morning, I saw Kael leaving. I contemplated turning around, but he spotted me immediately, only offering a vicious curl of his lips. I've only seen him a few times since Amaund was killed, and each time, he gave me a stare that could curdle blood. Morwen has assured that if he wanted me dead, I would be already. Knowing that somehow doesn't make me feel any better.

"You're distracted," Morwen calls from her corner of the garden. Her dark hair is wrapped tightly into a bun at the crown of her head. For today's training session, she decided to forego her usual librarian attire for a pair of joggers and a black rain jacket. We are working on increasing the intensity of my fire magic. According to Morwen, the rain will help prevent any unwanted, potentially hazardous outbursts.

Despite being a vampire, the cool bite of the air and the cold rain makes me shiver. I rub the palms of my hands together and shake the rainwater from them. "I'm sorry." It has been raining since yesterday morning and the ground is soaked. The center of the garden is inundated with a decent-sized puddle. I wouldn't be surprised if my toes have wrinkled from being submerged for so long. The sun, still hidden behind dark clouds, has sunk toward the horizon. The space is illuminated by iron candlelit lanterns.

"What's on your mind?" she asks, making her way to the center of the garden. She stops just before the edge of the puddle.

That's a loaded question. What *isn't* on my mind these days? I look toward the castle as I reach out with my beta ability, checking to see if it can sense anyone's energy. We are alone. Still, I keep my voice low. "Have you ever looked into who the King is?"

Morwen stiffens, her blue eyes shifting to our surroundings. A grim expression flashes across her face when they settle back on me. "It doesn't end well for those who get curious and find out."

I furrow my brows, nostrils flaring. "What do you mean?"

She closes her eyes for a moment, then, she pulls the neckline of her raincoat away from her skin. There is a blotch of black ink just above her collarbone. "The moment someone learns the King's identity, they receive this mark. It is a spell, or curse rather, to keep any mention of who the King is..." she swallows, wincing as she does so, "quiet. Its either that or death. Like I constantly have a blade at my throat waiting for me to say the wrong thing."

I walk to her, my steps slow. The coolness of the water at my feet, and the drops from the sky keep the growing anger at bay. There is visible pain on her face. "This spell hurts you?" I say through gritted teeth. It looks like someone pressed the image of a yellow flower on her skin. The ink is raised and appears rough to the touch. The brown twig begins at her shoulder and forks into two, the stems curving away from each other, as pale yellow, stringy flowers emerge at the top. I get the sense that I've seen this tattoo before, but I cannot recall from where.

"When I talk about this topic, yes." She covers the mark with her jacket collar again and straightens the coat on her body. Pooled rainwater runs down the sides, getting lost in the streams made from the increasing output from the clouds. She squints and looks to the sky. "Let's get inside."

I nod and fall into step beside her, our pace steady. We can't really get any wetter from the rain. I feel my nails digging into the flesh of my palms. "It makes me so angry, that he did that to you." I point to her neck.

She keeps her head forward, her face soft. "It is what it is. I recommend not doing anything that puts you at risk of receiving one. The King has dominion over those with the mark. No one can fight against it." Her voice is hollow. Is that why she stays with the Brais? She can't fight against the King. If she were an Essite with that mark and came face to face with him…

I stop walking as we pass under a tree, and Morwen turns to face me, brows furrowed with confusion. Rain pelts the ground as the storm increases. Hate burns so deep within that cage that I just stand there, my mind reeling. If the Brais have no regard for human life, their King has no regard for his subjects. And that is dangerous. For not just the vampires and humans but for every species. If someone who is in charge of others cares only for themselves, they taint the world they live in. There can't be any growth or peace in life, only despair and darkness.

"What is it?" Morwen wonders, her eyebrows turn up in concern.

"I can't," I breathe. "I can't sit by while others are tormented or not even in full control of their own bodies." The mark on her neck, though hidden underneath her coat, seems to hum at my words. "The—" I search her face, unsure if I should continue the thought emptying from my mouth. She didn't say that she couldn't listen to a conversation about the topic. And if the slate-gray whirls of energy around her are any indication, she isn't happy. But are her emotions directed at the Brais, the King, or this conversation?

"Thea?" she asks, placing a gentle hand on my arm. "You can trust me." Her lips turn down with worry. "I know some-times it might not seem that way, that I am fully committed to the Brais, but," she lightly caresses the scar underneath her sleeve. Until now, I don't think I've ever noticed her Brais mark. "You give me hope, Thea. It's true that I've only ever known and been with the Brais, but you give me hope for something better."

A wave of calm washes over me, and I place my hand on hers that still rests on my arm. Part of me hates that I still doubt her intentions even when the energy says otherwise. I extend my beta ability one more time to our surroundings. Still, there is no one else but us out here in this miserable weather. "The Commander. I think Kael is the King."

She drops her hand from my arm, her eyes wide.

"You don't have to say anything," I urge, sensing the worry pouring from her shaky movements. "I'm not certain, but I think that he is. It would make sense." I bite the inside of my cheek as thoughts race through my mind. "He tries to hide who he really is for both protection and to incite fear. But those who work as sentries have his back. He also is the only one who ever receives commands from the King. Also—"

"Thea," Morwen cuts in. "I believe you." She pauses, and I

can't help but wonder if it's because she is expecting the pain from the mark to come. The thought sends a flare of magic sizzling in my veins. "Please, be careful."

TODAY'S SESSION in the library was put on hold. Morwen wanted to rest before doing whatever it was that the King has her doing. She couldn't tell me what that was, of course. At least now I know that there is a reason why she becomes secretive about things. I wonder how many other vampires here have that mark on their collarbones. And if I were to find concrete evidence regarding the King's identity, would I receive that mark?

Since Morwen is busy, we'll have to put off our rescue of the humans another night. The rescue is not something that I want to do alone, so waiting it is. Spending time alone in the library is also not high on my list.

I watch Morwen escape to the stairs that lead to her room, a sadness tugging at my heart, before turning to the hall that leads to my own room. I desperately need to get a drink, but first, I want to get out of these soaked clothes. My legs shake with each step and my feet slosh in the sneakers. Everything about me is uncomfortable at the moment. I pass by many other vampires, none who I have ever spoken to. Many of them glance at me briefly before continuing their trek to wherever they're going.

A throbbing pain intensifies in my gut, and I grip the railing as I stumble up another flight of stairs. Maybe I should have gotten a drink first. The closest storage room is down two flights of stairs and down a corridor that runs almost the length of the castle. The cellars with the humans…that's just at the bottom of three flights of stairs.

I clutch the wet shirt that sticks to my stomach, nails

digging into my skin. The pain clears a bit of the fog that pushes against the hunger that fights to take control. I should have taken a bag of blood with me to train this afternoon. Using my magic has drained so much of me. Just one more set of stairs until I'm on the same floor of my room.

The flickering light of the candles along the wall brighten. I can see the subtle changes of where the paint along the stone has been redone. Strange that it is in blotches. The sharpness of my teeth poke at my bottom lip. With a shake of my head, I dig my nails in deeper. My vampiric vision and pointed teeth recede, plunging me back into the dim light.

When I get to the landing, hunger rolls through my body. The throbbing pain becomes sharp, and I double over. I didn't realize how hungry I've been getting. I bite down on a gasp, my tongue catching underneath my sharpened teeth. Warm blood leaks from my tongue, the taste turning my stomach. I should have just gone to the storage room.

After a moment of consuming pain, it subsides enough for me to straighten, using the wall as support. My hand cracks the stone, and I just stand there, staring as the rest of the pain sizzles down to a bearable ache. When I remove my hand from the wall, chipped fragments fall to the ground.

With an exasperated sigh, I rub a hand on my face and make for the corridor. The wound on my stomach from my nails and tongue already healed.

One step at a time. Get to my room, change, go to the storage room.

I only pass a few other vampires on the way to my room, my mind still struggling to focus on anything but how hungry I am. And as I turn the knob on my door, I let the calming scent of my lavender plant wash away the rest of the discomfort.

I focused so hard on the sensations and thoughts that I didn't notice who was in my room before I almost finished closing the door.

Commander Kael stands by my bedside, the lush lavender plant in his hand. Somehow, his usual black armor seems more menacing in my small room. He turns at the sound of the door, his dark blue eyes devoid of emotion. The deep brown stubble around his chin is longer than I've seen it before. "Close the door, Thea," he says coolly.

CHAPTER EIGHTEEN

THEA

With Kael standing in my room, I no longer feel the hunger ravaging my insides. His ominous presence is only heightened by the dull, flickering light from the candles and darkness on the other side of the window. Clad in his black armor and sword, my body screams to run. For days, he has hardly been around. And now he is in my room.

And we are alone.

Did he somehow evade my magic earlier when I was searching for another's presence? If he somehow hid himself, then he heard everything. And if he truly is the King…

The ghost of an invisible sting burns in my throat.

The sword at his hip is long, almost touching the floor. He could probably unsheathe it and plunge it into my body before I could even reach the training shortsword in my closet. It would be a stupid move—a gamble that I surely would not win. Morwen has praised me for how fast I am, despite being a Kindria. The King is an experienced vampire. He must be able to move at least twice my speed.

Magic heats underneath my palms, eager to be of use. Too much training with Morwen has left me depleted, otherwise I might be able to use my magic as a distraction. Would I even be able to do any damage to him in that armor? I doubt my dull sword could. But running would likely not turn out in my favor either. Especially since I haven't discovered the words needed to use the portal. I would be trapped.

I am trapped.

I close the gap between my palms and my soaked pants, splaying my fingers. My magic disperses at the touch. The movement catches Kael's eyes, but he just stands there. I close the door behind me, swallowing the rising fear.

"A lovely day, isn't it?" He places the lavender plant on the cold windowsill. Dread explodes in my chest at the book sitting next to the crumbs of soil on the nightstand. The book from the library written in Latin.

A flash of lightning streaks across the sky, illuminating the forest beyond. It casts a frightening silhouette of Kael, making him look like a shadow. An old memory of watching a thunderstorm claim a sky over a dense mountain with my mother filters into my muddled brain. And as the lightning cleared the darkness, it also cleared my thoughts.

I will not bend to fear.

"Hardly," I say, intentionally keeping my response short.

He studies me for a moment, his face still emotionless. "I was curious how training with Morwen is going."

"It's going well."

"Good." He shifts his body so that he is facing me fully. Sometimes, I forget how big he is. His broad muscles seem to take up most of the width of the room, the top of his head almost to the ceiling. The sight is intimidating, threatening to bring me back to that frozen state of terror. "I would like to see for myself tomorrow. Morwen can have a break from training you."

The mix of confusion and horror must be written on my face. A short burst of air exhales from his nose, and he crosses his arms over his chest. "The magic that runs in your blood is not something that should be idled so you can gallivant in the library every day. It would be a waste."

The words *during a war* were left from the end of his last sentence. My magic does not awaken to his claim. And because I'm foolish, I open my mouth and say, "I will not fight for the Brais." My body braces, expecting a blow from his fist or sword.

He doesn't move. He remains standing with his arms crossed, his gaze locked on to mine. It is more unnerving than having him explode in anger. His dark blue eyes pierce mine, and I fight the urge to look at my feet. I feel the prickling sensation of sweat on my back, but it is lost in the wet clothing that still clings uncomfortably to my skin.

Kael drops his arms and takes the few steps necessary for him to be within striking distance. He leans in, and I am hit with the stale scent of blood. "You are a Brais. Will you not fight for yourself?" As if it was connected to him, the scar he imprinted on my wrist starts to burn. A reminder that I am, indeed, a Brais. Something like fury or challenge glimmers in his eyes. "Would you not fight for your friends here?" He flashes a wicked grin, lethal fangs protruding from his upper lip.

Morwen's gentle face crosses my mind, followed by Sarah's and then Cole's. "I will *always* protect them," I snarl.

He laughs and straightens his posture so that he looks down his nose at me. Though he wears a smug smile, a flash of sorrow flickers in his eyes. My energy manipulation flares to life and reaches for him, not to heal his sorrows but to test my curiosity of whether he can feel anything other than fury. His energy is stiff and thick, like cement before it dries. A layer of bright red anger sits as the outlier of his emotions. It feels fragile in some spots, as if it were tired. By his heart, it is the thinnest. I almost gasp at what I feel. There is so much sorrow and grief. My finger twitches with the automatic desire to send him comforting emotions to soothe the ache there.

Like the flip of a switch, my magic snaps back into me. Its retreat leaves me heaving, a dizziness threatening to knock me to the ground. As much as I would prefer to not let him see me like this, I can't support myself and brace myself on the door-frame. The stone is cool to the touch.

Confusion flickers to realization as he tenses and puts a hand on the hilt of his sword. He could slice my head off before I would even register him unsheathing his weapon. Rage dances so slightly on his features.

A wave of hunger washes over me again, the pain crippling. This time, I can't hold myself up. A gnawing pain ripples through me like an earthquake, and I collapse to one knee. My nails dig into the floor, scraping wood as they curl. My teeth slowly emerge from my gums as if it were their first time. I stifle a cry as it feels like knives tearing through my mouth.

The sound of the floorboards creaking screech into my ears. Kael crouches next to me. "I suppose it is a good thing that I took the liberty to call for a human to your room."

The space around me bristles, colors pulsing as my vision shifts from normal to vampiric. A throbbing ache pounds behind my eyes, followed by a numbness. "No," I force out through gritted teeth.

"When our bodies are so low on nutrients, it pushes us to feed. That drive is so excruciating, we lash out at anything with a heartbeat." The triumph in his tone is evident. He relishes in vampires killing humans. A cold hand grasps my chin and forces my head upward. His eyes dart between mine and his smile grows even wider.

There is a knock on the door before it opens without invitation. Kael grabs my arm and pulls me to my feet, keeping hold so that I don't fall again. His touch is like the first step in ice cold water. The sting travels to all parts of my body.

Just inside the room stands a dirt-covered woman, led in by a vampire in leather armor. The woman's vibrant red hair is matted to her face with mud and her clothes reek. By the look of her, she must have been here for a long time. Her body is on the thinner side, though not as much as I would have expected it to be. Though the scent of fear lingers on her, there is only tiredness etched into her face.

"Do it," he says.

"No," I say through gritted teeth. "I want a bag."

Kael's eyes gleam with an emotion I can't pinpoint. "Why do you deny yourself that which your body craves?" He lifts his chin so that he looks down his nose at me.

I match his posture and his eyes narrow. "A blood bag or nothing at all." I grind my teeth as red slips into my vision. On this, I will not budge. A low rumble in my stomach awakens that primal hunger deep within, eliciting a response from my fangs. They slowly slide further from my gums, but I retract them back, reminding myself that I don't need to feed on an innocent human to live.

A growing silence hums between the Commander and me, neither of us willing to change our stances on this. Kael's gaze flicks to the woman behind me, a spark of red forming in his irises. His nostrils flare slightly and his expression becomes hard. A lock of his brown hair falls from its place behind an ear.

I'm about to demand a bag again when I smell it. That tantalizing, honeyed aroma. I turn to the woman and see that she has cut herself on the neck with a small pocketknife clasped in her hands.

A part of my brain recoils at the thought that she would do that to herself, but then I remember that some vampires can control a human's mind to a greater degree than just erasing their memories of being fed upon.

I have already taken two steps toward her before I realized

what I was doing, my gaze locked on to that glorious crimson liquid dripping down her neck. The sound of her heartbeat pounds in my ear like an enchanted song. As if on instinct, she tilts her head, exposing the wound. My mouth waters at the sight, and I take another slow step.

Morwen's words flash across the part of my mind that is still fighting. I swallow, still watching the woman's blood as it stains her already soiled shirt. From all the debris caked on the material, it is impossible to tell what color it once was. "I don't have to feed from a human again if I don't want to," I say in a raspy, low voice and the woman's dull eyes move behind me. I swallow, ignoring the fogginess entering my brain. "I want a blood bag."

"You are limiting your abilities, Thea. Compared to drinking from a vein, blood bags offer significantly less nutrients. You'll need more, and even then, you'll never reach your true potential in magic or strength." The scuff of his boot on the floor sends an alarming jolt down my spine. "Drink from a human and you could be unstoppable. Didn't you say you wanted to save people?" he asks in my ear as the woman moves closer to me. Does she want to be fed from?

"I won't drink from her." My lips quiver because I know that he speaks the truth. The memory of the rush of power that comes with feeding from a human ignites the hunger pangs in my stomach. Still, I don't move for her.

"Please," the woman breathes, her voice weak. Water lines her light brown eyes. Staring into her weary expression pulls my beta ability to her. Sorrow blooms from her heart and ripples outward, the emotion so intense my knees wobble just from sensing it. Her plea for me to feed seems to come from this place of extreme sadness. Like she doesn't want to be here anymore. Doesn't want to *live* anymore. Something in my heart shatters at that thought. If I can't save the people in front of me, what hope do I have at saving others?

Kael whispers in my ear again, his breath like ice against my skin. "The human is asking to be fed from. She *wants* it, Thea. Indulge her."

"No," I whisper.

"Then I guess she's mine."

The sweetened scent of her blood travels into my nose and all the way to my stomach, eliciting another wave of hunger. I am starving, and the use of my magic has left a ravenous void in my gut. Kael did not say that I have to kill her. If he feeds from her, I have no doubt that he would end her life. "I'll feed from her."

His hand on my back pushes me forward. I follow the momentum and take the last few steps to her. She tilts her head more, opening the wound wider. The drum of her heart beats with each wave of hunger within my body. It calls to me, to my senses. My teeth slide from my gums like shards of glass, but I'm too focused on her blood to register the pain.

The woman braces as I grab ahold of her arm and chin. I tilt her head up and back. Her neck is the only part of her body that I can see that isn't smeared with dirt, as if the Brais make sure to keep it clean. The woman gasps as my teeth sink into her neck. More blood flows from the openings, and I drink as if I have never consumed anything in my life. I greedily take from her body, each drink more needy than the last.

Honey and cinnamon and vanilla.

The gilded cage within me shakes with exhilaration. It asks for more, and I oblige. My magic runs along my skin like electricity as it wakes up. And my body shivers with a fresh burst of life—of power.

I sink my teeth in even harder, liquid pouring into my mouth like a roaring river. And the human's grip on this world slips.

CHAPTER NINETEEN

THEA

The woman trembles underneath my grasp. Her teeth chatter as if she were out in a snowstorm. The movement pulls me from the intoxicating adventure of euphoria. I become aware that her heartbeat is slowing and that her posture is beginning to slouch. If I continue, I'll kill her.

A person. She's a person.

Kael's approving presence lingers in the corner of my room. I feel his gaze on me, on the tight grip I still have on the woman's body. He wants me to keep drinking, otherwise he would have stopped me by now. I'm reminded, once again, how little value a human's life is to him.

To the potential King of the Brais.

I remove my mouth from her neck and quickly catch her before she falls onto the floor. With more tenderness, I put my lips back on her throat, leaving them just on the unbroken skin. Nerves prick on my spine when I feel no heartbeat.

Please be alive.

I'm so sorry.

Then, ever so subtly, there is a beat. It is so faint, and I'm not entirely sure if I just imagined it, so I wait for another. I almost sigh in relief when the next one comes, no fainter than the last. It is so quiet that my ears did not hear it. I could only feel it through my lips.

I place her gently down onto the cold floor. For anyone looking, or listening, she appears dead. Her body is limp and only a soft touch can sense any pulse.

"Good," Kael says into the silence as he walks to the door. He puts a hand on my shoulder as he passes. The touch, though brief, leaves a stain on my skin. I want to burn it off. "I'll have someone come and clean it up. See you tomorrow, Thea."

I look up just as he is exiting and see a satisfied smirk on his face.

Time moves so slowly as I wait for his cleaner to arrive. Each second that she is prone on the floor is a risk. I may have some time to make her stronger. My blood heats as my beta ability flares to life, eager to heal. I study my tingling palm as a faint blue glow forms along the veins underneath.

Kneeling beside the woman, I place one hand on her neck wound and another on her chest and unleash my energy manipulation. The healing magic flows easily into her body, seeking out what needs to be mended like a missile to its target. My right hand warms on her chest, the magic aiming to soothe. The magic under my palm on her neck intensifies as it attaches to the broken vessels. The inside heals first before restoring the visible parts. My magic cures the broken skin of her wound, pulling them together like it were a stitch and needle.

As I feel the magic pour out of my hands, something enters at the same time. Another sort of magic that doesn't feel as warm as my own. It reminds me of the cold bite of metal on my skin after it's been left out in the winter. More noticeable in my left hand, it travels from my palm up my arm. Then, it passes through my shoulder. As if someone drags a knife across the side of my neck, a slicing pain burns where the strange magic touches. I lift my right hand to the throbbing spot and pull away red stained fingers.

The sight roots me in place, my beta ability staggering. How am I bleeding? The woman's chest heaves with a deep breath, her heartbeat gaining a healthy rhythm.

Removing my hand, I stand and turn to the old, cloudy mirror inside my closet. My neck is bleeding. The wound looks exactly like the one that was just on her neck. A deep slice with a pinprick on each side. And it isn't healing.

I look at my hands, still tingling with the residual magic that makes me a unique vampire. When I healed those plants while training with Cole and Sarah, there were no aftereffects. But healing a human…did the wound transfer to me? I flex my hand, the blood already dried and cracking. Like all other vampires, I could have tried healing her with my blood first, as I did with those hikers in the forest all those weeks ago. But she was hardly holding on to her life because I drank too much. I couldn't risk healing her with my blood then her turning into a vampire because of that. I will not force this lifestyle upon anyone.

"W-what happened?" a hoarse voice says. I turn and see the woman slowly rising, a hand on her forehead. Her eyes move to my neck and widen at the sight of blood running down my skin. With trembling lips, she says, "Did you—did you turn me?"

I blink at her, my hand still raised in front of my chest. "No, I didn't. I healed you."

Her alarmed expression doesn't change. "Why?" she whispers softly. Color has returned to her face, a lovely rosy stain on her cheeks. She looks so much younger now than when she shuffled into my room earlier.

I wonder how long she has been here for and how much she has suffered. I clench my fingers into a fist. "Because I care." The next thoughts race through my mind so fast that I hardly have time to register them before I speak. "I'm going to get you out of this place, okay?"

Water lines her eyes and she forces herself to stand. "Thank you," she whispers.

I offer a small smile and reach for the glass of water on my nightstand. It has been sitting there for a week, but that most likely means nothing to someone who is thirsty. And by the way her eyes light up when I hand it to her, she must be parched. "Here." She takes the glass with a shaky hand. "What's your name?"

"Riley."

"Nice to meet you, Riley. I'm Thea." I almost cry at the genuine smile she gives me. In just a short time, she looks nothing like the frail human who walked into my room just moments ago.

As she sips the water, I pack a few things into a bag. Her light brown eyes follow me around the room as I shove random things inside. A change of clothes, worn shoes, a small pillow, and blanket. I even throw in one of the fantasy books I took from the library that I've been meaning to put back.

A knock at the door has both of us freezing in place. The doorknob turns, but I am quick to run and grab it, cracking the door open just enough to see into the hallway. A stout vampire stands with one hand at his side and the other dropping from the knob. There is a tired expression on his face. "I've come to retrieve your indulgences," he says.

I blink at him for a moment before I shake my head and run a hand down my hair, making sure the long length covers my bloody neck. "I'll take care of it, actually. I wanted to get outside anyway."

One of his thick dark brows turns up. "It's raining."

I shrug. "My favorite kind of weather."

He narrows his eyes, his gaze shifting to any space behind

me that my body does not conceal. "Listen, I'm just trying to do what the Commander ordered me to." Irritation seeps into his tone, and he straightens his posture.

I close the door a little more, the knob pressing against my hip. "Right, and the Commander told me I could take care of it if I wanted to." The lie rolls off of my tongue easily. Anything to save a human.

Doubt billows from the vampire in front of me, slamming into my still-humming beta ability like a raging plume of smoke against glass. He takes a step forward, his hand moving up to the center of the door.

Without thinking, I let my beta ability free. Conjuring images of Kael and his fury, panic crashes into the vampire's distrust. My forced emotions weave around his easily, and he hesitates as his palm flattens against the wood of the door. "I don't know about you, but I wouldn't want to question Kael and risk his wrath. He told me I could do it if I wanted to." I push another sliver of my magic into his emotions for good measure.

The vampire takes a couple of steps back, the candles along the hall illuminating his features better. Though he still manages to keep a neutral expression, there are hints of growing distress in his face. "All right, all right. Just be quick about it. Bodies are dumped to the western border, off the cliffs."

I reel back the cringe bubbling up in my chest. "Great."

He nods curtly before sauntering down the hall, his heels scuffing against the floor. The sound echoes, and I leave my door cracked in order to keep track of how far he has moved. Silence takes over after the sound of a door closing.

"Let's go," I say to Riley after a few minutes of quiet.

"We are leaving now?" She glances to the window that is being pelted with rain.

"Not yet. We are going to the library. There is a room in

the back that you can hide in for a bit." I take the empty glass from her and place it on the nightstand. "There are portals to this realm that I don't know how to use. A friend of mine does, though." Morwen will help, I know it. If she's been too busy for rescuing more humans from the cellars, then freeing one that has already been released will hopefully be quicker.

THE PAST TWO straight days have been nothing but heavy rain and dangerous winds. Now, the clouds finally break away. It's like the dimension knew that we needed to get Riley safely out as soon as possible. Stars dot the darkened sky as we emerge into a circular meadow far from the castle. I'll never get used to the silence of the forests in this dimension. Or the strange emptiness. In the forests back home, there is a life within the plants and animals that scurry about. Here, it is utterly still.

Riley and I both stop in our tracks at what lies in the center of the meadow. An arched portal of black stone, smaller and narrower than the one that I entered through, which stands with an omnipresence amongst the trees. Though the nature here looks ordinary, even a human can tell that this portal was constructed by something other. The energy surrounding it hums and the hairs on my arms stand.

"I knew that there was another portal, but this is the first time I'm looking at it," I whisper. The portal Amaund took me through that day was larger and of weathered grey stone.

Morwen continues forward. "This one doesn't get used as much due to its size and distance from the castle." Indeed, it was a trek to get here and looks like only one person at a time can pass through.

"Where does it lead?" I ask out of plain curiosity.

Morwen steps over a small branch that sits in her path. "It could take you anywhere. But without guidance, it would take the traveler to an old manor in Europe." She turns her vibrant gaze to Riley. "Where would you like to go, Riley?"

"I have family in upstate New York," she answers timidly.

The corners of Morwen's lips pull upward. "That didn't answer my question, Riley."

A red tint creeps into Riley's cheeks and she glances to me. "I'd like to go there, please."

"As you wish," Morwen responds. We watch as she steps closer to the portal and pulls out a small dagger from the brown cloak around her shoulders. If it were possible for the forest to become even more silent, it did. I feel like I can hear all the leaves rustling on the farthest corners of the dimension and the sound of feet shuffling somewhere in the gardens. She looks over her shoulder at Riley. "Step in front of the portal, please."

Riley follows Morwen's command, stepping so that she stands between the portal and Morwen. The temperature seems to drop as Morwen holds her hand in front of her and places the dagger on her palm. She doesn't even wince as she slides the blade along her skin. Crimson liquid pools into the cup of her palm. I strain myself closer in order to hear the incantation.

"*Sol Invictus redit cum duobus.*"

With a twist of her hand, she squeezes her pooled blood onto the grass. Like before, a black velvety curtain ripples from the space between the pillars. A salty, metallic tang fills the air and coats my tongue. As if she could read the confusion on my face, Morwen says, "This portal is old, and you're sensing that by the magic it gives off. Think of it like a layer of dust covering the portal space."

That actually makes me more confused.

Morwen drops her hand once the veil stops moving. A thin sheet of opaque magic hangs from the arch. The trees beyond it become more visible the longer it sits. "Go ahead, Riley."

Riley turns to look at Morwen first then to me. Her features soften as she says, "Thank you, Thea and Morwen. For everything."

I offer a smile, hiding the sadness looming in my heart. I wish that she was never put into this horrific place. The Brais and their disregard for human life needs to be put to an end. "Be safe, Riley."

She smiles before turning and facing her new life.

CHAPTER TWENTY

THEA

This morning was a compilation of failed attempts at meditating and researching. My nerves are too great for any sort of stillness. Morwen gave up and had me practicing stances and combinations for fighting with swords. That sort of practicing helped subside the jitters for what is to come. We were both surprised at how natural it all came to me.

"Maybe you were a swordsperson in your past life," Morwen muses, stealing a glance at the rare blue expanse above. Only a few clouds dot the sky, making it feel like a completely different place.

I chuckle, smiling at her glimmering stare. "Do you believe in that stuff?" The concept of reincarnation has always fascinated me, and I've babbled to Sarah countless times about it. Knowing now that she is a witch who is deeply connected to the earth, it makes sense that she always latched on to every word. I've fantasized about how our bodies are just recycled elements from beings of the past and that our souls live with the wind before settling down somewhere new.

Morwen stretches her arms above her and tilts her head

back, soaking in the sunlight before we enter the castle. "I do." She moves her sparkling gaze to me. "Imagine how sad it would be if we only had a small amount of time to experience its magnificence. There are so many things to see and lessons to learn."

We pass a cracked marble statue of a bird with its wings spread. It appears there was something hanging from the wings, but it has since broken off. Jagged shards are left behind, giving the bird a wicked look. I shrug and say, "I don't know. Vampires go against that argument though."

"But vampires weren't always a thing on this world. Compared to all the other supernatural races, we are babies." She cocks her head. "Though you are right. Out of the others, we are the only race who could essentially live forever. Which is perfect for wanderlusts and curious minds, like me." A toothy grin spreads across her face.

In the weeks that I have been here, I have never known her to leave this dimension. Unlike Mica and many other Brais, Morwen remains here, mostly in the library or in the garden with me. "When was the last time that you went through the portal?"

She runs a hand through her long hair. The deep red color catches in the sunlight, imitating a smoldering flame. "That was a strange statement to make, I'll admit. I can't remember the last time I walked through the portal. It's been decades, most likely." There is an underlying mixture of emotions layered within her words. My beta ability senses her usual calm smothered in a sadness, though I could have sworn there was a hint of anger laced in her last sentence.

"Why don't you leave?"

Her usual blue, calm aura covers her body again as she lets out a long breath. "The war has kept me in here." She glances sidelong at me.

"If the war were over, you would leave?" I put my hands in the pockets of my loose pants as we walk under a drooping willow tree.

"I would, I think." She raises an arm so that tendrils of the tree caress her skin. "Though," she continues, her expression thoughtful, "depending on who wins, living out there might be too frightening."

If the Brais win, the real world would undoubtedly plunge into chaos. Would other supernatural races step in to put them down? Or is it solely the responsibility of the Essites to stop them. The Minuit coven has taken a stand against them. Maybe others would follow suit. Surely, if the Brais won, it would not just affect the humans, but them as well.

Still under the protection of the tree, I stop walking. Nerves prick at my spine and travel all the way down to my tapping foot. Leaning against the rough trunk, I take a shaky breath.

Morwen walks to me and places a hand on my shoulder. Concern clouds her usual vibrant eyes. "What's wrong?"

I stare at her for a moment before reaching out with my magic to sense any other vampire's presence. My fingers clutch the trunk, scraping as I struggle to comprehend all the thoughts racing through my mind. Just when I convince myself to not divulge my ideas to her, for both her safety and mine, a flash of memories coat all other thoughts. Memories that prove I can trust her.

I straighten from the tree and lean closer, lowering my voice. "Do you think there are vampires within this castle who would rebel against the King?"

Morwen blinks at me but keeps the space between us close, her hand sliding down my arm. She opens her mouth but shuts it before saying anything. Then, she opens it again. "That is an incredibly dangerous thought to have, Thea." I almost sink away at her response, but she adds, "But yes, I do. And you can trust me with that idea you have, you know that, right?"

"I do, thank you," I say with a small smile.

"Good," she says, returning the expression. "I don't think there has been any vampire who tried to execute a coup d'état against the King. At least, not one I am aware of."

"I don't even know where I would start. Or if I could pull it off." A shudder crawls down my spine. In the last few months, I went from a traveling artist to a vampire spy in a deadly court. I'm not even sure how I've pulled it off this long.

Morwen runs a finger over her chin. "Most vampires here might know of you, but none know you enough to follow you into something so dangerous."

In other words, none would follow me to their deaths. Because this would most likely be a one way ticket to a shortened immortal life. But the possible outcome vastly outweighs the risk. For some reason, the King has yet to make any significantly grand moves against the Essites in a long time. But the constant ball of dread that lives in my gut tells me that he has been planning something big that will be executed soon.

Most likely to retaliate for Amaund's death.

Which could possibly put his aim right at Sarah and Cole.

Even if starting a coup only distracts him long enough that the others can move against him, it would be worth it.

"Everyone knows you," I blurt.

Fear and nervousness poke into her aura, the emotions prickly against my magic. She waves her hands in front of her, the loose sleeves around her elbows swaying with the movement. "No, no. I would be the worst to start a coup against the King. You should talk to Mica. Though he has this mark too." She points to the inked part of her neck, hidden under her blouse. "I think he would help you."

My eyes widen with realization. I remember seeing the tattoo on his neck and wondering about it. He also pushed me that day to look to the library for my answers to everything.

"He should be back," she adds. "He was one of the few Brais survivors of the attack at Amaund's manor."

I open my mouth but am cut off by the tingling sensation of someone coming within earshot of us. A rigid, cement-like energy bounces against my magic. Morwen looks a moment before me in the direction of the side door that leads to the garden. One of the silent sentries is making his way toward us, a rolled-up scroll in his hand.

We break away from each other, positioning ourselves to receive the sentry and the note he bears. I have a feeling the note is for me. Training with Morwen pushed a little too close to my session with Kael and he sent one of his guards to retrieve me. From what I've heard and witnessed, he isn't one to appreciate waiting.

Which means, he will be in a lovely mood for our session.

Morwen crosses her arms as the sentry dips under the dangling branches. His armor clinks in the silence as he hands the scroll to me. The sun filters through the tree just enough that it gleams on his upper body. Though his armor wraps loosely around his neck, I can see between his skin and the metal. I suppose that there is no need for a binding spell to keep one silent if they have no tongue to speak secrets.

The sentry waits as I open the scroll and read it. Morwen, though standing right beside me, doesn't lean over to read it. Out of the corner of my eye, I can tell that she is glaring at the sentry.

Thea,

Per our conversation yesterday, I am to assess where you are with your training. Come to the training room the moment you finish reading this note. Do not keep me waiting any longer.

Your Commander,

K

"Lead the way," I say to the sentry, who appears to be unfazed by Morwen's glower. He takes the scroll, turns, and walks back to the castle, not bothering to check if I am behind him.

"Good luck," Morwen offers with a frown. "I'll be in the library if you feel up to joining me afterward."

I take a step after the sentry before turning back to her. If Kael wants to make me miserable, I'll do the same to him. Lowering my voice to barely a whisper, I say, "Maybe we can finally do that thing?" Rescuing more humans.

Her frown deepens, regret showing in her blue eyes. "I can't. I'm sorry, Thea."

I wave her off. "It's okay. See you later."

The sentry is almost to the door, so I rush to catch up. I'm tired of waiting. Tired of knowing that the humans in the cellars have been nothing but fodder for the Brais. I know that Morwen feels bad, but each night that they are there, they suffer. According to her, the humans currently in the castle have been here for at least a few months.

Months.

Months of being imprisoned and kept in a dark cellar where their only source of light are flickering candles. From what Morwen told me, the General in charge of replacing and handling the humans has been too preoccupied to notice the ones she freed before. Perhaps that General is the only one with that job.

So, if something should happen to her...

The wooden, double doors to the large indoor training room are pulled open. Flickering sconces line the wall at eye level, their light swallowed by the dim glow from the windows. The ceiling is high and devoid of candles, so it is hard to see just how tall it is. Vampires grunt as they face and fight each other with all sorts of weapons. Fists, magic, swords. There is a dozen here, all keeping their attention on their opponent rather than the bulky vampire standing in the back. Kael.

He is standing, a sword in his hand, with his piercing gaze locked on to me.

CHAPTER TWENTY-ONE

THEA

"Pick up your sword," Kael growls. He traded his black armor for brown leathers. An empty bandolier is stretched across his front and golden stitching and buttons accentuate the pristine piece. Luckily, he also swapped out his terrifying metal sword for one that is made of bamboo. Unfortunately, it is still incredibly sharp.

The Commander wasted no time in showing me how poor my sword fighting skills are. Rather, how poor my speed is compared to his. The past thirty minutes have consisted of me trying, and failing, at evading his swift movements. The moment I stepped onto the mat, he struck fast and hard, knocking my weapon from my hands.

Now, I kneel on the cold gray mat, breath heavy as I grab my own bamboo sword. Blood coats the grip, stained from an already healed wound on the back of my hand.

Kael moves the moment I stand. His right foot glides silently over the mat as his arms carry his weapon in an arch over his head. It is the same strike he just used to disarm me. He will swing the sword around and bring it toward my hands at an angle.

I bring my weapon up to the right to try and block his blow, twisting my blade so that the flat side will catch the edge of his. Our swords clank as they collide, the sound echoing into the darkness of the high ceiling. Vibrations ripple from the wood and into my hands that clutch the grip so tightly.

If he is surprised that I stopped his attack, he doesn't show it. Instead, he slides his sword down, the edge of it scraping against mine. The sound is quick but abhorrent, rattling my spine. My block doesn't stop the fluidity of his movements and he steps backward and out of the reach of my sword. In a single breath, his body spins toward mine. Unable to predict his move, I bring my weapon back in front of me to protect my center, but not quick enough. As he stops just a foot away, he brings the pommel of his sword slamming into the back of my left hand in an unforgiving crack.

The sharp pain causes me to instinctively release the sword and bring that injured hand in to my abdomen, leaving another opening for him to strike. I move just in time to dodge his left elbow colliding with my jaw and the smooth leather of his sleeves slides against my right cheek.

When my father was alive, he would drill into my head during his self-defense training to use my opponent's movements against them. That's easier said than done when the person you are facing is an experienced supernatural being. Before becoming a vampire, I've never had to use any of his teachings in a real situation. It turns out that recalling what he taught is like remembering the combination for my high school locker. Everything still resides in my mind like an ice-covered stream. After years of unuse, I just needed to melt the blockages a little.

With Kael's elbow angled upward, his sword hand hangs in front of my face. Biting down the pain, I wrap my injured hand around his wrist and dig my nails into the leather hard enough to feel the outlines of his tendons. If I can squeeze hard enough, perhaps I can get his weapon to drop to the floor.

He snarls and is lightning quick with a retaliation strike. Candlelight glints on a silver ring upon a finger on his right hand. It is the only thing I see before his fist collides with the bridge of my nose. Obliterating pain erupts from the impact and clatters in my head. I collapse to the mat again, holding my face as blood pours from my nostrils.

His footsteps on the mat send explosions of pain into my pounding skull. "Pick up your sword," he demands again, his temper exponentially higher.

This makes the fourth time that he disarmed me, each by hitting precisely the same spot. He seems to revel in knocking weapons from his enemies. With vampiric strength, I'm surprised that getting a cut is the only thing to come from each hit.

If he decides to put more strength into his moves, I'll be lucky to not lose a limb.

Ignoring the onlookers—who, at this point, are only pretending to train with each other—I force my shaky legs to stand. Kael's sneer doesn't go away as I grip the sword tighter and position myself for another round of assaults. If we were sparring with magic instead of swords, maybe I could actually protect myself. Instead, I look like a fool who has never even held a weapon. It doesn't help that he isn't holding back. Or at least, he doesn't seem to be.

The moment my hands rise, Kael strikes. With only one hand holding his weapon, he again spins the sword over his head in an embellished arch. He brings the blade down, aiming to slash it across my chest. The movement was fast, but I was able to catch it early enough to move my own blade. I shift my feet and arm so that his attack hits flat on my sword. The reverberations vibrate into my already aching body. Blackness seeps into my vision as the movements rattle my injured face.

I hardly have enough time to collect myself before he is moving to strike again. Kael steps back and slides his sword away from mine. In a fluid movement, he brings it back as he advances. The sword smacks me right in the left side of my abdomen, knocking the breath from my lungs.

He then, with vampiric speed, spins and brings the sword down on my head. It connects with a ringing thud that I feel it all the way to my feet. I drop to the floor, the sword falling from my hands. Blood oozes from the wound and drips down my eye.

"You're lucky I hit you with the flat side. Both of those blows would have incapacitated or killed you otherwise." He walks to a bench just outside of the mat and picks up a towel. "Even a bamboo or wooden sword can do damage."

"Yeah, I know," I grit out. "I've only had a few weeks of training." An ache is thundering in my head, my nose stings with each breath, and my side is throbbing. Kael tosses me the rag, and I wipe the blood away. He watches me impatiently and with disgust. When his gaze flicks to those around us, I hear a sudden burst of activity.

"Get up," he says as he returns to the mat. I throw the rag on the ground and stand. "Your movements with a sword are good, but you are stuck in a human's way of moving. I could have hit you ten times before you even saw my sword move."

I don't know what to react to, his compliment of my skill or the boast of his. I take a deep breath, reveling in the slow mending of my body, and shake out my hands before grabbing the sword still lying on the mat. If the issue is of my slowness in perception, then I'll try Cole's advice. Instead of imagining only my hearing is on a dial, perhaps it will work with all my senses. With another deep intake of air, I close my eyes and imagine everything linked to a knob within my mind. I increase what is needed: my hearing, sight, and speed. I open my eyes with the exhale and lift the sword.

A slight tug on Kael's lips indicates that he noticed a change. This time, when he lunges, I am ready. He is still extremely quick, but at least my brain can register his movements faster. I parry his forward attack and shift on my feet in time to block his next move that hits my sword right above the hilt. I ignore the disrupting vibrations and step forward with my own lunging attack. He evades easily, sidestepping and using his change of position to swipe at my back.

This time, he uses the point of the sword. I try to turn around and block it but am too slow. His weapon cuts into my shoulder and slides across my upper back. I disregard the tickle of liquid streaming down my back, and the acrid aroma created from it.

"Still not good enough," he says, poising for another strike, this time for my legs.

I want to ask him to explain. Good enough for what? The Brais or something else? Why is he so adamant about me training so hard? But the flow of the session is moving too fast for my brain to be able to ask questions. Another old lesson from my dad emerges from my cobwebbed memory. A move to deflect an attacker from behind. But with my own vampiric twist. I rotate my body as my beta ability flares to life and stretches toward Kael, connecting with his jagged energy. As if in slow motion, I can sense the exact positioning of his feet, body, and weapon, as well as how they are moving. In response, I twist my wrist so that my own sword is level with his hand.

Two can play at the game of disarming. With a step to close the gap between us, I flick my wrist, the flat side of my sword pushing against the end of his with as much strength I can pull. His sword bounces away from me, giving me space for another move. As I take another step, I bring my elbow up and aim it right for his throat, using both of our momentums to my advantage.

I'm too locked into my attack when I notice the grim satisfaction cross his features. A flash of scarlet in his irises causes a wave of gooseflesh to travel down my entire body. With such a fluid movement, he lifts his free hand and grabs my elbow, rising it enough that I become unstable. At the same time, he pulls his weapon arm back, bent at the elbow, and lunges forward. It was so fast that even my magic couldn't pick up the flow of his energy.

His sword pierces my abdomen. The splintering pain causes me to drop my weapon and grab ahold of his out of instinct. I feel my blood pouring from the front and back, staining my already soiled clothing. A pained cry escapes my throat, which only widens his feral grin.

I strangely become aware of my heart, beating out of fear, as the bamboo sword scrapes against it. Nausea turns in my gut and the sharpness of the wound becomes the only thing I know.

"Never drop your weapon," Kael chides, clicking his tongue and leaning forward. He pushes the sword in a little more, dragging another cry from deep within me. The sensation of it against my heart is like scraping nails on a chalkboard.

Before I have a moment to protest, he slides the sharp blade into my pounding heart. Pain explodes like fireworks in my chest and courses to the rest of my body in tendrils. A stale, metallic tang coats my tongue. And as quick as he slid it upward, Kael pulls the sword out.

I don't even feel myself hit the floor.

I see nothing. I am nothing.

~

A PULSING, blue light reaches forward, grasping at my limbs. Not grasping, entering. It enters my body with intention and comes from a place born of love.

To protect.

It feels like…family. There is the hint of those soft rose petals from the plant that my mother always loved. And the smell of warm chocolate chip cookies that my father made. Their strength manifested into a glowing light.

Something materializes in front of my eyes and the light weaves around it in a curious fashion. A sword, crafted from golden fire and crimson blood. The light pours from its point and flows into my chest.

The blade then tilts, aiming right at me. It speeds forward and connects with my heart. Brilliant golden light explodes all around me, revealing the silhouette of a person's small figure far in the distance. They turn, and I can feel the hatred dripping from their shadow.

Their darkness overwhelms the light, swallowing it with such ferocity that everything around me quakes.

Then, the darkness swallows me.

~

I AM STARING at the darkened ceiling as I awake, sprawled on the mat of the training room where other vampires are still practicing. My body is stiff, limbs bent in awkward angles.

"Welcome back," that daunting voice says from behind me.

I sit up quickly. Kael is standing off to the side with his arms crossed. He must have been conversing with someone because one of the other Brais is walking away, keeping his gaze averted. I swallow and notice my sandpaper of a tongue, still coated with the stale taste of my blood. The wound in my chest, as well as my broken nose, is fully healed, but I gasp at the sight. My clothing is absolutely drenched with my own blood.

"Seventeen minutes," he says. "That's all it took for you to heal your heart and regain consciousness. Not enough to prevent an enemy from finishing you off, but quite impressive, given you being a Kindria." He makes the compliment sound like an insult with that last word.

My head is pounding, and his voice is not helping. Nor does the sound of all the others grunting in the room. I force myself to stand despite the protesting from my legs. My entire body feels heavy, and my stomach is rumbling. "I wasn't aware that you can heal while you're dead," I snipe back and immediately curse my brashness.

Kael walks over to me, his feet gliding silently on the floor in an even stride. The sound resembles the pulsing of that blue glow from the dream. And though Kael isn't wearing his black armor, there seems to be a dangerous shadow surrounding his figure, as if that unnerving armor is a part of him. He doesn't appear fazed by my sharp tone. "Morwen must be training your *anima.*"

The hunger and tiredness dissolve, and I meet his gaze. There is a knowing sparkle to his eyes that chills my blood. All thoughts leave my mind and, I scramble for something to say. "My soul?"

A muscle feathers in his cheek as he crosses his arms. The ghost of a smile that makes me want to jump from a window. Instead, I school my trembling bones and hold his dark eyes. "When we strengthen our souls, we can withstand the impossible."

Vampires are the experts at being ambiguous.

"Your Latin must be impeccable, given your choice of reading material," he adds, his finger tapping slowly against the leather sleeve. So, he definitely noticed the book on my night-stand yesterday. It was hopeful thinking that he didn't. Somehow, I don't think that many things slip by his awareness.

I shrug, exaggerating the gesture to convey boredom. "My parents taught me." In a swooping motion, I pick up the bamboo sword at my feet. A flicker of candlelight catches on the blade, and I see the sword from the dream. Shimmering and alive. When I stand, Kael is watching me with an unreadable stare. "Another round?"

Under his unmoving expression, I feel the need to fidget. It takes all of my strength to remain as poised as he is. "No. We are done. I'll have Morwen keep training you in sword fighting. It is as important as learning how to wield your magic."

I don't understand why he thinks that, but I don't say anything. With a nod, I put the sword back into the rack next to the array of other weapons. Crossbows, maces, axes, daggers. Some made of wood, others of different metals. I feel the gaze of Kael and the rest of the vampires on my back as I walk to the door and close it behind me.

No one saw me grab a small wooden dagger.

Even if it can incapacitate a stronger vampire for just a few minutes, that is all my fire will need to consume them. Because as the sun begins to set, I won't be in the library researching or in my room sleeping. I'll be in my room, planning to free those humans.

And to secure that no others are brought here until the Essites can infiltrate, I might need to kill a General of the Brais.

CHAPTER TWENTY-TWO

COLE

"Your pacing is making me uneasy," Oba says, his brown eyes piercing mine as I stop in the kitchen. He sits on my dark green couch, his hands clasped together as he leans over his knees. Helios is curled on the cushion next to him, eyes slowly closing as if he is fighting sleep. Oba reaches out and scratches underneath the cat's chin, his dark skin a contrast to the light orange fur. A smile spreads on Oba's lips as Helios' purr vibrates into the cabin.

It has been a couple days since the fight with Amaund, but Oba still wears his leathers and a fully stocked bandolier as if a battle could break out at any moment. I suppose one could. The thought is distressing, and I start pacing again.

Oba groans and turns, placing a hand on the back of the couch. "Are you serious?"

"You're the reason I'm pacing," I chide as I grab on to the handle of the refrigerator, contemplating if I need a drink. I release the cool metal and walk back toward the dining area. The night presses against the windows, and I pull the kitchen curtains closed. "You invited a Brais vampire to my cabin." Not that the location of my home is unknown to the Brais. At least the barrier that Sarah and Valeria still holds. The only reason Oba was able to enter was because he is my ally. Sarah said the magic knows Oba has no ill intentions toward Thea or me.

"I told you, he's the contact I have inside the Brais." Oba stands and stretches. He pulls his phone out from his pocket and glances at the screen. "This is the safest place to have this meeting."

My eyes flick to Helios who takes in Oba's stature. The cat looks like he is contemplating jumping on Oba's shoulders or wanting to disappear. I wouldn't blame him for running, Oba is a giant. I narrow my eyes at my friend. "Yeah, but I am still not a fan."

Oba chuckles. "We'll have to meet him on the outskirts anyway. He won't really be in your house," he teases.

I press my lips together in a tight line before a knock on the door has us both tossing apprehensive glances at each other. Helios darts off the couch and into my bedroom.

There is another knock.

Oba gestures to the door, his phone forgotten in his hand. "It's your house."

I keep my feet planted on the tile in the kitchen and jerk my chin. "It's your contact."

With a huff, Oba walks over to the green front door, taking one last glance at his phone before shoving it into his pocket with a frown. Oba's magic stirs the air around us, mixing with my own. He creaks open the door slowly and peers through the crack before sighing and opening the door wider.

I feel Oba's magic simmering back to a slumber as his contact steps through the threshold. My own magic rises, causing papers and curtains to ruffle and sway. "Are you serious?" I ask to my friend with a growl, never taking my sight off from the pale-haired vampire standing in the doorway.

"So good to see you again, Tempest." Mica says with a

wicked grin. His tall and slender build makes him appear small next to Oba. His white hair is pulled back, and he dons a pair of black pants and a white dress shirt. No weapons that I can see. Not that he needs any. The magic that runs in his veins is deadly enough. His green eyes look around the interior and his grin widens. "You are making a mess of your home."

My magic reacts with my emotions and increases. A few papers from the counter behind me roll onto the floor. "This is your contact, Oba? You should have said that." I all but snarl.

Mica doesn't move from the threshold and Oba just stands a few feet to his side.

"'*He* is your contact, Oba?' is what you should have said, Cole. I am a being after all, not some object." Mica's tone is teasing, though it riles my magic up more.

"Sounds like you two know each other," Oba cuts in. He calls on his own magic, not to challenge but to calm. "You're going to scare the cat."

Mica lifts a brow at that. "I didn't know you're an animal lover."

My nostrils flare and my teeth grind together, but I take a deep breath and straighten my posture. With the calming breath, my magic recedes, though I keep it at the ready should I need it. "I knew him when I was a Brais."

Mica takes that as an invitation and steps fully in my home before closing the door. "We were comrades once."

That time seems like so long ago. Mica was always stationed at the castle dimension, but he would occasionally stay in the Brais camp that I remained in. We had an extreme falling out shortly before I left, when I killed Valeria's best friend and coven mate. "How did you get past the barrier?" At this, even Oba sidesteps, his expression shifting from calm to wary. Even if he doesn't have any ill intentions, he would still need to be considered my ally to get through. My fingers twitch with the tingling magic, a wish. I always perceived Mica as one of the few Brais who was close to the King. The mark on his collarbone glimmers in the dim light, as if it could hear my thoughts. I'm an idiot for not mentioning the King's marks to Thea. Somehow, in my decades of fighting for the Essites, I have forgotten.

Mica simply shrugs. "I assumed the barrier was tethered to you and Thea. And I'm assuming, by your oh so grateful demeanor, that it isn't your trust in me that let me through."

I blink at him, a mix of confusion and rage roaring in my mind at Thea's name on his tongue. I don't know why I never connected them being in the same place, and that he might know her. The casual way that he suggests Thea's trust in him makes my blood boil. Magic like knives slithers under my skin. It wants to tear everything down to nothing. I should have talked Thea down from her mission at infiltrating the Brais ranks and pushed for her to lie low. Sarah and I would find a way to get her out of there. With Mica here, I can't help but imagine Thea already in the clutches of the King. Is he poisoning her mind with his cunning words, or has she been locked away and tortured? At the thought of her in pain, my magic drums violently with my pulse. It pounds in my ears, threatening to explode.

"Cole," Oba says softly.

My friend's voice cuts into the storm in my heart, and I force my gaze to him. His expression is full of worry and his palms are out, as if he thought he was the one my brain considers a threat and is trying to diffuse that. I glance back to Mica and notice thin shards of ice forming around his fingers, though the rest of his posture is relaxed.

"We are on the same side," Mica says, his teasing tone replaced with a cautious one. The ice on his skin slowly melts away. "But if you want me to leave, I will."

Out of the corner of my eye, I see Oba take a half step forward. "No," I grit out, forcing my magic down. It seems to recoil at being shoved away. With a deep breath, I rub my hands on my face, trying to hide their shakiness. "That mark." I jerk my chin at Mica. "You are aligned with the King, aren't you?" I let some of the residual anger seep into my tone.

Mica shoves his hands in the pockets of his pants. "I have had this mark for centuries but I have never been aligned with the Brais' leader."

I frown. "And I am supposed to just trust you?"

Mica dips his chin, though doesn't avert his gaze. "I never told you this, Cole, so let me tell you now." His chest rises with a deep inhale. "Centuries ago, I was desperate for answers and made a bargain with someone who was said to be knowledge-able with curses. At the time, I just thought—" Mica winces, his hand latching onto the place underneath his shirt collar where the mark is. Whatever he was about to say was apparently not permitted through the magic that resides in the mark. He clears his throat before continuing. "The King wanted my magic, and I wanted to save someone I loved who was cursed. The King promised to help." Now his eyes fall to the floor. "I failed, but the King didn't. The help the King gave to the one I loved—" Mica pauses and swallows. "The help *I* sought out, resulted in her death." The anguish in his voice is heavy, slicing through the air and stabbing at my own heart. "I was young and naïve and didn't quite understand the bargain I made at the time. The moment I found out it was the King of the Brais who I was dealing with, this mark etched itself on my collarbone."

The hum in my veins lessens. "So, you know who the King is," I breathe, swallowing my frustration. "And you can't tell us anything?"

He shakes his head. "No." He holds a palm up as I open my mouth. "And before you ask anything else, I can't tell you. I know that it may be hard to trust those of us who have this mark, but just know that having it doesn't equal unconditional devotion." A lock of his pale hair falls into his face and he tucks it behind his ear. "I wish I could tell you more, but I figured you should know at least this." He fixes his shirt, smoothing out the collar. His voice quiets. There is a strand of venom woven into his next words. "If there is anything I can do to get back at the King for killing the woman I loved, no matter how small, I'll do it."

Even though Mica cannot fight against the King, he does what he can to hinder him and the Brais. He trusted the King when he was younger, and it got his lover killed. And now he fights for revenge in any way that doesn't trigger the curse mark on his collarbone. I study him for a moment, observing any indication of deceit. The story could be fabricated. He could have been sent here by the King to try and earn our trust or to kill us. But, he did get through the barrier. Which means Thea does trust him. Or could there be a part of me that still trusts him? Despite not seeing him that often when I was a Brais, we were close. He was always a genuine person back then. And his somber body language suggests that his story is true. If Thea were here, she would tell me that he is on our side. I let a long breath out. "I'm sorry I reacted the way I did. I just—"

Mica waves me off. "To be fair, I did try to kill you the last time we saw each other."

"Second to last time, actually," I correct. "You saved me at the fight against Amaund." The vampire who turned my attacker into a popsicle. He was hooded, but I knew it was him.

A corner of Mica's lips turn up. "So, you did notice then."

"I hate to break up this reunion," Oba interrupts. He is leaning against the wall beside the stone fireplace. "But, isn't that mark supposed to prevent you from moving against the King?"

"Yes and no," Mica answers. "It won't allow me to speak about the King's identity, or any related information, and should I try to physically harm against the King, it would kill me." He runs a hand over his smoothed hair and tucks a strand into his bun. "There is nothing stopping me from divulging other secrets, however."

"What do you have?" I ask. Something nudges against my ankle. I look down and see Helios looking up at me with his round, golden stare. His tail flicks up when I reach down to pet his head, and he rubs his head on my palm.

"You really do have a cat, Cole," Mica says, his tone turning almost childlike.

"I wasn't lying," Oba chimes in.

Mica shrugs before crouching down and sticking his hand out to get Helios' attention. The cat trots over to him and sniffs his fingers cautiously before rubbing the side of his face on them. Mica smiles and runs his hand down the length of the cat. "He's soft."

A part of me doesn't want him touching something of Thea's. "What information do you have, Mica?" I ask again.

Mica scratches the top of Helios' head before standing and turning his attention back to Oba and me. "I've learned that the Brais are going to move on the Essites soon."

"We already know they are planning something for the next full moon," I say, realizing that maybe I shouldn't have a moment too late. Mica knows that I turned Thea, but he most likely doesn't know that she has been feeding me information. Even though he comes here to do just that, I don't want anyone knowing that she is as well.

Mica lifts a curious brow and clears his throat. "They are gathering to attack earlier than that. I don't think they expected the Essites to rally so quickly, nor did they expect an alliance with the witches. Your coalition killed Amaund, and they want to retaliate."

"When?" Oba asks, pushing away from the wall.

"In three days."

Color blanches from my face. I look to Oba, whose complexion also pales. We knew that this was a possibility, but we still weren't ready. Oba has been trying to get a hold of more Essites to fight, but it is hard to find all the ones who scattered after Eero was killed.

"They're gathering their forces quickly." Mica shakes his head, a look of frustration crossing his face. "I don't know their specific plans, but based on things I've overheard, it sounds like they are planning something large."

"Is the King himself going to fight?" Oba asks. It is hard to miss the bit of dread that slips into his voice. Since the death of Eero, no Essites have reported seeing the King. No one knows what to make of that.

Mica just looks at him for a moment, an unreadable expression on his tan features. "I can't answer that." He must notice our tenseness because he continues. "I'm sorry. I can offer you something else though," he pulls out a small, empty vial from the pocket of his pants and rolls it between his palms. "First," he looks to me, his hands pausing, "you should know that given everything, Thea is okay. She's strong."

"Thank you, Mica." I didn't know how much I needed to hear those words from someone. I've known how strong Thea is, but somehow it's better when someone else confirms it. I have told it to myself so many times that I wasn't sure if I was just trying to convince myself anymore, or if I truly knew it.

"I'll tell you everyone that I know who has the mark of the King." He looks to the glass in his hands. "And I can get you inside the Brais dimension."

CHAPTER TWENTY-THREE

THEA

After two days, the only thing I confirmed was that Elisz, the Brais General, is a horrible person. Morwen has been so busy that she gives me instructions for training I can do alone. The practices are quick and easy, giving me ample time to trail the General. She is too consumed in her aggression toward her soldiers and humans that she doesn't notice me standing down the hall, my face in a leather-bound story.

My book of choice is one that looks old and important but is, in fact, the retelling of a fairytale. Someone must have read it so many times that the binding has frayed and the cover is torn. I read it fairly quickly and have since designated it as my undercover disguise.

This afternoon, she is training in one of the smaller rooms with her soldiers, most of whom look exhausted. I found a secluded room next door, the walls thin enough that my beta ability has no issue reaching inside. I can only hold my magic through the wall for a few minutes at a time before I get tired. The blood bags I brought with me help keep my body satiated, and thus, I am able to keep pushing on.

"Do you want me to get a chair for you, Kindria?" A familiar, amused voice calls from the doorway.

I fight the groan that tries to escape my lips as I peer over the pages that I've been staring at. "What do you want, Mica?" I shift on the hardwood floor, my body numb from sitting so long. Maybe a chair would have been a smart idea.

He grins, strands of his pale hair falling into his face. He leans against the doorless entrance of the room, his arms crossed loosely across his chest. "Not a place I would choose to get some reading done, but to each their own."

I haven't seen much of him lately. After getting humbled by Kael in the training room, I saw Mica in the busy halls when I was trudging to the cellar. He took one look at my tired face and stained clothes and turned in the other direction. I could have sworn there was a combination of anger and worry on in his expression, but it disappeared so fast I couldn't be sure. Then, he vanished from my sight. "It looked inviting," I answer, lifting my shoulder in a shrug.

He laughs and looks down at the floor, and I take a moment to study him. Today, he wears a button-down, black shirt. The top buttons are undone, and I can see the hint of that mark along his collarbone. Morwen suggested that I talk to Mica about fighting the King from within. How does one have that conversation with someone? Especially someone who can't talk about the King.

"Enjoying what you see, Kindria?" Mica watches me, his burning gaze full of some emotion I can't figure out. I could reach out with my beta ability, but I don't think that I want to. This room feels too small at this moment. Despite his ability of water manipulation, the temperature rises, and I know it isn't my magic.

A blooming heat spreads across my cheeks when I realize that to him, it looked like I was staring at the bare skin visible in his open shirt. I clear my throat and close the book propped up against my knees and fidget with the binding. "That mark. On your collarbone. I thought it was a tattoo when I first saw it."

He tenses, the smirk on his lips faltering. Mica looks behind him, into the hall beyond. Another reason I like this room is because it is off of one of the quieter corridors. The room that Elisz is in currently can only be entered through the hallway that runs perpendicular to the one Mica is looking into, but it's a bit busier.

Mica takes a few steps into the room and crouches so that he is eye level with me. When he speaks, his voice is considerably lower, and apprehensive. "And now?"

He wants me to say it. To confirm that I know not everything is as it seems here. "I know that it isn't. It tethers you to the—"

"Thea," his voice is a whisper, but it stops me from continuing. There is fear in him. I can hear it in the slight tremble of my name, and I can see it in the nervous swallow afterward.

It is a strange time to realize that for once, he said my name.

"I know I was pushing you to look into the things you were curious about, but," his nostrils flare and he closes his eyes. One of his hands moves to the mark, his fingers digging into the skin. "Things are getting more intense here."

Annoyance floods my thoughts. "If you are about to ask me to sit back, then don't bother."

He stares at me for a moment, his green gaze so piercing. There is a knowing in them. I feel like I'm in a different time, a different place, staring into those same eyes. There is a slight tug on my memory, like I am about to be pulled into a vision, but he chuckles, the sound erasing everything. "I know."

I narrow my eyes at him. "Why do you seem so invested in my safety?"

He cocks his head. "I do not wish to see the Brais become conquerors."

There it is. My opening for what I'd really like to ask of him. He didn't quite answer my question, but I'll take it. "Help me. We can fight the King from inside the Brais. Morwen said others would follow you."

His eyes widen. "Morwen?" It sounds like he was about to say something else but stopped himself. "Thea, it is too dangerous to move on the King from within the castle." With that, he stands. Again, it looks like he wants to say more but is holding himself back. Is it because of the mark, or does he not trust me? His gaze flicks to the wall behind me. As if he could see right through the stone and to the Brais General that I've been stalking. "Be careful."

He turns to leave, but I stand abruptly, gripping the book so tightly in my ire that I almost dig my fingers through it. I'm tired of people telling me that I don't know anything or that I need to sit back and let others handle things. I'm in this life, and I want to help. I *can* help. "Why are you being a coward? There are innocent people getting hurt and killed. And there will be more to come. Do you even care?" There is a feral rage building in my chest that I didn't intend to let seep into my words. Now that it has, I don't care. I want Mica to know how mad I am. I want all the Brais to know.

He turns slowly back around, his expression so devoid of emotion that I slide my foot back as if to take a step. The heel of my shoe touches the wall. He notices the movement, his cold stare moving from it back to my face as he says, so quietly that I hardly hear him say, "I care too much." And then, he walks away, leaving me alone with my simmering rage.

CHAPTER TWENTY-FOUR

THEA

I missed the last bit of Elisz and her vampires training. My mind was too occupied with everything Mica said. *I do not wish to see the Brais become conquerors.* His words imply that he is not aligned with the Brais, and yet, refuses to help me fight them from within. When I first came here, he seemed so insistent that I stick my nose in the Brais' business, but now it appears to be that he wants the opposite. It is making me not trust him at all.

Dwelling on what he wants or doesn't want is not my mission. I think about all that I have learned regarding Elisz so far. She is very strict with her training. When Mica told me that she was once one of the Brais' best fighters, he was not exaggerating. Not a single vampire in her ranks has been able to land a blow against her. If fighting Kael was hard, could I win against her if it came down to it? Most likely not.

And the fact that the King pulled her from the front lines of the war is intriguing. It is good for the Essites, no doubt. She appears to be taking her anger over being demoted out on her subjects.

I'll have to be stealthy if I am to stand any sort of chance against her. The first night that I was following her, she slept in a room on the second floor in the western wing. Since then, she has been awake. If I am going to go through with my plan to bring her to justice, the best chance I have is if she is sleeping.

But can I kill another vampire? Sure, I have killed others already, but that was in the heat of battle. Elisz is not kind and there is no doubt in my mind that the world would be better off without her. But should I be the one to make the judgement of her fate? Perhaps I could just send her to the Essites. Use this stake to incapacitate her and throw her through the portal. Hopefully, they would understand who she is and why she was sent to them.

Outside, the daylight is receding, and rain falls in sparce beats against the glass as it finally gives way to open sky. There will be no trailing Elisz tonight. Morwen left a note, asking for some training under the moon.

The cool evening air on the walk to the garden is refreshing. The rain from earlier left an earthy scent in the air that hugs my nose. After days of relentless rain, the clouds finally gave way to the sky above, gracing us with a glorious sunset. A magenta-and-tangerine-stained canvas stretches from one end of the dimension to the other. The dark castle looks absolutely stunning against the tranquility of the sky. Like a picture in one of my old travel scrapbooks. An entire section was dedicated to places that have a fantasy feel. Only a handful of times has the sun—or moon—appeared for a training session, granting us the ability to do so comfortably. Meditation always comes easier when we are surrounded by nature. Albeit, magically-induced nature.

I'm thankful for the long walk from the castle to the western gardens. Though I saw them from a window, I have yet to visit them. Morwen said the swirling hedges and black roses make this one prettier than our usual spot in the eastern gardens. She also mentioned there's an old water fountain sculpted in the garden's center to look like the crest of the first vampire's family. Now, however, it is too aged and eroded to be able to decipher what it once looked like but is still pretty in its own way.

The gravel beneath my feet turns to cracked pavement as I cross into an old driveway. Weeds have proved their invulnerability through resilience by making the holes in the asphalt home. Humankind—and supernatural kind—could learn a thing or two from plants like these. Plants considered unwanted or ugly by standards set by those within, typically pulled away or burned for ones considered more desirable. Like the standards that society puts on its people, shoving falsehoods down their throats. It isn't much different here, I've realized. The vampire factions and their desire to be the ones in control of the other. The praise for one element over another. Then, there are the witches and their secrets. What would happen, I wonder, if there were no secrets between creatures of the supernatural world and the humans?

My foot catches a beautiful turquoise stone, and it skids across the uneven surface of the driveway, clinking against something as it passes under the half open garage door. Do vampires even need vehicles? We can run as fast as a car can drive, though I suppose our magic and endurance wouldn't be able to handle long treks. Not to mention, traveling would become tiresome if we had any amount of luggage.

The light of the setting sun catches on one of the facets of the stone, sparkling like the tendrils of a flame. Entranced by it, I bend down and reach under the wooden door to pick it up and see the massive front end of a black vehicle a few feet from my face. What catches my eye first is the dent along the side of the bumper. Then, I see the engraving of the Brais sigil on the hood and the world spins under my feet.

The headlights of a huge vehicle blinded me that night— both nights—as it barreled into our lane. It looked bigger than this though, when I was younger and in the back seat of my parent's car. The one that struck Sarah's friend and me off the road just recently looked like this. Though it was dark outside, I can still remember seeing something etched on the vehicle's front end. I thought it was just a triangular design then. Now, I know in my bones that it was the Brais' crest. The shield with three peaks on the top, meeting in a single point on the bottom. And a golden embossed letter "B" in the center.

It's because of this car that I'm a vampire.

My hearth thunders in my chest as everything else becomes silent, allowing the roaring in my head to explode.

Were the Brais the ones who forced us off the road?

The Brais almost killed me when I was little.

The Brais killed me this summer, setting me on this path to become a vampire.

The Brais killed my parents.

It replays in my head as if on a theater screen. Their hands clasped together and the lovely shade of blue that glowed between. I always thought it was the oncoming headlights. But, just like those two burnt corpses in the vision, the light pulsed from their hands, held together in their last moments of unconditional love.

The temperature inside the garage skyrockets. Flames, angry and wrathful, engulf my hands, mirroring the emotions ravaging my mind. They burn hotter as I stare at the emblem on the metal of the car, a cobalt blue flame dancing in their center.

Everything. Everything that has been wrong in my life is because of them.

The Brais killed my parents. They set me on a downward, grief-induced spiral. They are the reason why that terrifying, gilded cage sits at the center of my soul, consuming and holding all the thoughts and emotions I could never handle. If it were not for the love and care of Sarah and Valeria—

Valeria is dead.

Again, because of them.

They'll regret interjecting themselves into my life. The King will burn. *Kael* will burn. No one hurts my family without repercussion.

A piece of crumpled paper on the floor catches on fire as my magic pours from my skin like molten lava. I am faintly aware of someone yelling my name from far behind. The voice sounds deeply concerned, afraid even.

I catch the glimpse of glowing orange eyes reflecting in the window of the SUV. Like smoldering embers. A scream roars from my throat as I punch the vehicle with all the hatred bottled up in my body. All the hatred that has settled and lived in my soul.

The Brais will burn.

I don't even care if they all know.

Flames extend from my fists and eat away at the car, melting the metal as if it were ice. The walls of the garage burn next. The fire consumes the old photos hung in disarray, spreading like a starved wildfire.

I punch the car again, my fist colliding with red hot metal. The bite of the melting car stings my knuckles, but I don't care. Someone could throw a dozen wooden stakes into my back, and I would welcome that pain. Nothing compares to the pain felt at the death of those I love.

Dead because of the Brais.

My arms stretch out on either side of me, palms facing outward, as a roar of flames explode from them. Wood crunches and cracks from their intensity. A gust of air tries to enter through the new holes in the walls but is quickly consumed by the raging fires.

Someone yells my name again, the sound closer.

The Brais were there the night I almost died.

I have murdered humans because I became a vampire.

Because they ran me off the road.

I tilt my head back, the euphoria of letting go completely building in every cell of my body. It's as if every bad emotion, every terrible memory, fuels the magic that is flooding my veins. The heat seeping from my skin is glorious and pure. It seeks to devour, and I want nothing more than to let it.

"Thea!" The frantic voice becomes familiar now. Morwen. Her footsteps are loud on the pavement of the driveway. "Thea, please!"

"Stay away, Morwen!" I yell, my voice hardly recognizable. I am transported back to the night that I destroyed my family's manor. To Cole when he tried to calm me down. To the sight of Valeria's lifeless body that triggered my explosion. To that dark family secret hidden in the walls of the basement.

Morwen may be a friend, and she may even dislike the Brais, but she hardly does anything to hinder them in the war. Destroying the garage might alarm those close to Kael, or even Kael himself, that I know this secret.

Then, I'll go right to him after this.

The fire in my body seems to agree as it shoots to the back of the garage, striking a wooden cabinet. The furniture shatters, sending shards everywhere.

"Thea!" A cool hand grabs my arm. I hear Morwen hiss, followed by the sizzling of her skin. "Thea, please," her tone is softer. "If you want to destroy them, this is not the way."

Warmth spreads through my body. Not the heat from my magic, but that of a comforting calm. Of Morwen's calm. It flows through me, eliciting images that diffuse the erupting magic. Memories of my family, of Sarah and Valeria, Helios and Cole. Of that quiet meadow sanctuary.

And as if my magic were a stitched-together dam holding back years of shoved away memories, Morwen's presence is the gentle touch that melts it away. One look at her concerned face has my magic running. She doesn't balk at my golden eyes either. Just a worried expression for her friend. Tears threaten to break free as I collapse onto my knees, from both exhaustion and grief.

Morwen holds my shivering body, pulling me into an embrace so that I face away from the interior of the garage. "You're okay," she whispers. "You're okay."

The tears fall rapidly down my cheek, my breathing coming in uneven sobs. The fire behind us still crackles, but with less ferocity now. The floor is ice beneath me. We sit there in silence for long enough that the sun dips below the tree line. Morwen just holds me, her palm moving in circles on my back.

I have learned during these past few weeks that not all the Brais crave destruction. Morwen has been so kind and open with me, yet I have not been so. Some things I have left out during our conversations and research. The guilt weighs heavy on my broken soul. I pull away from her comfort and her gaze searches my face, concern still written in every curve of her lips and eyes. If we are to rebel against the King, then there should be no secrets between us.

"I need to tell you some things about my past. About things that I have done and have experienced."

Morwen tilts her head slightly, a curious but sad expression. She wipes a lone tear from my cheek. "I will listen to anything you want to say. I am here for *you*, Thea."

So, as the sun completes its descent, I tell her everything.

# CHAPTER TWENTY-FIVE

COLE

The moss-covered building across the street stands with an intimidating presence. The structure itself has seen better days, some of the bricks are chipped, the glass storefront is cloudy, and the paint is peeling back from the purple door. Earthy perfumes waft from cracks in the door and walls, blanketing the street in the essence of natural magic. There is no mistaking what lies inside.

The Demoix Apothecary sits as a lone building at the end of the old main street. And though it is midafternoon, the closed sign hangs vibrant on the door. With a sigh, I shove my hands in the pockets of my black jacket and make my way to the quiet building.

The last time that I was anywhere near the Demoix coven's apothecary…the scars from my actions are still fresh in my mind. The ache in my chest still burns when I think of the last words that Valeria spoke to me. If she were still alive, would our relationship slowly have returned to civility? It could never have returned to what it was. Not after what I did, nor could it with Thea now in my life.

The door opens before I reach the curb and one of the

coven members steps out. She holds the door when she notices me approaching, and I offer her a nod of thanks.

Entering is like walking back in time. Dried herbs hang from beams along the high ceiling. Elaborately carved chests sit against the wall with the large, cloudy window that looks onto the street. Not that anyone can look out or in, unless their face was pressed against the glass. A wooden armoire towers over the other furniture, stocked full of tinctures and salves. A table set in the center of the room is mostly covered in plants, some potted and some cut and chopped. On the counter in the back, more supplies sit on shelves and a stick of incense burns, the smoke moving idly into the still air.

"You're late," Sarah says from behind the counter, her displeased attention set on a piece of paper. It is a handwritten note inked in straight lines. She folds it when she looks up to me and tucks it under a jar of what appears to be herbs soaking in oil, her expression now blank.

"I was busy," I respond, glancing at the worn rug underneath my feet. The floorboards creak with each step to the back. Sarah has been busy since Mica came to offer his information yesterday. We couldn't find a time to meet, but I was at least able to inform her that the Brais were moving up their timeline. "You wanted to know how I came across that new information. A contact from within the Brais came to visit."

She looks up at me, a single brow lifted. "Oh? Who?"

Her questions sound more like demands, and I fight the urge to remind her about our allyship. Ever since her mother died, her demeanor has changed. It is completely understandable, given the circumstances, but sometimes I wonder if she still truly considers me—and the rest of the Essites—an ally. "An old friend. He expressed that he is an ally of Thea's."

Her fingers still, frozen in the middle of tying a handful of herbs together. "Is she all right?"

Despite my uneasiness about Sarah, I know that she would

still do anything to protect Thea. Not being able to check in has been hard on the both of us. "Yes." I won't mention that I wouldn't be so calm if it were otherwise.

"Then what other information did he give?"

Witches love keeping secrets from others, but apparently hate when others keep secrets from them. "He gave us the words needed to get through the portal." That gets her full attention, her wide eyes snapping up. My hand pats the pocket of my jacket. "And a vial of his blood that he claims will work in opening it. So long as we use it within the next couple of days."

"He just…gave it to you? No conditions?" Her tone is wary, borderline accusing.

"He wants the Brais defeated as much as we do." When her suspicious gaze doesn't leave mine, I add, "I didn't sense any ill intention from him."

A short, bitter laugh. "Am I supposed to trust just your instincts? What if this is a trap, Cole?"

I breathe through clenched teeth, magic whirring in my veins. It connects with the air around us. "He gave me his sun totem to hold onto as a token of his trust."

She opens her mouth to retaliate again, but I hold up a hand. "I can tell the magic of a sun totem and the vampire it's linked to from a random object, thanks."

Her nostrils flare, but she doesn't say anything. A chill runs down my spine, and I blame it on both of our rising tempers. This shop is a dangerous one for a vampire to be in. Walking in, I counted numerous herbs that could knock anyone out, regardless of species. Then, there is the amount of wood in here, many of which have decorations shaped into sharp spikes. And if all of that wasn't enough of a deterrent, the witch who runs the shop would be.

"All right," she says finally, tightening the lid on the glass jar and placing it next to the antique register. "Then, I guess we should start making an official plan."

I nod. "I agree. If the Brais are planning to hit us tomorrow, and we need to use this blood soon, then we need to strike. Tonight. We could catch them off guard." Nerves that come at the promise of a fight prick along my back. This could very well be the fight to end the war. The list of vampires that Mica offered put them all in the castle dimension. It would make sense for the King to surround himself with those who are bound to him. Bringing an army to him is most likely our best plan. Strike our enemies at their heart.

"I'll call upon the witches and wolves. We can meet in an hour to begin discussing specifics."

"Okay. And I'll—" The strong, jagged presence of a vampire stabs at my awareness. My blood chills and magic pools into my palms.

"What is it?" Sarah asks, though I hardly hear her. I strain my hearing to listen to anything outside. The only sounds I hear are the voices of distant people going about their day, and…the scuff of a foot stopping just short of the building.

Someone is standing on the other side of the window, blocked by its cloudiness and the beams of sunlight overhead. The sound of something crunching fills my ears. The feeling of dread washes over me.

Sarah is still recovering from our last battle. And if we are to go up against the Brais tonight, she'll need all the strength she has. "Is there another exit? Something safe?" I ask in a hushed tone.

Her eyes narrow suspiciously before she realizes why I am asking, and they widen. "Yes."

"Get out of here." The vampire outside clearly knows what this place is, and who is inside. Someone needs to keep them preoccupied while Sarah gets to safety. If we both ran, that vampire would no doubt follow, putting Sarah in harm's way.

She glances to the door then back to me. "But if there are many—"

I turn to face the entrance. "There is only one." The herbs hanging from the ceiling sway. I breathe in deeply, feeling the air fusing with my magic.

"I'll fight them with you."

Without looking at her again, I hiss, "Your magic regenerates slower than mine. Get out of here." There is a brief moment of stillness before I hear glass clinking and her footsteps scurrying toward the back.

There is hardly any time for me to readjust my attention when the glass to the front window shatters. Instinctively, I crouch to avoid any shards, ducking behind a small table cluttered with bowls. Something small and hard hits me in the hand while protecting my face, the impact brutal.

In response, my magic hums and a growing wind blows within the shop. People outside are yelling, confused and scared.

"Come on out, Tempest," a voice growls from the entrance. When I stand, pebbles of glass fall to the floor. A vampire I do not recognize has jumped through the window, landing just inside the apothecary. He is short with dark hair tied into a bun. A crooked nose sits on his angular face. In one of his hands is a wooden stake, the other engulfed in a violently churning flame. "I've always wanted to be the one to bring you down. Traitor."

My fangs come out, pumping my blood with heightened vampiric senses. "You can try," I say with a taunting grin.

The vampire snarls and hurls a ball of fire at me. There are so many knickknacks in here that could get destroyed in this fight. I need to try and move to the secluded ally outside. It is strange, and bold, that the Brais are picking a fight in broad daylight.

The heat from the fire grows intense as it moves through

the space. With a slash of air, the fire hurdling is extinguished. A second blast was thrown at me in succession. I hardly have enough time to dodge it, and I cringe when I hear things breaking behind me.

"It was noble of you to fight and let the witch escape." Two other vampires emerge from the blinding sunlight outside, glass crunching beneath their boots as they jump into the apothecary. Each one a fire wielder, their fingertips or arms covered with the lethal element. "But ultimately, you will both die here."

A male's scream bellows from the back room where Sarah ran. I risk looking as some movement catches in my peripheral. Sarah has her hands up, a medallion hanging from one palm. I smell it before I see it. Blood pours down the side of her head. The enticing sweet scent is tainted with the sourness of anger.

How did I not sense all the others? How many more could be outside? Focus, Cole. I turn my attention back to the three in front of me just in time to see a massive fireball forming in front of them. They are combining their magic to create a destructive force.

With a deep breath, I swing my arms out in front of me and pull the air to my palms like a magnet, depleting the fire and its wielders of oxygen. With careful movements so as to not drag the fire toward me, I put all my magic into creating a dome. A barrier. The hanging herbs within my magic stop swinging from the beams. The fireball stops growing and begins to shrink. The smug expressions on the Brais vampires contort into something of fear. They grab at their throats, and one even drops to a knee.

Sweat beads on my forehead and my limbs shake as I strain my magic, pushing it past its limit. Darkness creeps into my vision and a dizziness washes over me as I push through the quickly approaching end to my stored magic. The fireball consumed so much already, and it holds steady against me.

Despite his loss of air, the vampire who entered first still holds his own hand up, keeping the fire magic alive.

Out of the corner of my eye, I see Sarah move into the main area of the apothecary. She is still concentrated on an attacker. I grunt and widen my area of magic. The fireball loses its hold on the outside air and diminishes quickly. One of the vampires collapses, knocking into a table.

The lead vampire falls to a knee, his skin turning blueish with lack of oxygen. Despite it, a smirk pulls at his lips. Before I have a chance to wipe it off his face, a hole is blown into the wall to my right. Splinters of wood and herb and glass spray everywhere.

And a fireball half the size of the building explodes inside, crashing with an unknown golden light.

And then everything spins. The floor beneath my feet, the herb-covered ceiling, the flames that were about to devour me whole, and my mind. They seemingly blend together like a whirlpool of chaos, though stay separate altogether. Then everything but my mind disappears and my body feels as though it was ripped apart molecule by molecule before forming again like a jigsaw puzzle. My feet hit something solid, and I drop to a surface like I am made of liquid.

With a gasp, I brace my hands on what appears to be a hardwood floor. I look up, breaths coming heavy, and notice that instead of the Demoix Apothecary, I'm in the living room in my cabin. Sarah stands with her body braced against the wall, her chest heaving as sweat drips down her brow.

"What the hell was that?" I ask as I try to stand but think better of it when my legs wobble. Instead, I sit on the floor beside my coffee table. Right where Thea taught me how to play a card game the night that we found out Valeria and Sarah were taken. I comb my fingers through my hair and look up at the witch again. That's when I notice that it isn't all sweat beading on her face. Tears rim her eyes and slide down her cheeks.

Her empty gaze on my floor shifts to me and when she notices me staring, she wipes her cheeks quickly. "Sorry," she says as she takes a deep breath. "I didn't have time to warn you before teleporting." She's winded. It's amazing that she was even able to use her magic like that. Her hands clench into fists as she rights herself and pushes off from the wall.

I don't see Helios and figured we must have spooked him with our entrance. With a sigh, I brace my palm on the coffee table and push myself to my feet, fighting the churning in my stomach. "I'm sorry," I offer.

"For what?"

"For your family's apothecary."

I watch as her jaw clenches, her brown eyes locked on mine. I get the sense that she is battling with herself with how to answer. But it doesn't need an answer, not really. I know grief, and sometimes all you need is someone to acknowledge it.

I open my mouth to say something else but am cut off by a thud at the door, my blood turning to ice. Only a few weeks ago, a similar sound crashed at my front door when Amaund threw someone's head onto my front porch. But where that made a large thump followed by the sound of it rolling, this noise only made one clean whack.

Sarah's wide eyes don't help the increasing tempo in my chest. My magic pools in my hands as I slowly turn to face my door. The silver tip of an arrow pokes through the painted wood.

CHAPTER TWENTY-SIX

COLE

"Wait," Sarah calls out. "They're allies."

"That doesn't seem like something an ally would do," I growl, pointing to the lethal arrow tip. It was a clean shot, hitting between two of the vertical planks. My magic roared the moment I saw the arrow. I've never run into a vampire hunter before, but from the stories I have heard, it's a damn good thing. With magic of their own and elite weapons and fighting skills, they are a force to be reckoned with. I suppose that makes sense, given their prey. They tend to live in closed knit societies governed by a council. That day Thea and I broke into her family's old manor, we came across a stash of weapons fit for a vampire hunting party. They were stored in a hidden panel in the basement, and it made me wonder if her parents left that life behind. If so, why?

"Cole, trust me," Sarah says carefully, her eyes darting to the papers and curtains that are flapping in my magic.

The way she says those words has me reeling back on the wind. It was like her old self, back when she and I decided we weren't going to carry on with the usual vampire and witch feud. Another memory of a place that became consumed by fire.

"I'm not opening that door," I grind out. Ripping an arrow from my chest is certainly not how I intend to spend my afternoon.

She moves past me and places a hand on the doorknob, pausing for a moment as she examines the arrow. Then without a word, she opens the door, and I almost brace myself for an onset of arrows.

The afternoon sun shines brightly into the clearing around my house, giving the area an enchanted look. It is one of the reasons why I chose this place. I'll also never forget the expression on Thea's face when she saw it for the first time. Or the way my nerves pounded at the thought of her spending the night in my cabin.

Just beyond the tree line, where the outskirt of the barrier sits, is a group of people armed to the teeth with vampire-killing weapons. Though none of their weapons are drawn, I still feel wary about stepping outside and giving them a clear shot at me.

Sarah makes her way toward them, and I fight the urge to rush out there and protect her. I doubt that is something she would take kindly to. Her mother was a strong witch, but I think Sarah might be stronger. She stops when there is about ten feet between her and the hunters.

The one in front is tall with tan skin and carries a large crossbow strapped to his back. Despite the chill in the air, he wears a short-sleeved, dark green shirt, showing off a multitude of tattoos along his arms. He jerks his chin to the cabin. "Is your vampire friend going to join us?" His deep voice carries to my ears with little effort from my heightened senses.

Sarah shrugs and looks over her shoulder. "They won't harm you, Cole. Like I said, they are allies."

The group of them watch me as I cautiously step through

the threshold. The nausea from teleporting still hasn't completely subsided, made only worse with the magic I used at the shop and with what stands before me. The fact that they wanted me to come out here was either because they do actually plan to try and stake me, or they really intend to share their allyship. Though I don't let any of it show, I pool my magic into my palms in order to be ready for anything disconcerting. "You shot my house," I say as I stop next to Sarah.

The man in the center snorts a laugh. "How else would you expect me to announce my arrival with that barrier spell." He looks around, as if he could indeed see that invisible wall the spell created. "It was hard to knock. How do you have visitors with such uninviting protections?"

"I don't," I grumble.

The vampire hunter tips his head back and laughs, his throat barred toward me. A daring position to put yourself in while there is a vampire around. The movement causes a chain around his neck to sway, and I lower my gaze to a medallion that hangs from it, a circular shape is etched into its golden facet.

Sarah shifts on her feet. "Why are you here, Isaiah?"

I snap my gaze to the witch beside me. How long have these two been allies? Was it before the coven decided to fight against the Brais or after? And why didn't she ever mention them before?

Isaiah looks to Sarah, his amusement still twinkling in his smile and brown eyes. "I heard you killed Amaund." The smile on his lips shifts from amused to approving before it disappears, followed by a long sigh. "I ran into him and his group of bloodsuckers—" He flicks his gaze to me. "No offense. It was a couple weeks ago and right around here, actually."

"He let you live?" I ask, growing a bit more wary.

Isaiah snorts and a few of his comrades share glances with each other. "Because we had a truce."

I blink at him and open my mouth, just to close it again. A vampire hunter and a Brais general with a truce? The magic in my blood stirs.

"A truce? I thought you vowed to destroy vampires who kill, not ally with them." Anger drips from Sarah's words.

Isaiah surveys her in a way that a predator would size up another. He shoves his hands in the pockets of his jeans. "A temporary truce. We were working with him and another of his kind to kill their King."

My jaw might have smacked the grass beneath my feet if I wasn't too stunned to move a muscle. Neither Sarah nor I say anything, too shocked at his words.

A smirk tugs at his lips, as if he is pleased to see that expression on her face. "Your mother knew."

And that is all it takes for Sarah's magic to pour out of her. Ghostly golden light slithers from her body like smoke. The pressure from her magic feels like it is pushing against my soul. The power that flows from her could rattle the entire Earth. "Explain," she says, her voice like a promise of death.

"First, tell me who that brown-haired vampire was that Amaund was traveling with. The one who was shackled," Isaiah says.

A muscle feathers in her lip, and I get the vague sense that I should take a step away. The moment I do, the ground around her cracks, splinters of earth running in jagged lines a few feet in front of her. The hunters don't even flinch.

Sarah flexes her hands, the tension of her magic rolling off her shoulders. "A friend. They took her, and we are trying to get her back."

"Interesting," he responds.

Before he can say anything else, I interrupt. "Why are you interested in her?" I ask, letting the bite in my words be a warning.

Isaiah looks me over. "You must be the one who created

her." He gestures to the cabin. "Her magical signature is all over this place. We followed its trail from a clearing only ten minutes from here, where all the trees are scorched. It brought us here, but also to her being escorted by Amaund and his group. We've been searching for a similar magical signature for years."

"Why?" Sarah asks before I can, her voice clipped. She may have stamped out her magic, but I can tell that it wouldn't take much to let it out again.

"I think you know," he responds, the smirk growing again.

"What does that mean? Sarah?" I ask, my anger rising as I turn my gaze to the witch beside me. She just keeps her focus on Isaiah, her posture unnervingly calm.

After a moment, as I was about to explode with fury from her silence, she turns to me. "I'm sorry, Cole. I can't tell you."

A sickening lump forms in my throat and a tingling sensation creeps up my back. My magic begs to be released, threatened by what only feels like betrayal. "What the fuck, Sarah?" I hardly get the words out without slurring them together from the rage. I can feel Sarah's power shrinking until it is hardly felt.

"She can't tell you anything, nor can I," Isaiah adds. "We're cursed into silence."

"By whom?" I can hardly keep from shaking, a mix of anger, frustration, and betrayal bounces in my mind. The tops of the trees start swaying from a natural wind, and I latch onto it, braiding my magic with nature.

"The King of the Brais," Sarah says quietly, her light brown eyes soft. She hangs her head slightly.

I gape at her with an expression that probably isn't too kind. This whole time, Thea has been risking her life to gather information on the Brais and their King, and Sarah has known all along? Curse be damned. Sarah is letting Thea put herself in danger for information that is already known. I pull the wind to me, creating a barrier between myself and the others. Leaves littered on the ground spin around me as they are picked up. I feel Isaiah's comrades tense, a couple even reaching for their weapons. But their leader holds his hand up to stop them.

"You've known all along?" I seethe at Sarah.

"I'm sorry," she says again. "It is the curse of my coven. We—" she winces.

"An old, powerful curse, cast hundreds of years ago. It latches on to anyone unfortunate enough to learn who the King is." Isaiah points to Sarah. "For her, anyone of Demoix blood is cursed at birth."

The growing fury disperses a little, replaced with a sort of pity. I school my expression so neither of them see that. "Is that why you haven't said anything to Thea?"

She nods slowly, as if she were nervous the affirmation would trigger whatever pain this curse of silence causes.

"Should your vampire discover who the King is, or you for that matter, you'll receive the curse as well." Isaiah's words are a warning, one that comes from a point of concern.

I swallow as a small cloud passes over the sun. With any passing moment, Thea could figure out who the King is and suffer the consequences of that knowledge. A living, snarling fury rises in my chest at the thought. "How do you fight against something like that?"

"It's why—" Isaiah pauses for a moment, contemplation written on his face. "It's how the King has evaded hunters and witches for so long. You can't." A defeated breath spews from his mouth.

"Then why the truce?" Sarah asks, bringing the discussion back to the first topic. "I doubt that Amaund was not without the mark either."

Isaiah shakes his head and glances to his comrades. A

couple of them bow their heads after he looks away. "I would lead them to the King. They could fight while I…"

"While you die," Sarah finishes. She turns to me. "Those cursed cannot fight against the King, lest we forfeit our lives."

"I'd get one good shot in first, I think," Isaiah adds with a grin, trying to bring some lightness into the conversation.

"How can a single curse be so powerful as to affect anyone who stumbles on the right information and also kill?" I ask, unsure if I want that answer, but I know I should hear it. Maybe I can reach out to Thea and warn her. Try and convince her to stop her search.

Sarah and Isaiah look at each other, frowns forming on their faces. Sarah tilts her head and gazes at the sky, letting out a long breath, as Isaiah replies, "That isn't something we can answer, I'm afraid."

I shake my head, the earlier frustration coming back. Not at them, but at this entire mess. "There has to be a way. Something that doesn't involve sacrificing ourselves."

"I think there might be." Sarah brightens, her fingers tapping on her chin.

"Care to elaborate?" Isaiah asks.

She grimaces. "I can't, really. I've been reading the Minuit coven grimoire and various notes have been added about the curse and the King. Unfortunately, I haven't been able to make much sense of anything." She digs her toes into the disheveled ground. "I've torn through the book so many times and haven't been able to find anything written by my mom. I don't think she would have agreed with what our ancestors wrote."

Before I can inquire what that meant, Isaiah speaks. "Oh, right. That reminds me." He reaches behind him, and for a moment I tense, ready to defend. But instead of a weapon, his hands are gripping a brown satchel. "Valeria left this in my protection not too long before she was killed." When he pulls out a black tome, I hear the sharp intake of a breath.

Sarah's eyes twinkle with something that is a mix of sadness and hope. "Is that my mother's grimoire?"

Isaiah nods and holds it out for her to grab. "She thought that the Brais were after her, so she gave this to me to hold onto so I could make sure it safely got into your hands. I never opened it."

Sarah walks to the hunters and reaches for that piece of her mother. Her arms tremble as she regards the book like a fragile relic that could turn to ash at any moment.

"She gave it to you to keep safe even though you were allied with some of the Brais?" I ask, knowing that Sarah is too engrossed in the grimoire and what it represents.

Isaiah's lips press into a line. "We had a truce. We were not allies. There is a difference." He dips his chin at us. "I hope that book has what you need," Isaiah says as he takes a step back. "We should get going."

Sarah doesn't respond, her attention fixed wholly on the book. Her hands rove over the cover.

"Hey, vamp?" Isaiah calls out as his comrades keep moving.

"It's Cole," I offer.

"Cole," he corrects with a pull of a grin. "I'd like to call a truce with you, too. I suppose I can trust you, since the Minuit coven does."

I don't dare say that I have my doubts with how far the coven's trust goes. So I nod at the departing vampire hunters. "Likewise, Isaiah."

And so, our forces against the Brais became a bit heftier.

CHAPTER TWENTY-SEVEN

THEA

The sun passes its apex in the afternoon sky as I make my way through the quiet halls of the castle. Strangely, there seems to be almost no one here. All the better for this plan. As the sun rose, I tracked Elisz to her room on the second floor after hearing her tell a comrade she was getting rest. I can feel the two wooden stakes strapped to my belt with each casual step down the stairs. A storm rages outside, drenching the windows in a pelting rain that echoes through the tower stairwell.

I might have lost complete control of my anger yesterday if Morwen were not there to bring me out of its destructive embrace. I would have destroyed that garage then made my way to Kael's study. If I made it all the way there, I would have unleased the rest of the magic inside my body on him. Even if it would kill me.

But it was only Morwen's kind and loving words that steadied my hand. After listening to me babble about all the wrong in my life, she just continued to sit there with me, listening to the sobs. I didn't need to use my beta ability to sense her anger with each story I told. By the time we walked back to the castle, arms interlocked, we vowed to destroy our enemies.

And my first enemy is the one who steals innocent humans and brings them to this forsaken dimension. To a place so dreadful and nightmarish, the place where they will likely die. No human deserves to die so that a vampire may live.

With each step, I go over the simple plan in my mind. Sneak into her room, drive a stake through her chest. Easy, more or less. First, I'll have to affirm that she is asleep. Which is why I am holding a small, fabric cooler of blood bags. Should she be awake, I was simply sent to deliver these to her. I've camped out near her door enough to know that sometimes she calls for it. Though, most of the time, she calls for a human from the cellars. And I only see them leave when the cleaner collects their body.

The door to her bedroom is just as simple as the others. The only indication that it is her room is the golden, italicized *'Gen'* written on the top panel. A General of the Brais, who loves showing off her fighting prowess, stripped of her ability to be on the front lines.

The knob turns silently as I open the door. The moment it is cracked, the smell of stale blood slams into me. I hesitate for just a moment, clutching the cooler tightly, and continue inside.

If the state of her room was any indication of her mind, I would be frightened. The entry foyer is immaculate but coated with the scent of blood. I would think her an orderly systematic person if I only saw this room. Her outward appearance portrays that as well, with her combed dark hair and stain-free, leather armor.

Beyond the foyer, past the closed door, there is hardly a path to walk on. A voice inside screams for me to get out of here. Clothing, weapons, papers, and books litter the floor. Her bed is toward the back of the room, underneath a slim window that appears to look out onto the western gardens. The memories from last night propel me forward. Elisz is one of the worst parts of the Brais.

I quietly make my way to the back of the room where she is sprawled on her bed. My foot catches on something soft and stiff. Risking a glance, I peer down. A person's foot sticks out from a pile of freshly sweat-stained clothing. Red dances into my vision at the thought of her absolute carelessness. She might even be worse than Kael.

Her eyes fly open as her arm moves fast to mine. The back of her hand smacks the inside of my wrist and knocks the stake free. It hits the wall behind her bed and lands in the disheveled blankets. I quickly step back and grapple with the second stake.

A fiendish grin cuts into her sharp features. "I was wondering when you would finally make your move. Not a bad time to strike, I'll give you that." She brushes a lock of her dark hair behind an ear. Her blue eyes change to a menacing crimson.

Nerves mix with fury, calling my magic. "You are going to answer for all the horrendous things you've done." My magic manifests into flames that swirl around my free hand.

She watches me with a predator's gaze, the promise of a fight exciting. A low laugh comes from her lips before she says, "You are in way over your head, Kindria." With that, she lunges. No weapon, no magic.

I strike first with the flames, my fist aiming for her head. Like before, she knocks it out of the way. With a strong blow, she punches my arm away, the motion sending my limb snapping back. I grit my teeth and continue forward with my other hand. Her block of the first attack set her up to be hit with this one. The wooden stake is positioned at her heart. Her eyes widen as it comes within a few inches of her torso. But then a grin replaces her surprise.

One breath she is in front of me, the next she vanishes. The strike with the stake connects only with air. I blink at the spot where she was just standing when I sense her behind me. I try and whirl around but am stopped by her grasp. She positions me so that my arms are trapped between her elbow and chest, her hands on my neck. It catches me by surprise, and I lose the hold on my magic for a moment but regain it quickly. Fire leaks from my arms and slowly spreads to my back, where she is pressed against.

Her voice whispers in my ear like the breaking of bones. "I could snap your neck before your fire reaches me, Kindria. Then, I think I'll hand you over to the King as a traitor." Her tone is amused, eager even.

I release my magic and fight against her grip, which only makes her laugh and clutch tighter. Her hold on my neck becomes uncomfortable. "Only those who are weak attack a sleeping enemy." She croons, "What was your plan?"

I turn my head slightly so that her finger isn't pushing on my throat. "A stake to the heart."

She laughs, a cold, amused sound that sends shivers down my spine. "Your weapons wouldn't have killed me. Didn't anyone teach you that?"

"I wasn't done," I grit out. My magic flares and my skin burns. "I'll burn you to ashes. No one would ever find your remains."

"Vicious," she says almost approvingly. I don't think I like that response from her. She leans closer, and I can feel her hot breath on my neck. "You are more like the Brais than I thought. It's a good thing your Essites have crumbled."

"What?" I seethe, fighting again to break free. She only grips tighter, and I wince at her strength. The arm that still holds the stake is immobilized in her hold.

She laughs, a cruel, awful sound. "I never trusted you, Kindria." I can feel the smile on her lips as she says, "The Brais began their assault this morning."

Blood drains from my body, dread threatening to pull me

into a mindless fury. That is why I didn't run into a single vampire on my way here. They were all called to fight. I didn't even see Morwen. Everyone is fighting, except for the Kindria who's alliance is shaky and the General who is banned.

I have been sitting idly by while everyone here was gearing up for war. The Essites were expecting an attack, but not this soon. Were they able to gather enough defenses and allies? What if they were taken by surprise and can't handle the numbers?

Cole and Sarah…are they safe?

As if she were able to read my mind, she leans in closer. "Your traitor creator and witch friend were among the first to go down."

No longer do I feel the floor beneath my feet or the smell of blood coating the air. No more is the vampire General holding me. I am falling through a darkness so quiet and empty. Deep, deep, deep. The world slips from view as that caged part of my soul rips free, the metal bars melting into nothingness. There is no beginning and no end to my body. Here, there are only emotions and the energies that they produce. They hum into the deafening silence. Fury, grief, and fear sing the loudest. Emotions so bottomless and primal devour my very being.

They can't be dead.

They just can't be. Everything that I have done was to protect them. To protect the world from the Brais and their destructive path of domination. It couldn't have been for nothing.

A blue glow pulses above from within that writhing darkness. All my vicious emotions hiss and shrink away from its brightness. It plummets downward, sending waves of light out into the shadows of my mind. It calls to those energies that desire the same destruction always enticing the Brais. It doesn't mend the cage that held them. It caresses them, like the love from someone close to you.

When the light ceases, I see the form that it takes. A sword so beautifully crafted it appears like a sculpture. It seems sentient, like it has been searching for me. Waiting for so long.

A voice so familiar yet unknown at the same time speaks from that sword. It warms my heart but chills me to the bone. Ordo ab choa, *change is born from chaos. One must feel all there is to feel, to sense all things inside and all things outside, to know where to go. Let it hurt, then heal and let it go.*

The pain from my past slams into my mind. For the first time, it doesn't feel harmful and destructive. It doesn't seem like a separate entity living within my body, one that I have shoved deep down and ignored. The emotions feel like an extension, one of protection and familial love. All this time, those terrifying emotions have only desired to protect me from the outside world. From those who have threatened and harmed. Who still threaten and harm not just me, but so many others.

I never asked to become a part of this war, but I couldn't imagine going about a normal life without fighting against it. Had I been given the option all those weeks ago, I would have chosen whatever path that would lead to the dismantling of the Brais. Even if it meant losing the parts of me that I grew to accept, even admire. Like a forest that undergoes a fire or ferocious storm, I will regrow. My roots in this world have gone too deep to give up now.

The emotions of the Brais General pokes at the wall of my mind. She holds her own hatred, resentment, and sadness. Small blotches of black sit beyond the other emotions. She suppresses her fear, masking it with the others. I reach into that chasm and latch onto those hidden emotions, then I pull with all my strength so that the fear overpowers the others. Tugging on her fear and feeding her some of mine, I feel the hold she has on my physical body loosen as her body shakes.

I grip the stake tighter in my hand. No, not a wooden stake, but a sword. The one that I just saw in that vision. The sword that resembles the painting in the library.

Elisz scrambles away from me, her heartbeat erratic and breathing ragged. She presses her back against the wall. "The sword! H-how?"

"It came to me," I say. One of the two stakes I brought with me rests at my feet.

Her gaze holds mine and some of her fear recedes. She bears her fangs at me, blue eyes returning to a deep red. "I'll slaughter every last one of you traitors to the King." Despite the overwhelming amount of fear radiating from her, she lunges.

I lift my hand that holds the sword. I plunge the blade into her heart. The red in her irises return to their indigo blue. Her eyes widen as I slowly lower her to the floor. A wave of relief, mossy green in color, washes into her other emotions until it is the dominant one. Her skin pales to a sickening color as she takes her last breath.

I pull the blade out of her and stare at it, coated in her blood. The sword, though made of metal, killed a vampire.

CHAPTER TWENTY-EIGHT

THEA

*L*eaving her body, I rush from the cluttered rooms. I don't know if what Elisz said about the Brais beginning their attacks and what happened to Cole and Sarah is true, but it is the only information I have at the moment. And while most, if not all of the Brais are away from this dimension, I need to begin my own assault.

I'll start with the humans. Get them out and into the safety of the real world. Then, I'll burn this place to the ground. I have no more time or energy to look into the unknown revolving my past and the visions from within the library.

From the past twenty-four hours, I have learned enough that I can piece things together with what I already know. As crazy as it seems. My family—at least those on my father's side—were vampire hunters or worked with them. Given the number of weapons stashed in my parent's manor, I would say it was the former. Which might explain why they were targeted by the Brais. But why keep me alive? The vision I had in the library is eerily similar to what I experienced the night of that first car accident. Mica told me that some vampire hunters have magic. So, does that mean that my parents performed magic that night? Is that what the blue glow was? I was spared in an accident that should have left no survivors. And whoever's eyes I was looking through in that vision was also spared in that fire. Maybe that blue glow was—

"Thea, thank the goddess. You weren't in your room," Morwen says as I turn a corner and slam into her on the landing of the stairs adjacent to the meeting hall.

"Morwen? I thought you went to fight with the rest of the Brais." I strain my ears for any sounds of others as I look beyond her into the corridor. There is no one else that my senses perceive.

She frowns and shakes her head, but asks instead, "How did you know?" She takes a moment to actually assess me, her eyes widening when she spots the sword clutched in my hand. I could swear her hand moved slightly to reach for it, but she remains still. "Where did you get that? Thea, what did you do? Please tell me you didn't attack Kael."

The crackling from the fireplace down the hall and the dripping of the rain from on the windowsill stop. A familiar silence rings in my ears. It is consuming. "Kael is here?" All the magic within me stirs at the thought. The sword seems to hum in the palm of my hand. A foreign, friendly power vibrates from it into my body and mingles with my own magic. If Kael is alone, with the help of this weapon, I might be able to put up a fight. My grip on the sword tightens.

Her frown deepens. "He's in his study. Thea, what—"

I grab her by the shoulder, her gaze unflinching. "Morwen, I need you to get the rest of the humans out of here. Can you do that?"

Her beautiful ice blue eyes narrow. "What are you planning?"

"Please, Morwen." I feel time slipping away from me. The longer we stand in this stairwell, the more Essites are in danger and the less time I will have alone with Kael, with the potential King.

She nods curtly. "I will free them from here." She reaches into an inside pocket of her leather jacket. "Take this." In her hand is a silvered dagger, the blade and hilt curving into a tilde. "For whatever you are about to do. It's poisoned, so be careful."

I take the blade from her and strap it into my bandolier where the stakes were. It is significantly heavier. "Thank you." I step away from her, motioning to return up the steps I just came from. "And Morwen?"

She turns back to me, already a foot on the steps to the cellars. "Yes?"

I don't let myself think about how she might be my last living ally. The last person to truly know me and who understands how I see the world. A friend found in the most unlikely of places. I swallow the lump forming in my throat. "Thank you," is all I manage to say. There would be so much more if we had time.

She offers a genuine smile. "I'll see you soon, Thea." Then, she vanishes behind the banister, her feet pounding on the steps.

The trek to the third floor isn't long, but it feels as though it were. I feel like I have already ascended dozens of flights of stairs by the time I reach the one his study is on. Like the rest of the castle, there is no one present. No guards, no sentries, just silence. As I step into the corridor, I notice that the sun is peaking out of the clouds, casting a golden glow on everything.

My left hand tingles, and I rub it on my pants. I should have gone to the storage room for a drink first or consumed the bags I brought into Elisz's room. Such a stupid mistake. But who knows when the Brais will return. I can't waste any time.

The last time I stood in front of his ornate curved door, I was minutes away from killing a human. A memory that I will never allow myself to forget. The deaths of everyone, whether I caused it or not, sits within me. Their memories fuel my magic. No longer am I frightened of releasing those emotions, nor am I afraid that they will control me.

I let the tension wash away with a final deep breath and open the doors. Kael stands ominously in the center of the room as he did those first few days I was here. He wears his black armor, his sword on his hip, and his arms crossed at his chest. He blocks the view of his cluttered desk and the weapons hanging on the wall. Sunlight stains the floor, illuminating the room.

"Welcome, Thea," Kael says as if he were expecting me. The door closes behind me as I take a few steps inside.

I call upon my magic, feeling for its humming energy. Just like me, it is eager for a fight. Though he still frightens me, I no longer find it hard to resist. Instead, the fear feeds my magic, my cells and bones.

When I don't respond, he fills the silence. "Do you remember that day in the library when I told you to be careful?"

The tingling in my right hand increases, and I fight the urge to rub it on my pants again. He might mistake that as nervousness, and I don't want that at all. "Yes."

A burst of air is exhaled from his nose. "You do? Because ever since then, you might as well have been screaming all the plans running through your mind." He drops his arms, one resting at his side and the other on the pommel of his sword. The sun seems to shine brighter.

"I have no plans," I lie, forcing my voice to remain steady. "Only a curious mind."

Another harsh laugh. "If you are going to lie, Thea, you should at least bend a little bit of the truth into your words." He assesses me, his gaze falling first on the sword in my hand, stained red with blood, then the dagger strapped to my bandolier. There is a flash of anger that crosses his features, but it vanishes so quickly that I couldn't be sure of it. "If you had no plans, then why are you here?" He bobs his head at me, eyes pinned on my silver sword. "And with that?" His lips curve in a knowing smile. A fly caught in a web.

If I summon all of my magic to one blast of fire, I might be able to catch him off-guard. Even if it doesn't kill him, but simply distracts, I could slice him with Morwen's dagger. Since it is poisoned, just one cut from it could mean death. Then, I can use the sword to finish. I'm sure having no head would kill him for good.

Fast. Too fast. He moves, pinning me against the wall, his burning hand on my throat, his other on the sword. There isn't enough space for me to grab the dagger. "I never wanted to kill you, Thea. I wanted to help you," he says harshly. "But it seems someone else has their claws in you."

I snarl at him and fight against his hold. "Help me? How is anything that you did helpful to me?" The words are mumbled, a mix between a growl and rasp with his tight grip.

His cobalt eyes flash a threatening scarlet. "You may be a vampire, but you are still ignorant of this world." As quickly as he grabbed me, he releases me and takes the sword with him, his long, braided hair swaying with each slow step. The sudden removal of his hand causes me to slump, and I grasp the door-frame to keep myself from collapsing onto the floor.

"I'm tired of hearing that," I mumble as my throat hurries to heal. Kael walks back to his desk, completely writing me off as a threat. "Fight me, Kael." Fire churns in my veins, energizing my body. "As the King, you have to fulfill a request for a *Necaut Necare*."

Kael stops then turns slowly back around to face me. "A phrase you learned in that book on your nightstand, no doubt." He swipes the sword through the air, his chin lifting as he looks me over again. During sword training, he always had the upper hand. Unlike now, we weren't using any magic. Nor did my life hang in the balance. Not just my life, but the lives of so many others are riding on me winning. Morwen and maybe Mica. Any surviving Essites and witches. "I am not bound by this request," he continues, "but I will honor it."

I yank Morwen's dagger from its holster. The weight of it is comfortable, reminiscent of the friend who lent it to me. In my other hand, flames spread and creep up to my elbow.

He grins, a dark expression that ignites the magic inside me. "Oh, no. A true *Necaut Necare* is fought only with metal."

My jaw tightens with my rising anger. "Then, I believe that is mine." I gesture to the weapon in his hands. When I held it, there was a sense of sentience emanating from it. Standing away from it, I can't even feel a spark of its consciousness. My beta ability touches only that of Kael's energy, which is wholly solid, a threatening wall of power.

"Indulge me for a moment, Thea." Kael turns his back to me and places the sword on his desk. When he takes a step back, the blade rests in golden curved arches. The sun catches on the pommel and light reflects onto the flat guard, illuminating the circular symbols etched into the metal. "Do you know what sword this is?"

"The Sword of all Swords," I whisper, recalling the time he cornered me in the library.

"To its original owner, it was called Vitamors. It means the sword of life and death." He jerks his chin at me. "If it truly has called to you, it will come when you summon it."

"And if it doesn't?"

That terrifying grin again, the one that alone would be an answer to my question. "Then you are not who I thought you were."

For some reason, that answer is more unnerving than anything else he could have said. I don't know who he expects me to be, but once I kill him, he won't need to worry any longer. I glance at the sword in his scabbard. At least he is waiting to start the fight. Morwen's dagger would be no match against him and his sword.

As he said, I stick my hand out to summon Vitamors. There is no glow to this sword, and for all I know, it could be a normal weapon. Perhaps it is. Maybe it is just a replica to the Vitamors, and Kael knows that it won't come to me. The thought sends unpleasant prickles down to my toes. But it had come to me once already. That I know. So why isn't it doing anything now?

There is no tug of energy, no glow that indicates its sentience I felt earlier. The sword isn't even buzzing on the desk. With each passing second, I fear I will have to face him with only a dagger. During the fight, I'll have to try and get to the Vitamors.

"A pity," Kael says, and I have just enough time to jump back as his sword cuts into the wooden floor where I was standing. "I was truly hoping you were the one."

Ignoring his words, I clutch the dagger in one hand and summon my magic to take form of a fiery blade in the other. The moment the fire sword manifests, a stabbing pain erupts in my chest. It is so extreme that I can't help but fall to the floor, grasping for breath. My magic vanishes at the intensity of whatever is happening. Did his sword get me? Is it poisoned, and this is what the poison does?

Kael clicks his tongue. "A *Necaut Necare* is meant to be a battle between swordsmen. No magic. Your request and my acceptance created a binding contract between the two of us." He moves so that he is in front of me and grabs me by the throat, ripping the poisoned dagger from my grasp. "You should have done better research."

Then, I am being hurled through the air. My back slams against the wall, a crunch following. Exploding pain radiates from my skull, and I slide to the floor, writhing. All the weapons in this room are still too far to get a hold of, but I force myself to stand, using the wall as support. My hand dips into a dent of where my body made contact. I can feel blood trickling from a wound on the back of my head, my vampiric healing coming too slow.

Kael throws the dagger into the wooden floor before he lunges forward, his sword aiming for my stomach. I dodge just in time and hear it stick into the already broken wall. As I sidestep away, I throw a fist at his head, the only place not covered in armor. He hunches over to avoid the blow and shoves his shoulder into my chest, sending me onto my back. I gasp for air as I quickly get to my feet again, not letting him out of my sight.

If I can get around him, I could grab the dagger. The sword would be better, but I would have to move through him to reach it. A small table sits in the corner next to me, and I move to grab it. Kael stands still, allowing me a moment to smash the table and use a broken leg as a weapon. It won't pierce his armor, so my target is still his head and neck. Definitely not easy, but it will have to do.

He swings his sword in a sweeping motion that could slice me in half, but I slide back on my toes to avoid it. I take advantage of being on the outside of his attacking arm to jab the makeshift stake at his face. But he is faster, and he brings his sword up as he twists away and repositions himself behind me. I jump and roll away, which puts me right at the desk.

The sword seems to hum to me, asking for me to pick it up. I reach for it as I see Kael out of the corner of my eye. To avoid a direct hit, I jump to the side. But I am not fast enough for his angle readjustment. The blade cuts through my body, leaving a gash from my shoulder to my hip. My blood pours out of the wound and down my clothes. He kicks me in the chest, and the blow causes me to release the table leg. I slam against the side wall and slide to a knee, my body aching.

Kael walks toward Morwen's poisoned dagger and pulls it free from the floorboard. "The poison in this dagger ensures a slow, painful death. It's a rarity even among the supernatural community." He flips it, catching it easily by the grip, before positioning himself to strike with both weapons.

Ordo ab choa.

I stand again, lifting the only weapons I have. My fingers tighten into fists as I step away from the wall. Kael laughs and darts forward, his intent to end this evident.

But, I am not going to lose.

I focus on that dial inside my mind, the one responsible for my vampiric senses, and turn it as high as possible, cursing myself for not doing this earlier. There is a blinding ring in my head but not distracting enough to get in the way. Kael moves in slow motion, and I analyze for a counter or dodge. As he begins moving the dagger arm, I lunge forward and drop so that I can slide out from under him. I am up and behind him before he even turns around, a look of fury on his face. Kael moves in front of the Vitamors, making sure that I have no chance at grabbing a weapon.

He lunges again, keeping both weapons at the ready so that I can't predict his attack. Again, his movements are slow enough that I can look for an opening. If my senses have heightened, perhaps my strength has too. I close my hands into fists and turn so I can twist around him.

I didn't notice his movement speed increasing. Didn't prepare to adjust my dodge as he swings both weapons at me. My brain doesn't even register both of them slicing into my body. The sword went into my thigh and the dagger into my gut.

I can already feel the poison slithering into my organs.

CHAPTER TWENTY-NINE

THEA

The room spins as red seeps into my vision, dotted by black at the corners. Kael pulls the weapons out from my body, and I drop to my knees. The pain is an intense throb that makes me nauseous. Or perhaps that's the poison.

"It really was a pity, you know." His voice sounds odd, as if he were talking through an old electronic device. He is standing a few feet away, both weapons staining the floor crimson.

On the floor where there once was the blood of humans that I killed, my blood now spreads over the wood. Their faces still come to me when I sleep. They never say anything, only stare at me with a hollow emptiness.

The metallic tang of blood coats my tongue, and I heave, hunching over. I can feel the toxin slowly working its way toward my heart. It seems to spread slowly and quickly at the same time. My limbs turn cold, the kind of cold when you dip your feet into the freezing waters of the ocean. I brace a shaky hand on the floor as I cough, blood splattering with each forceful breath. That same hand starts feeling fuzzy, like small tendrils of electricity are buzzing through it.

Kael crouches so he is eye level with me. "I wish your creator were still alive." He smiles when I snap my head to him, the movement causing a blur of images. "Then he would know how it feels when your lover dies, just as I did."

His lover? "Amaund?" I ask through coughs. My ears are pounding, making it difficult to hear.

"Well, I suppose you hearing about his death will have to be enough." Still crouched, he drags the dagger along the floor, the sound sending waves of nausea roiling through my body. "It felt good blowing him up."

That numbing silence floods my mind. I've been so worried because he hasn't appeared in my dreams in while. I reach out with my beta ability, trying to sense any deceit. My heart cracks a little when there isn't any to detect. A thread of my magic stretches far beyond the terror in front of me. It searches frantically for that warmth that only comes from Cole. Despite being in a different dimension, despite the poison and lack of strength, it searches to no avail. The cage inside my mind is gone, and my magic hides. There is nothing but blinding, consuming pain.

Cole is dead.

Cole is dead.

Cole is dead.

The words repeat over and over in my mind, each time more of a hiss than the last. My hand feels as though it were on fire. I scrape my nails along the wood, welcoming the pain it causes.

Ordo ab choa.

A feral, absolutely wild part of me claws its way out. Not my fire magic or beta ability, but something much more savage. Everything in the room brightens as my features shift. When I snap my head up at Kael, he blinks but doesn't flinch.

Then, I reach my burning hand out.

And Vitamors hears the call.

Kael flinches at my palm rising. He barely gets out of the way as Vitamors whizzes past him, the blade scratching his armor. The moment it is in my grasp, I feel a familial warmth spreading into my body from the humming sword. It feels like the same magic that flowed from my hands when I healed Riley. It travels right to the wounds where a heat simmers. The pounding in my head subsides and the darkness in my vision sizzles away. The sword is healing my wounds and purifying the poison.

"So, it *did* choose you," Kael says, astonished. His gaze roves over the sword in my hand. "You are a descendant of the first vampire, another child from sacrifice." His tone softens and he almost seems disappointed. His chin dips to his chest as a flash of annoyance crosses his expression as if he were struggling with an internal battle. He opens his mouth to say something else, only to be stifled by my attack.

I bring the sword down, but he blocks it with his, slashing at me with the dagger to counter. I bend back, dodging the blade, and swipe the sword to his left hand. The blade slices into his fingers, causing him to drop the poisoned weapon. He hisses and plunges his sword at me. I dodge but catch my back on the inside corner of the room. The light from the sun catches in my eye, blinding me.

Kael growls as he plunges his sword into my stomach. I grunt as he pushes farther, inclining it up to my heart. This blade won't kill me, but it won't feel pleasant if it were to reach my heart. Still unable to see, I swing my sword wildly at him. One of the attacks hits his arm, and he pulls his sword out of my torso, eliciting another cry from me.

I move to his desk and out of the path of the sunlight. Kael rounds so that he is between me and the door. His irises have completely changed to red, and his fangs protrude from his lip.

I lunge at him, swinging Vitamors in a rapid spin around my head and down at his chest diagonally. I see him angle himself to parry, but in this moment, I am faster. The sword comes down at full force on his free arm, severing his hand from the rest. His blood pours from the wound, pooling on the floor at our feet.

A blood-curdling growl escapes his lips, and he pushes forward, swinging his weapon so fast that I have trouble keeping up. I get lucky with the first few blows, parrying them at the last minute. But his fourth strike hits, cutting so deep across my chest that I stumble back, clutching at my torn clothes and bleeding body. He slams the pommel of his sword down onto my weapon, forcing me to drop it. Vitamors clashes onto the floor, the sound ringing in my head. He stabs his sword into the floor beside him, picks up Vitamors and throws it hard against the far wall next to the door.

"I would prefer you to suffer, but I want to get this over with," he grumbles, his voice pained. "I have a meeting with the King."

The wound across my chest is healing slowly. Too slowly. Only then do I realize that the lethal wounds from his earlier strike have mended completely. The Vitamors' magic heals.

His words hit me like a rock to the head. *I have a meeting with the King.* Earlier, he said he was not bound by my declaration of a *Necaut Necare* with the King. I was wrong. He could be lying. But why lie to a person who is about to die?

Kael grips his sword and yanks it from the floor. "I know you sought to rebel against the King. As a Brais, that is treason." The metal is cold against my neck, my blood already dried. "You know I'm a fan of decapitations."

There is too much pain. Too much grief keeping me on my knees on the floor, awaiting the strike of certainty.

Cole is dead.

And maybe Sarah too.

I was so certain that I could be this person who secretly infiltrates the evil vampires, feeding information to my friends on the outside. Perhaps if I just accepted death the numerous times it called to me, they would still be alive.

Ordo ab choa.

Nothing will change. The Brais are too powerful to be stopped. If the Essites were taken out, is there anyone left to stand against them? Would other covens convene to avenge the Minuit coven? Indeed, there is so much about this supernatural world that I know nothing about. An ignorant Kindria to the end.

Kael pulls back on his sword, preparing to take off my head.

At least I will be able to see everyone again. The glimmer of the setting sun catches on the point of his sword. And at least I can die underneath a shining sun, not the dreary rainstorms that plague this dimension.

I brace myself for the killing blow.

CHAPTER THIRTY

THEA

K ael brings his sword down, and I keep my gaze on the golden light outside. The promise of rest after my death is enticing. But what about Helios? My poor cat is most likely still in Cole's cabin, wondering where all his people went. I know the blow is coming, but at the thought of my furry friend, I no longer want to leave the living.

The sound of bone crunching causes me to flinch. When I realize there is no pain, I know that Kael's strike never hit. I look up and see a familiar blade plunged fully through his heart, through the armor on both sides. Morwen stands behind Kael, Vitamors in her hands. A gurgling sound comes from his mouth as he drops his sword and shakily clutches Vitamors' blade.

I am kneeling still, my mouth agape at the sight. Her timing could not have been better.

"For *your* crimes against the Brais, Kael, your punishment is execution." She pushes the blade in farther, fear etched into Kael's features. "I told you not to kill her, and yet here you are."

"I'm sor—"

Morwen removes the sword from his back and in a clean, quick movement, spins it over her head and cuts through his neck. His body and head hit the floor at the same time, landing in a crumpled heap in front of me.

Morwen stands with Vitamors in her hand, leaning against it as if it were a crutch. There is no warmth on her face, none of the usual calm that radiates from her, the kind that makes you relax instantly. No, the calm that hangs around her now is cold and lethal.

"I'll have to thank you for finding this," she gestures to Vitamors. "I've been looking for it for centuries."

I rise slowly to my feet. The contract that bound us from using our magic has released its hold on me, and I can feel the wound on my chest healing faster. "What is going on?"

She smirks wickedly, the expression unnatural on her soft features. Or maybe it just looks strange to me. "I must have given you too much credit these past few weeks, Thea." She sighs, wiping the sword on a cloth from Kael's desk. I scoot away from her, putting as much distance between us as possible. "This sword is mine. It belonged to my family many years ago. See, these symbols are my family's crest." She points to the carved circles on the guard. Circles with a horizontal line through the middle.

I shake my head, not wanting any of this to make sense. "I don't understand. Morwen, what do you mean by that?" I run a hand through my disheveled hair. "The war is over. Kael was the King and you just killed him." Does that mean the war is over?

Morwen laughs deeply, her attention still on the sword in her hand. "Kael was not the King. I'm sure he was flattered that you thought that though."

"You told him not to kill me..." Morwen gave Kael an order? If Kael was the Commander who took orders from only the King... No. Morwen has always been gentle. She has told me over and over that she doesn't like conflict, right? I trusted her.

Trust.

The word bounces in my head like a jagged rock. I trusted her because my gut told me to, something that I always took pride in myself for being able to do. My mother always taught me to trust my gut.

Kael's head sits in a pool of crimson liquid. I feel like I'm going to get sick.

"I didn't want him to kill you because I need you alive." She just stands there, as nonchalant as she always has. "Just for a little longer, that is."

I step back from the desk, from her. "It was you. It has always been you. You're the King?" It comes out more of a question than a realization. I want her to laugh in my face and tell me I'm wrong. But there is none of that warmth that I've come to love in her expression.

She cocks her head, the gesture alone affirming everything that I am now suspecting. There is an ancient depth to her eyes, a void of hatred and fire that could petrify the bravest of souls. "I'm sure if you kept at your research in the library, you would have figured it out sooner."

All the answers you seek are in the library, Mica once said. He has that mark similar to the one on Morwen's neck. This whole time, he knew she was the King, and he practically told me. Almost every time I was in the library, I was in there with Morwen. *All the answers you seek are in the library.* He told me.

Morwen is the King of the Brais.

And I told her everything.

Despite her terrifying gaze, despite everything in my body screaming for me to run, I straighten my back and stare at her. "You've been lying to me." Fire churns in my veins.

She snorts, leaning against the desk. The sunlight catches in the golden medallion around her neck. The stone in her sun totem matches the one in the pommel of the Vitamors. Everything was screaming at me that she was my enemy, and I ignored it all. The opening in her blouse also reveals the plant tattoo on her neck and parts of another along her collarbone. "I have never lied to you, Thea. Everything that I have said has been true and with intention. Could you say the same about your allies?"

"Shut up," I seethe. If Kael was a hard opponent to fight, I can't even imagine fighting Morwen. I glance at the bright window. How fortunate that the sun is still shining. "You're a monster." Mustering all the speed and strength I can, I snatch her sun totem. The chain breaks easily and Morwen just stands there, somehow too slow to react.

And then I am running out of the room.

CHAPTER THIRTY-ONE

THEA

own the hall to the main stairs. Step after step. Don't look back. The main doors are just a few seconds away. If I can make it outside, I'll be safe. Luckily, the castle still seems to be empty.

Pass the meeting hall. Turn left. There, the doors are there.

I let out a long sigh as I enter the sun-lit pathway. Looking at her totem in my hand, I catch my breath and steady my dizzy head. There is no way that I could have fought her, especially not after fighting Kael and losing. My magic flares to life, engulfing the medallion. I watch until it turns to ash.

Now, to get to a portal. I take one step toward the main one before something slams me against the unforgiving wall of the castle. I taste blood in the back of my throat, my vision blurry as I look up.

Morwen is outside, Vitamors in her hand. She let me take her necklace, pretended to be too slow so that I would run, and she could chase. Now, she moves faster than I ever saw Kael move, her icy hand around my throat, the sword's point at my chest. "Did you think that you were the only vampire with an immunity to the sun?" She moves so close that I can feel her breath on my cheek. "We are the same."

Unable to breathe properly, I struggle against her grasp. With heated hands, I grab her wrist and summon my fire. It comes eagerly, ready to vanquish the one who fooled me. Only it doesn't manifest. I feel the magic rising to greet the air, but once it does, it disappears.

"I told you, we are the same," she says, pressing the point of the sword harder against my chest. I wince at the sharpness. "Our magic, our stories, everything."

"I—" my voice is raspy against her hold, "—am…nothing like you."

Her fangs flash in the sunlight, sharper and longer than any I have seen before. "You'll have long enough to figure out otherwise." Her nails dig into my neck. "I honed your skills, made you stronger for this very moment. I hope you'll loathe being trapped in this prison dimension as much as I have."

Before I can say anything, she speaks again, in a language I have only ever heard uttered from Sarah. As the words spill from her lips, she tilts her head back, eyes closed. A second tattoo along her collarbone, placed just to the outside of the one she showed me in the garden that day, glows. Morwen winces, though doesn't stop speaking. The symbol, still mostly hidden, slithers as if it were alive. It travels underneath her blouse, moving to her arm and down to her hand. It moves from her fingers to my neck.

Blinding pain. I let out a scream and try to claw at her hand around my throat. White dots form at the outskirts of my vision as a thundering ache blooms in my head. It feels like someone is taking a metal poker from a fire and impaling my shoulder while breaking all of my bones. The pain is concentrated on my collarbone but reverberates to every limb. I don't hear Morwen's voice anymore, only the rasping sound of my scream.

Then there is only blackness.

CHAPTER THIRTY-TWO

COLE

*L*ike stepping through a sand-filled lake, I finally make it through the portal. Mica pulled through after all. The phrase he offered in order to get to this dimension was correct.

"Oye, this dimension makes my skin crawl," Oba whispers from behind as he steps completely out of the portal. He wipes at his clothes as if he just walked through a tunnel of spiderwebs. Like myself, he is equipped with a dagger and multiple wooden stakes.

Indeed. This place feels like death is waiting at its borders. Though the sun shines, there is a darkness hovering around the castle, looming in the distance and the forest beyond. It would be more advantageous if it were cloudy though. This dimension is large, and I have no idea where I might find Thea.

I laugh, though no amusement comes with it. "You say that like you've visited another one before."

He gives me a serious look. "I have." His whole body shivers as he shakes his head. "But I don't ever want to go back to that one either." When he sees me open my mouth, he puts a palm out. "Nor do I want to talk about it."

"Okay." I jerk my head to the forest on our left. "Let's go." We depart, me in front and Oba at my back. The apartment building that he was residing in at the time was also attacked by a small group of Brais, though his attackers refrained from using magic.

When I told Sarah what I was planning, I was quite surprised that she didn't insist on coming along. Though, I suppose that the curse placed upon her bloodline would prevent her from fighting the King. Whatever plan she and the other witches are concocting, it may result in the destruction of the dimension's anchor, which she believes is the King himself. That or some artifact. Whichever it is, I need to get Thea out before then. Because without the anchor, this entire place will crumble. She didn't inform me how she came to this information, so I can only assume it was in her mother's grimoire. Another witch-only secret.

As if the weather listened, clouds move overhead, dark and angry. If a storm starts, all the better. I move quietly toward the castle, keeping to the trees as best I can. I don't know how many air wielders might be here, so I refrain from starting a windstorm.

"It would have been nice if Mica gave some idea as to where your vampire is," Oba says quietly. "Do you think she is still alive?"

I flinch at his question. It has been on my mind since the Brais so boldly attacked the Essites and Minuit coven. No one reported seeing the King during those attacks, which worries me more than if he was spotted. If the King truly wanted Thea for something, would he have done it while the rest of the Brais were waging his war?

"She has to be," I whisper.

If they did something to her…I wouldn't hesitate to use every drop of my magic to tear the Brais down. There wouldn't be a single one left.

It feels so long ago since the last time that I saw Thea. I think about it all the time, about her all the time. And the promise I made to her. Nothing in this world can keep me from fulfilling that promise. If not in this life, then the next.

Oba pulls me back abruptly just as the whistle of a dagger soars by us. The weapon was thrown with so much force that it embedded almost completely into a large tree. We both have our own drawn by the time we turn to face the person who threw it.

A woman stands in the path running parallel to the forest. Her black-red hair blows in the wind that Oba's anger started. Piercing blue eyes follow us as we step into the path. "Nicolai Moretti," she says. "What luck I have to be graced with your presence." She holds a sword in her hand, already stained with someone's blood.

"She knows your old name?" Oba whispers to me, his fists clenching tightly around his weapon.

I call upon the air, letting it encircle me in a protective barrier. "I have no idea who you are."

The smile on her lips seems to pull fear out of my body, as if it can remember her, but my mind cannot. "I figured you wouldn't."

"Let us pass or die," Oba yells, taking a step toward her and lifting his weapon. The wind around us intensifies, rustling decaying leaves on the forest floor.

Her gaze flicks to him, and she cocks her head, her tongue running over her bottom lip. "I would rather fight Nicolai alone, thank you." She raises her free hand and twists her wrist as she closes her fingers into a fist. I hear the snap of what sounds like a twig breaking just to see Oba's neck bent at an irregular angle. His body then flies into the forest as if it were attached to invisible strings. The wind stops abruptly, a blanket of silence covering us.

"Oba!" I cry out as the forest consumes him. "What did you do?" I feel my fangs slide from my gums.

She swings the sword up so that the blade sits on her shoulder. "Not that I think this will be much of a fight," she says, ignoring my question. With the hand that just snapped Oba's neck, she reaches behind her and pulls out a wooden stake. "I actually believed Kael when he said that he killed you. I should have known that wasn't true. Just another plan in his treason." She stabs the sword into the gravel and steps in front of it. "I never felt that glorious little prick of magic when your soul departs."

Enough of her nonsense. I form a sphere of violently churning air and hurl it at her. With a quick step, she moves out of the way. The blast hits the sword in the ground, and it wobbles a little. When my magic touches it, I get the sense that I have seen it before. Pain and death surround it.

"Are you remembering?" she asks, a brow raised.

With my beta ability, I connect to some small rocks littering the ground and lift them into the air. Her expression shifts to excitement as she poises herself to block. The rocks fly at her head, soaring through the air like baseballs. She dodges the first four, jumping from side to side with incredible speed. When the last one gets close, it stops in midair. Her hand isn't even raised. The rock drops to the ground, landing just in front of her boots.

"Who are you," I ask, my temper rising by the second. I need to finish this fight quickly so I can check on Oba.

She rubs the back of her neck. Her entire demeanor seems off. She doesn't appear to be someone you can predict, which is quite frightening. "Honestly, I'm not sure if I prefer you to remember or not."

Remember? Have I met her before? Her confidence appears genuine. I stare at her casual demeanor, digging through my memory for those striking blue eyes and reddish-black hair.

She flips the stake in her hand, dashing toward me once she catches it. Her speed is like nothing I have ever seen before. I almost miss her quick spin to get behind me. I blast air that knocks her strike off balance and the stake just misses my side.

With the momentum of my push, she twists her feet and spins, aiming to stab me in the heart. I dodge the stake, and I grab her wrist. Her eyes grow wild with fury. The amount of speed and strength she has before even tapping into her vampiric senses is troublesome. If she were to shift, I don't think that I would stand a chance.

I can't seem to recall her face, and I think it would be hard to forget those bright blue eyes. Was she a Brais while I was? There is no way that she transitioned after, not with this incredible strength. Though I suppose she might have always been here, in this dimension. I've only ever heard about it. This is the first time I've stepped foot inside. But how does she know me?

An icy cold sensation floods into the hand that is holding her wrist. Images flash before my mind. They feel like memories, but I don't recognize them. Death and blood. Screaming. Winds that destroy an entire village. Fires that consume people. My heart stops at one that pictures Thea, blood covering her abdomen as she lies on cold cobblestone unmoving.

I release her wrist, grasping at my hurting heart. Tears threaten to break free. "What was that?" I demand, my teeth barred.

She just lunges forward, her fist colliding with my face. The impact cracked something in my cheek and my jaw throbs. Shakily, I lift myself to my hands and knees. The woman runs at me again, though this time with less speed. I twist just in time to catch her by the ankle. As I stand, I pull her leg out from under her. Her head smacks the ground and I bring forth the air from around her body.

She gasps, her free hand grabbing at her throat. Violent winds blow in every direction, bending trees and rattling the rocks. They howl like a pack of wolves running through the forest. That part of my magic that transferred to Thea when I turned her has reached out. That tells me that she is at least still alive, and that I am close. This woman picked the wrong fight. I won't stop until Thea is safe.

I am the Tempest.

The howling turns into roaring as the winds churn into circular rotations. Trees crack at the intensity. The last time I let this much of my magic loose, I destroyed an entire small town. An order passed from the King of the Brais to the General that I worked under. The resulting catastrophe that earned me my nickname.

The woman smiles despite not being able to breathe. She raises her free hand with her palm facing me. She doesn't move, but something crashes into my chest. The force pushes me off my feet, and I stumble back, losing the concentration on my magic. The winds slow, strong enough to only rustle some leaves.

Again, she lunges with the stake aimed for my heart. Instead of grabbing her wrist, I use my beta ability to hold her right arm in place. She doesn't look surprised, only thrilled. It doesn't take long before sweat beads on my forehead and back, my hand trembling slightly at the exhaustion already building.

"I will admit, this has been the most exciting of our fights." She leans in, pushing against my psychic hold. "I always enjoy doing this to you two." And despite the grip my magic has on her, she drops the stake from her right hand.

Her left hand catches the stake, and she plunges it toward my chest.

CHAPTER THIRTY-THREE

THEA

I wake with a scream, though not my own. The pained voice roars in my head. It sounds like it is coming from all directions while also remaining in my mind. Rising to my feet, I look around and notice that I am still just outside the castle doors. I can somehow feel Morwen's sinister energy pulsing in every corner of the dimension.

Rain falls from the darkening sky, first as small inconsistent droplets, their coldness biting at my skin. In a few strides, the drops become heavy and pelt the top of my head as I run to that archway portal hidden in the southwestern part of the dimension. The fresh brand on my collarbone still sears, but I push through the pain. Something in my chest aches, and I'm not sure if it has to do with whatever spell that Morwen transferred to me. I hope it isn't the same mark those who know the King's identity receive.

I was so stupid. She knew every minute detail because I told her. I *trusted* her. I trusted too easily. A crack of thunder vibrates the ground as purple lightning streaks across the sky, racing toward my left. Panting, I come to a brief stop before turning to follow the storm, my feet pounding the earth once again. The lightning continues to point me eastward. If the King can control the weather here, then she must be over that way.

Fire builds under my palm. A promise.

Despite getting closer to the ocean that surrounds the dimension, a woodsy scent fills my nose, and I question the direction that I am traveling. There are only two portals on this isolated island, and I feel her presence at both. Between the lightning flashing this direction and the feeling in my gut, I know this is the way I need to go. The smaller portal is more hidden than the other, and it is closer from where we were. Wouldn't this be the logical choice?

That abandoned garage comes into view. It is half burned and half collapsed in on itself. I shove down the memories of what is inside and how Morwen comforted me. And shoving deep down the vow that we made with each other.

Testing my magic, I flex my hands, the veins within sizzle in response. I wish that I had that sword with me.

I blur past the garage, stumbling on a random dagger, when a loud crack of thunder vibrates through me. It causes me to stop and catch my footing. Only when I move my foot do I see the body lying prone on the ground twenty feet to my right. His dark hair tousled from an unknown force. Blood streaks down his chiseled, stubble-lined chin and coats his dark t-shirt.

"Cole!" I yell, my voice cracking like the clouds above. Nausea boils in my gut. I don't know if it was my scream or a clap of thunder that roared into the rain. Tears blur my vision as my eyes land on the stake that sticks out of his chest.

"No, no, no. Please, no." I skid to a stop and crumble to my knees. A cry bubbles in my throat as he moves his head slightly so that his pale gray eyes meet mine. A light brown maple leaf sticks in the curly strands of his obsidian hair. How long has he been here bleeding out in agony? "I'll get it out," I say, grabbing the wood with shaky hands.

He puts a bloody hand on mine. "No, Thea." His voice is hoarse, and he winces. There is blood pooling at the corners of his mouth. "The poison…its already gotten to my heart."

I shake my head, ignoring the numbness creeping into my limbs. This is not happening. Cole has always been a beacon to me. Even with the doubts that interjected themselves into my thoughts…deep down, I knew they weren't true. "Then let me heal you." My fangs sharpen as I bring my wrist to my mouth and bite down. The smell of his blood hits me, knocking me to the ground. Cole's blood. It stains the deep green of the grass.

"Thea," he breathes.

When my own blood trickles from the wound I made, I bring my wrist to his mouth. With trembling movements, he pushes it away, his smokey eyes never leaving mine. "It won't work." His skin is paling underneath the dark sky. Rain falls unforgivingly on us both, as if the sky was weeping too. A wielder of storms, caller of wind.

"You don't know that!" I shakily move my hand back to his mouth.

His expression twists in pain as he turns his head away from my offering. "I do, Thea." His voice is so quiet.

"I-I can't Cole." Tears stain my cheeks, mixing with those from the clouds. "I can't lose you."

He brings a hand to my cheek, and I lean into it. The usual warmth from his touch is fleeting, replaced by the inevitable coldness of death. "You can never lose me, Thea." His thumb strokes underneath my eye.

I savor the way my name sounds on his lips, forging it into my memory.

"There is no distance, time or otherwise, that can separate you from me." He shifts slightly, grunting as he does so, and brings his other hand up to cup my face. "I love you, Thea.

And I will love you for as long as stars shine over your head. For as long as Earth sits beneath your feet. My soul will find yours again, like it always has."

I sob into his hands, his grip loosening. Color is draining from his skin with each painful breath. If there was any doubt in my mind, in my heart, about how I felt about this man, it is gone now. That day he pulled me from the car accident, he saved me. Saved both my life and my heart. In him is that unconditional love I thought was lost once my parents died. Even when I didn't understand, or when I rejected him in the beginning, he was always there protecting me.

I can't imagine breathing a single breath without him at my side.

Warmth blooms in my hand as I bring it to his chest, positioning it so that my thumb and index fingers are encircling the stake. And with my other hand, I firmly grab the wood. "I can't lose you, Cole."

"Thea—" My name is but a whisper upon the wind carried by the storm that remains centered above us. The rain lightens just a little, as if it holds the hope that dwells in my own chest.

I pull the stake from his flesh. His cry is like a dagger to the heart. "I'm sorry," I say, closing my eyes and placing one hand on top of the other over his bleeding wound. As if it was waiting, my beta ability roars to life. Healing heat pools in my hands, and I feel it rushing into his body, traveling to every part infected with the poison of the live wood.

My smile falters at a subtle throb in my abdomen. Acutely aware of where my heart is, the pain pulses just underneath it. I open my eyes and stifle a cry of happiness at the color already returning to Cole's complexion. My magic pours into him, finding and eliminating anything that threatens his well-being. With each pulse of healing energy into his body, pain echoes in mine. A metallic tang coats my tongue.

"Thea, stop." Cole's voice is clearer than it just was. He

places his hands on mine, trying to pry them free from his body. "Please, Thea. You're killing yourself!"

I can still feel the poison inside his body, inside his heart. It wriggles around like it has a mind of its own, maneuvering to avoid my magic. Though the rest of my body is shaking, I keep my hands firm on his still bleeding chest. The world around us feels as though it were spinning too fast on its axis. My feet grow cold, invisible icy claws digging unforgivably into my skin. Something warm drips down my chin.

"Thea!" Cole's frantic cry is muffled, as if he were yelling through an ocean between us. A sharp pain erupts in my head. Somehow, he is now the one kneeling, and I'm looking up at him.

I smile weakly at him, at the healthy glow that encircles him. The wound on his chest has healed, the only indication that it was there is the drying blood on his skin and clothes. If it were not for such a worried expression on his face, I would think we were back at his cabin together, staring up at the stars. Back when we thought a bubble would keep us safe forever. Only us and the stars, a drink in one hand and our fingers urging to intertwine. My body feels heavy, like the earth is slowly embracing me in its eternal calm. Something coarse and thorny slithers into my heart. It is uncomfortable, but somehow painless. My magic healed Cole but transferred the inevitable death to me. Just like when I healed Riley and a wound appeared on my own neck. "I saved you," I say to him, my voice a cracked whisper.

Tears rim his smokey eyes. "But who saves you?" He searches my face, his fingers wrapped tightly around mine, his other hand on my cheek.

I lean into his touch, a beacon of light in the dimming world. "You are better for this world than I am." My chest rises in staggering breaths. I can tell that I am dying even though there is no pain. There is only the softness of the earth and the warmth of Cole.

He shakes his head, and a few tears fall down his face. "You're wrong, Thea. There is light in this world because of you. I know you fear the darkness in your heart, but it's that darkness that sets fire to the injustice. Your fire ignites change."

Ordo ab choa.

"You light the world, Thea." His thumb gently caresses my face. "You said you can't lose me. Well, I can't lose you either."

Everything slows as a light starts flickering behind his head. *Thea, my Thea.* I blink at the familiar voice that echoes into the silence. The orb separates into two beings who slowly take form. My heart shatters at the two people I have missed most in this world.

Mom? Dad?

CHAPTER THIRTY-FOUR

THEA

My parents catch me as I collapse on my knees, suddenly back at our old manor by the lake, the Brais dimension only a memory—or a fleeting nightmare. We hold each other momentarily before they pull away, their faces so full of love.

"Thea," my mom says again, her melodic voice soothing my entire being. A voice that I didn't think I would ever hear again. "I am so proud of you." Her brown hair is tied back into a ponytail with a single braid on the left side of her head. Her hazel eyes dance with the joy written in her soft features.

"I missed you," I say, happy to be reunited with them.

"You are not done yet, my sweet daughter." My dad brushes a tear from my cheek. His pale blue eyes sparkle brighter than I have ever seen them. A gentle smile rests on his face as he adds, "We have slept on this for too long, and I am sorry that it has fallen upon you to fix our mistakes."

My brows scrunch together. "I don't understand."

"Oh, my dear child," my mother croons, her gentle finger tracing along my collarbone.

"This began with our family, our ancestors, and must end

with you," my father continues. "You're stronger than you believe, Thea." A light hum sings from behind us, from somewhere outside this building. This home, where everything is where it is supposed to be. Including the scratches on the kitchen doorframe from when I fought an imaginary dragon in the house, or lines of paint underneath the table when I claimed to be a painter. "I'm sorry I never told you about our family's history. We were once powerful witches, cursed by the one who created the vampires." He looks to where the humming grows.

The sound is beckoning, but I can't leave them. I don't want to leave them. But that sound…

"He's calling for you, darling."

I shake my head, burying my face in my mother's shoulder. "I'm dying."

My dad places a hand on my arm, forcing me to turn to him. Though gentle, his face is hard and full of determination. "You are fire, Thea. It has been in your blood since you were born. Feel it, nourish it. Fire can heal as much as it can destroy. Magic of the sun once burned in our ancestor's blood. It was how we saved you."

They clasp their hands together and a faint blue light glows between their palms as if I needed a reminder. "You sacrificed yourselves…for me?"

My mother puts a hand on my cheek. "It was our duty to protect you."

"And our honor to have such a strong, powerful child." My father smiles warmly at me, the gesture mending broken pieces of my heart. "We knew the moment you were born that your future would be important for this world. The magic that was once prominent in my bloodline has manifested itself wholly in you."

"Feel it, sweetheart," my mother chimes in. "Trust it."

With their words, a soaring fervor pools in my chest. It was slumbering in the remnants of that cage, hidden beneath the fears and doubts. With each word from my parents, each breath in my lungs, it grows. The magic, embedded in the parts that have been with me long before becoming a vampire, roar to life. It clears away all the muddled thoughts, all the false influences stitched into my mind. It is innate. It is home.

It is fire. And it reaches for that beautiful humming song.

"I love you guys," I say with one last embrace.

"We love you too. And we will always be here."

The house fades into a wall of glorious fire. The flames aren't rigid and harsh but soft and inviting. As if they have been waiting patiently for me to realize their truth. I release my parents and stand, giving them one last glance. A vibrant aura of turquoise glows around them as they fade into brilliant orbs of warming light again. Their colorful love beams toward me, illuminating the path before me.

With each step, vibrations pulse from my chest. Every sure step embracing the fears and doubts still nestled into my soul. Like the brilliant rainbow that shines after a hurricane, those dark parts of me melt into the soothing love. When there are none left, I feel the explosion of pure natural energy.

I once said that I would not simply rise from the ashes the Brais create. I vowed to be the inferno who turns *them* into ashes. But what goal can be sustainable without a vision far beyond it?

Change is born from chaos.

Fire is change.

I am the Phoenix, but I am also the Inferno.

CHAPTER THIRTY-FIVE

THEA

My eyes fly open the moment before my body is engulfed in flame. Crimson tendrils flare from my skin, a turquoise green at their center. I can feel my parents' souls still watching over me. There is no pain, no heaviness.

"Thea?"

His voice sends shivers down my spine. "Cole." I motion to get up and run to him, but he takes another step back, having already taken a good few away from me.

"You're on fire, Thea."

"I—" The feeling of something cold in my grasp stops the words from leaving my lips. Looking down, I see the golden hilt of a sword clutched in my hand.

Vitamors.

My flames engulf it, and the sword seems to vibrate with anticipation at my magic. The ripple of energy on the outskirts of the dimension's barrier catches my attention. I know the iciness of who it belongs to.

Morwen. She is still here and about to open the portal. I can't let her escape out of this dimension. She needs to be stopped here. There's no way that I can catch up with her though. The sword in my hand all but wriggles in my grasp.

Cole jerks back, still wary of my magic. I would never let my flames harm him. "Thea, what are you doing?" he asks, concern flitting across his perfect features.

Still on fire, I stand. With an outstretched arm, I pull a vast amount of magic into my palm. Within seconds, a fireball grows with that same red and blue-green flame. I turn slightly to the right. As if he understood, Cole moves away from my hand.

Instead of a massive fireball, a beam shoots from my palm. My fire streams so fast that it is hard to see. It races across the forest, curving to avoid hitting any trees, just as a lightning bolt streaks across the sky. It crashes against something in the distance in a garish explosion. Black smoke pillows into the air.

My collarbone burns, and I am reminded of that symbol that transferred from Morwen's to mine. Ignoring the pain, I leap forward, rushing toward the smallest portal. Cole yelled something, but I was moving too fast to be able to understand him. I didn't have time to tell him what I am planning. I couldn't risk Morwen escaping.

The sword in my hand sings as it slices through the air with each rushed step. Colors and objects whir by in a blur. Morwen is still here, I can feel her energy stationed straight ahead of me. She hasn't tried to get to the other portal yet. Good. Crimson flames emerge from my body again, creeping over the sword. Stepping out into the clearing, she is hunched over a pile of obsidian rubble. Her head snaps up at me, her eyes widening.

I hurl the flaming sword at her head.

It was the portal that exploded. Charred earth encircles where it once stood, chunks and slivers of obsidian scattered about. Even with a few jagged pieces of the portal stuck into her abdomen and arm, Morwen ungracefully dodges the sword. She rolls to her left to avoid the attack, grunting with the movement. The sword sticks halfway into the tree just beyond her. Blood spills from the wounds where the debris hit her. When she steadies herself, her expression is lethal.

Morwen's bloodied hand yanks a stone from her gut and throws it like a dagger toward me. I sidestep and easily avoid the chunk. "Do you even know what you just did?" she says, her voice unnervingly calm despite almost blowing up.

"I think I destroyed one of your exits." I smirk. Fire pools in my hand, shaping itself into a spear, and I throw it at her.

Flames erupt from her body. Black, menacing flames. The sight catches me off guard and I stumble backward, grabbing a low-hanging branch to steady myself.

"That day in the garden," I whisper. "I thought that my magic was going to burn you. That the black swirls I saw was the manifestation of your fear…"

A malicious smile crosses her expression, and she brushes a wave of her black hair over a shoulder. "I let you think that. Let you think that I was afraid. I manipulated your emotions to make sure you felt guilty, though I'm sure you would have regardless. Just like I've been manipulating your emotions since the first day we met."

"What?" The word hardly has any sound. White hot fury festers in my chest.

Morwen takes a step forward as she pulls out the stone embedded in her arm. She examines the piece as if it were a sculpture on a pedestal. "I have many abilities, Thea. And just like you, I can use energy manipulation."

I stretch out my arm like I was readying for a handshake. "You made me doubt everyone! Cole, the witches, and the Essites." Vitamors vibrates in the trunk of the tree, fighting to free itself.

She laughs. "I've done more than that." She tilts her head, her expression consumed in feral delight. "I'm surprised that in all of your investigating of the castle, you never discovered what was at the end of the northern wing." Black flames engulf her hand, slithering like they were a liquid. Even from this distance, I can feel the intensity of their heat. Instead of throwing them at me, she aims for the ground where the debris from the portal are crumbled together. The pieces catch fire and burn away with a hiss.

My lips purse as I flex my burning hand. "What does—" As if someone slashed my body in half, I crumple to the ground, clutching at my chest. A searing pain spreads from the tattoo down to my toes. Thunder roars overhead, the drum harmonizing with the pain.

Her smile widens, a triumphant expression on her face. It no longer looks like the one that belonged to my gentle friend, the vampire who stayed with the Brais simply because she had no other choice. Like a switch was flipped, Morwen's face is dangerous, all sharp edges that have been honed from years—centuries—of power. "For so many years, I've tried to find a way to escape this dimension." She laughs, the sound rigid and cold. "I created this place to be a haven. I underestimated the vengeful wrath that the witches held against me. They tethered me here, made me become a physical anchor so that I could never leave." Her tone becomes animalistic, a mix of hatred and hunger. "I've tried to transfer that role onto so many other vampires, but they were never strong enough to withstand the spell."

Now her face twists with feral glee. "Imagine my delight when my vampires discovered a descendant of my bloodline, with a father who knew the sacred spell passed down that would protect the life of a loved one at the cost of his own. The same spell that created the concoction of magic that runs in my own veins." Images of that vision from the library play out in my head. Of the burnt corpses whose hands were clasped together. And that familiar glow between them. "All I had to do was put your parents in a position to use that spell." She takes a predatory step forward. "I felt them sacrifice themselves the night of that car accident. All to save you."

I shake my head, my teeth grinding together. "Shut up."

"I've shaped you. Together, we are the children born from sacrifice. A noble and rare power." A small twig snaps under her careful step. "Everything that you are is because of me. You should be grateful, the power that runs in your blood was perfected by a King." A low, harsh laugh rumbles in her chest. "Strong enough to withstand the transfer, but too weak to kill Kael."

Anger boils in my soul, and I let out a lethal growl, still clutching my side as I stand. When I lost control of my anger after finding out the Brais were responsible for the death of my parents, Morwen was there to soothe me. The person directly responsible for everything in my life…and she acted like a friend. A *friend*. Someone who cared.

A scream of pure rage boils in my throat, magic fueled with it. "You lied. About everything! And you said you never did. You sat there and consoled me about my grief as if you weren't the one responsible for all of it! You killed my parents. And me!"

"I never confirmed nor denied who was responsible for your so-called woes." She takes another step, the black flames on her arm becoming even hotter. "I made you strong. You are one of the most powerful creatures on this planet, Thea. Thanks to me. Be grateful."

I dig my nails into my side to steady the rising rage. I have loathed the Brais this whole time when it was Morwen who that hatred should have been directed at. She is the plague that is rotting this world. On the outskirts of my perception, I sense Cole running toward us. I need to end this before he gets here. I won't let her harm anyone else I care about. But I need the sword first. "And when I asked you about the King? You lied then!" I pull harder on that invisible string that connects Vita-mors to my hand. It shakes in the tree's hold, as if it under-stands my urgency for it.

I pull harder on the invisible tether to the sword as she takes another step. The stone in her hand hums the closer she gets to me. "Maybe if you weren't so adamant about wiping out the humans, the Essites and witches wouldn't be so pressed about your faction."

Her expression turns sour. "The humans, even the witches, deserve nothing but torment for everything they did to me." Her voice drips with poison.

"Sounds like a you problem," I retort. "Just because people wronged you doesn't make it right to destroy them and their descendants."

"It gives me *all* the right." Her energy teeters on her usual calm and the beginnings of becoming unhinged. The black flames swirl around her arms like living shadows. They watch me like a predator sizing up their prey.

The sword flies from the trunk, the handle aiming for my hand. Morwen moves so fast, and I curse myself for not think-ing. She snatches the sword from the air, continuing toward me, the point held forward. I move just in time for the sword to miss my heart. Instead, she plunges it into my shoulder. My beta ability flares to life and pools into my feet, magic rooting me in place to the grasses beneath. The earth is holding me, our energies becoming one.

A slicing throb burns from my shoulder outward. I grunt as Morwen pushes the blade so that the hilt is pressed against my body. She glances down, a slight upward tug on her lips. "Neat trick."

"Be creative, right?" I pant against her strength.

She holds the sword with one hand, the other still clutching that piece of the portal, her blood dripping from it. I bring both of my hands to her arm and struggle against her strength as I try to push her off me. Even with one hand, she is stronger. I call upon my vampiric strength, feeling the sharpness of my fangs as they grow and touch my bottom lip. Everything becomes clearer, the colors of the open meadow around us, the iridescence of the portal shards, Morwen's hair that sways in a growing wind. The color is extraordinarily beautiful and soft.

I push harder against her, ignoring the pain slicing through my body. A warm liquid streams down my side from the wound. With each breath, I force her back. The blade slides slowly from my body, sharp pains shooting down to my legs with each movement. With so much of my concentration on my beta ability keeping me upright, I can't muster enough magic to flare fire from my hands.

Her eyes grow wild with challenge, a sharp smile on her crimson lips. They change color to a deep garnet. Razor sharp teeth protrude from her upper lip. "Not being able to kill you because I needed you to get strong and take the mantle of anchor was difficult, but I knew it would be worth it. And now, since you have that mark," she jerks her chin at the symbol on my collarbone, "I am free to leave this dimension."

How would me receiving this mark allow her to leave the dimension? I thought this mark was for finding out her identity as the King. If that were the case, wouldn't the curse be trying to kill me for fighting her?

A wicked grin cuts across her expression. "That is not the mark you think it is." The smirk disappears, replaced with a snarl. "Infuriating as it is, you and your beloved are immune to the curse of silence." She gives one push on the sword and plunges it back to the hilt again, almost knocking me off balance. "But, now that you have it, and I do not, I am free to kill you."

I glance down to her hand and notice there is a subtle point to her nails, like claws have emerged from the tips of her fingers. Sensing that well of magic within, I pull more energy into my beta ability. My gaze flicks back to hers, and I almost release my grip. Instead of a deep red, her eyes glow a dark orange, reminding me of burning coals.

Morwen takes advantage of my slackened hold and pulls the sword free from my shoulder. With a swift spin, she brings the sword diagonally down, a direct line for my neck. The same move that she used to decapitate Kael. Shifting the magic from my feet to my hands, it sears underneath my skin, readying to be used offensively. Her movements are so fast. My magic is still traveling up my legs.

The violent energy from her strike travels faster than the blade. It hits my skin like a vanguard in an army, sure and lethal. My magic speeds down my arms now, flames emerging from my limbs and moving at her like arrows fired from a legion of bowmen.

Her swing doesn't falter. Not even as my magic reaches out for her, a fire so hot that it pulls the oxygen from the forest around us. An all-consuming inferno.

She's still faster. I should have tried to dodge instead of countering with my own attack.

It's only inches away from my neck. My flames still have at least a foot.

There is a gleam in her fiery eyes, like the glee on a child's face on a holiday morning.

I won't make it.

A violent gust of wind blows in a horizontal spiral, picking up leaves and small debris with it. It sends Morwen flying into a grove of slender trees. The whirlwind catches my flames and the two elements mix, forming a tornado of flame and wind. It roars into the silence, a lion intimidating an enemy who threatens their pride. I look to the direction it came from and find Cole standing at the edge of the clearing, his palms facing us, fingers crossed, creating a triangle. He catches my eyes and gives me a nod.

"It's a pity," Morwen pants as she shakily gets to her feet. The inferno tore into the trees, shattering them into splinters, and pinned her, though not enough to keep her down. I see the Vitamors glinting underneath a leafy branch, almost ten steps away from where she is. Burns on her face and arms are already healing, her clothes are blackened. She brushes dirt from her pant leg.

I don't dare make another move for the sword, not with Cole in her reach. "Care to elaborate?" I seethe. I feel Cole's protective presence as he steps beside me.

Morwen's gaze shifts between us and she releases an amused breath. Though she lost the sword in her fall, she still holds the chunk of the portal. As she speaks, she lifts it up. "That I couldn't relish in killing you two again. Not that either of you remember, but I have lost count of the number of times I've killed your reincarnations. Perhaps the next—"

The temperature around us plummets despite the flames of both Morwen's and my magic. Puffs of breath billow from our mouths. Fear flashes across Morwen's face. Her knuckles turn white as she grips the stone chunk harder, her dagger-like nails digging into the hard surface.

I lunge at her, grabbing the sword on my way, when she crumples to the ground, crying and writhing in pain. Her skin turns blue and ice forms along her arms and hair. Still, she manages to hold onto the piece of the portal. Morwen's blue eyes look up, beyond Cole and me.

Out of the trees emerges Mica, his fist raised. Ice hovers protectively around his body like tiny daggers. Water, he said was his element. And his only magical ability. Clearly his elemental magic makes up for no beta ability, if he can take down the King of the Brais.

Morwen lifts herself slowly, her entire body stiff. "You vowed to protect me." Her words come out slow and strained.

Mica steps into the clearing. With each step, water droplets rise from the ground, hardening into ice shards once they reach his knees. There is blood on his clothes and in his hair. None of it appears to be from him. A sword is sheathed at his side. "If it means your end, I will gladly sacrifice myself to see it through." He stifles a cough and there is a trickle of blood that drips out of his mouth.

Silence echoes all around as Mica glances to me. "I vowed to protect the anchor. I came to protect Thea."

CHAPTER THIRTY-SIX

THEA

"What?" Cole asks enraged. His emotions feel mostly centered on Morwen, but there seems to be some pointed at Mica as well.

I turn my burning stare at Morwen. "That spell." I trace a finger lightly over my collarbone. Outside the castle, after Morwen killed Kael, she whispered words in another language. A mark on her shoulder slithered to mine. The skin is tender, warm underneath my touch, and I hiss. "That is what you meant when you said you transferred it to me." I all but growl the words into the increasing winds.

Morwen's feral smile comes easily, unaffected by whatever icy torment Mica is inflicting on her. "Yes. You are trapped in this forsaken dimension, as I was for decades." With that, something snaps in the current of the air.

Mica winces, his hands grabbing at his head. He drops to a knee, crying out in pain. Morwen, color returning to her complexion, rises to her feet. Her hands are outstretched, fingers curled as if she were holding a ball.

"Release his mind," Cole sneers and the wind howls, leaves

blowing around aggressively. Rocks and shards of the portal begin hovering in the air as he takes a step forward.

Morwen only holds the chunk of stone in her other hand high above her head. "See you in your next lives," she says with a toothy grin.

Morwen is distracted with the piece of the portal, and I use that to my advantage. I call to the sword, and it answers with an electrifying hum, lifting from the rubble quickly. I don't call it to my hand, but instead let it aim for Morwen. Though the smug grin never leaves her face, her eyes widen at the point of the sword.

Then, she breaks the stone chunk. A misty black void appears in a spiral from where Morwen stands. The mark on my collarbone sears, sending sharp bolts through my entire body.

"Thea!" Cole cries out, his hand on my back.

"I'm okay," I answer through gritted teeth.

"She's creating a portal," Mica yells.

I gasp and clutch at the burning mark underneath my tattered shirt as I release the sword. Like a racecar, it flies from its starting gate of branches and debris.

Morwen moves so fast into that inky murkiness that the sword sticks into the tree behind where she stood. Her body fades like a rock sinking into a lake, golden eyes the last to disappear. The portal vanishes.

"Is there another portal we can use to go after her?" Cole asks hurriedly.

"There is, but Thea can't leave now," Mica says, jerking his chin at me as he stands shakily. "She's the anchor to this dimension now. Besides, Morwen could open that portal to any place in the world."

We lost. The King was in our grasp, and we let her slip away. The King of the Brais, stuck in a dimension where no harm could come to a human. Now she could wreak havoc on everything.

"England," I say. "I think—"

Blinding pain. In my head, in my chest. It sends me to the cold ground, heaving in between rolling throbs. The metallic tang of blood coats my tongue like a flooding river. I cough it onto the grass, unable to take a breath. The ground is shaking violently, and I get the vague sense that it is splitting some-where. Either that or it is my mind that is tearing down the center.

"Thea? What's happening?" Cole is by my side in an instant. His hand is on my back, moving in comforting circles. A light shines from my chest, and Cole helps me onto my back, my head resting on his legs. "What is happening?" he repeats with an urgency.

Mica's face turns ghostly white. "This dimension is being torn down."

I gasp for breath in a gurgled sound. "Cole…" The sword doesn't come to heal me like it did before.

"What? How?" Cole's hand is on my cheek, brushing the blood away.

Mica kneels on the ground, the look of defeat etched into his tense expression. "Either someone has destroyed the last portal or the connection between anchor and dimension is being severed."

Cole's eyes widen at that. "I need you to watch Thea." He gently places a kiss on my forehead before placing my head on the ground, his fingers gently cupping my cheeks before he stands. I grab at his foot as he backs away, grief and wrath mixed on his features. "I need to stop the Minuit Coven. They're destroying the dimension."

ACKNOWLEDGMENTS

And here we are! On to the list of wonderful souls that helped put this book together. Truly grateful for everyone!

First, of course, my family. You all have been so supportive of me on this journey. I could totally dedicate each book I write to you guys, but I have to share the love, so I hope you're okay with a section all the way back here. Do you even read this part though? Truly, I am thankful for your unconditional love.

An enormous shout out to one of my best friends, Sam. You endured through a very rough draft of this book and somehow still enjoyed it. Honestly, when I was reading through the manuscript with your notes I just kept cringing. Thanks for not giving up on me or the story, ha!

To Nicolette, my oh-so-absolutely-amazing editor. Not only have you helped with both books in this series, but you have also helped immensely with my writing. The drawings and notes you leave as you read are my favorite things ever. I am so incredibly thankful to have found you in the sea of editors. I truly lucked out! You are the best.

To Brittany! Here you are again, being amazing. Honestly, I don't know where I would be in my writing career without you. I am extremely grateful that you took time to look through and proofread the book before it went out into the world. Step by step, I'm getting the hang of this book writing and publishing nonsense, and you are one of the reasons, so thank you!

A shout out to the creator behind the cover, Natália. I'm starting to think that you are a mind reader. I just have to mention a couple things and you blow my expectations out of the water. You help bring Thea and the book to life with your artwork on the covers! I can't even count how many times people have gasped over the beauty of the cover art. In this, I have also truly lucked out! Thank you so much!

And of course, Franziska Stern! Thank you so much for the amazing cover design and all the beautiful artwork in the chapters. It is like the cherry on top of a delicious ice cream or the beautiful gift wrapping on a present.

Thank you to every person who has pledged in the Kickstarter project! You all are truly amazing and I can't even express how much you helped! So thank you: Sergey, Cindi, Molly, Ryan, Sara, Henry, Ginger, Kelly, Debbi, Laura, Paula, Sam, Mark, and Tina. And to every other pledger who didn't want to be named, thank you!

A truly special shoutout and gratitude mention to all of my friends, advanced readers, readers, social media followers, and newsletter subscribers! You all are the reason I keep going!

ABOUT THE AUTHOR

Arleta Rae is a first time author living in the beautiful hills of New England. Her debut novel, RISING EMBER, came from her love of writing, the supernatural, and nature. She has a BS in environmental studies and a MA in ecopsychology and she hopes to open a nature retreat in the future. Arleta weaves her enthusiasm for fantasy and nature into her books. When she isn't writing, she can be found hiking, working in a greenhouse, sipping a latte, or reading.

facebook.com/araebooks

twitter.com/authorarletarae

instagram.com/authorarletarae

tiktok.com/@authorarletarae